COLONIAL MURDER

ERIC THOMSON

A Colonial Murder
Copyright 2020 Eric Thomson
First paperback printing August 2020

Published in Canada
By Sanddiver Books Inc.
ISBN: 978-1-989314-28-9

— One —

Sometimes, the enjoyment I derived from my job felt unseemly. The looks my team and I earned as we swept into the headquarters of the Cimmerian Gendarmerie triggered a disturbing power rush. As usual, we wore what looked like tailored civilian business suits instead of gray Constabulary uniforms. But they were, in fact, made with a material capable of stopping knives, slugs, and even small caliber plasma rounds. However, the next senior officer I met who didn't know who and what I was would be the first.

Sure, planetary police forces had their own internal affairs departments. But when cops with stars on the collar were suspected of corruption, smart public safety ministers called in the feds. And in the Rim Sector, that meant me.

I headed the Commonwealth Constabulary's Professional Compliance Bureau in the Rim Sector. My boss was at Constabulary Headquarters on Wyvern, several dozen light-years away, and that made me, a mere chief superintendent, the equivalent of a Marine Corps lieutenant colonel, something of a free agent in the badge and gun community. As usual, I wore one and didn't bother carrying the other.

When making high profile arrests, I brought Master Sergeant Destine Bonta along. A muscular woman with a drill instructor's charm, she could display an attitude capable of stripping paint from a starship's hull. And for all that Inspector Arno Galdi passed as everyone's favorite grandfather, mostly because of a legendary beard, no one looking into his eyes during a takedown mistook him for a fool.

Gendarmerie officers, whether in blue uniforms or civilian suits, scurried out of our way, though they stared at us until we vanished from sight around the next corner. None were foolish enough to speak, let alone demand we state our business. And since I knew where we could find Lieutenant General Gytha Goresson's office, we didn't need a guide. No one in the building expected us, and that's how I liked it.

There was nothing better than catching a bent cop off balance. It helped get a confession even the most incompetent prosecutor could turn into a life sentence on Parth. Goresson was the Cimmerian Gendarmerie's Chief of Operations, second only to General Dubnikov, the star system's top police officer. This arrest was one of my most high profile yet.

Not that it meant anything. Constabulary officers transferred to the Professional Compliance Bureau stayed there for the rest of their careers. We investigate other cops, Constabulary and planetary, the military, and politicians of every stripe. It meant we had to be the incorruptibles, the ones with nothing left to lose, the ones who weren't afraid of getting on anyone's wrong side and didn't care about consequences. We were the ones with no qualms about traveling from planet to planet and star system to star system, arresting those who should know better than to break the law.

Promotion meant leaving the Rim Sector, and I liked it here. I was particularly fond of my independence. My team and I shared space with the Constabulary's Rim Sector Headquarters at the heart of Howard's Landing, Cimmeria's capital, but I didn't take orders from the deputy chief constable, though I did my best to keep her sweet.

This investigation was one she really tried to ignore. Her mandate included making nice with star system police chiefs in the sector, and a Constabulary internal affairs officer arresting the Cimmerian Gendarmerie's number two would put a chill on that relationship.

General Dubnikov wouldn't enjoy us dragging his second in command out of Gendarmerie Headquarters in shackles. Still, he was smart enough to take it up with the star system's minister of public safety. Or he might remember that when a sniper assassinated Louis Sorne, the closest thing to living evil I've ever met, many in his service were revealed as irreparably corrupt.

Of course, he didn't know the shooter belonged to the Commonwealth Marine Corps and had, along with his partner, saved the better part of the Cimmerian government and the senior officials of most Rim Sector worlds from certain death. Lieutenant General Goresson being part of the anti-terrorism effort while secretly taking money from the terrorists' backers, only made it worse.

Everyone could be corrupted. The only difference between Goresson and me was the asking price. Mine would be a different outcome at age seventeen when the Pacifican State Security Police picked up my parents and younger brothers and 'disappeared' them into the detention system without a trace. Turn back time, spare my family, and promise me I'll finish growing up with them instead of running for sanctuary, and I'd sell out the Chief Constable himself.

Lieutenant General Goresson's price had been considerably lower. Family debts covered by back-channel payments, children admitted to elite schools, and private retirement funds topped up so she could live in enviable comfort.

She'd sold the three gold stars on her uniform collar to the highest bidder. Never mind it could have meant the end of Cimmeria's legally elected government.

Goresson didn't deserve a shred of pity, let alone respect. Perhaps that's why I felt such a rush. Arresting her after months of painstaking, covert investigation which uncovered the full depth of her depravity felt like a climax, though I knew her downfall was merely the start.

Most of my unit's teams were even now hunting down Goresson's co-conspirators, though my brief from the Cimmerian government stopped with the Gendarmerie's number two. Another advantage of working for a deputy chief constable trillions of kilometers away. I decided where

I stuck my nose. If high-ranking individuals dabbled in federal crimes, they became fair game.

The door to Goresson's office was open when we arrived. She sat behind her desk, comfortable as you please, chatting amiably with a pair of officers wearing a brigadier general's star on their collars. The sight made me smile even more because it proved she didn't have the slightest inkling her career was over, and with it, a privileged life as one of the star system's elite. It also meant my office and that of Deputy Chief Constable Maras, the Rim Sector commander who I kept appraised of my investigations out of enlightened self-interest, remained leak-free.

When she caught sight of me standing in the doorway, framed by Sergeant Bonta and Arno Galdi, her round face lost its color while her porcine eyes widened almost comically. It was the expression I usually saw on someone with a bad conscience. Innocent people and those with excellent acting skills tended to look puzzled. Both brigadier generals, a man and a woman, turned their heads to see what attracted Goresson's attention. They weren't on the bent cops list, at least not the one I was working from, and clearly did not understand why internal affairs officers from the federal police were standing at the door.

I pointed at them with splayed index and middle fingers. "Please leave. Now."

The man opened his mouth to protest, but when his eyes shifted, I knew Sergeant Bonta was slowly shaking her head and scowling. Arno stepped in to make room and gestured at the doorway.

"Best do what the chief wants. Otherwise, she might take an interest in your personal bank accounts. It could make your lives more interesting than you want."

I didn't know whether to laugh at the alacrity with which they obeyed or wonder whether we should see if they too were bent on a police general's salary. Once they'd left, I stepped in and looked Goresson straight in the eyes.

"I'm Chief Superintendent Caelin—"

"Everyone knows who the hell you are. How dare you intrude with such a lack of courtesy?"

She'd obviously decided to brazen it out now that the initial shock was wearing off. The higher up they were in the food chain, the more they tried that old ploy.

"—Morrow, Commanding Officer of the Commonwealth Constabulary's Rim Sector Professional Compliance Bureau. I am arresting you on charges of corruption, perverting the course of justice, and abuse of office. You do not have to say anything. But it may harm your defense if you do not mention when questioned something which you later rely on in court. Anything you do say may be given in evidence. You have the right to ask for assistance from the Cimmerian Gendarmerie Senior Officers' Association."

"Those charges are bullshit, Morrow."

"Do you understand what I just said?" She eventually gave me a curt nod after a long staring contest, which I won because I had more practice. "You can either come quietly, or Sergeant Bonta will shackle your wrists, after which she'll perp walk you to our car out front."

"I will do no such thing. And if you figure on perp walking me, think again."

"Surely an officer of your rank and decades in uniform must realize I'm here at the orders of the Rim Sector's Director of Prosecutions. Orders which, moreover, were countersigned by a federal judge, and with the full knowledge of Cimmerian Public Safety Minister Brunsvold. The evidence against you is incontrovertible and overwhelming. You're headed for pre-trial detention without bail in the naval base cellblock since the charges are federal, so you can forget about calling on your connections. I'm asking one last time. Will you come quietly, or would you rather do the perp walk? I don't care either way. Once we deliver you to the provost marshal, our job is done."

As I expected, Goresson chose dignity over a symbolic protest and walked out with us wearing her kepi and overcoat, as if we were heading to the Howard's Landing Inter-Service Club for drinks and a natter. We didn't stick around to see what she looked like in a detainee's orange jumpsuit, graciously provided by the base's military police contingent, after a full body cavity search.

Brunsvold, embarrassed that the Gendarmerie's second highest-ranking general proved to be thoroughly corrupt, wanted the federal justice system to make an example of her. Between today and when she left for a federal penitentiary after sentencing, Goresson would share her pre-trial detention with Army, Navy, and Marine Corps personnel serving time for minor infractions or waiting for their turn in front of a court-martial. It was a precipitous drop in living conditions.

Did I mention that some days I worried about enjoying my job too much?

— Two —

The Rim Sector Constabulary Group's headquarters was once the colonial government house before Cimmeria gained its independence. After the Cimmerian bureaucracy moved into newer accommodations, the Constabulary inherited a ten-story structure with offices designed to impress the peasantry when this place was still under Earth's direct rule.

My unit owned the tenth floor, or at least those parts not occupied by the building's environmental systems. Being summoned to the tenth was a signal for career-ending trouble since long before my arrival.

Our isolation from the rest of the Sector HQ staff and the subtle dread it engendered suited me. We lived under the same roof as the other Rim Sector divisions, but we were not part of their family. On the contrary.

I reported directly to Constabulary HQ just like Deputy Chief Constable Maras and could ignore her — provided I was prepared for greater ostracism and precious little by way of support. As a result, I treated her like a stand-in for my actual boss, DCC Hammett, which was why I stepped off the lift on the executive floor and let Arno and Sergeant Bonta head up to the tenth without me.

Maras' adjutant looked up as I entered the antechamber to her office. Though he didn't smile, neither did he give me the vaguely annoyed look any other chief superintendent would receive upon entering the holy of holies unbidden and unannounced.

I was the only senior officer in the building who enjoyed unfettered access to the DCC, something which irked my so-called colleagues just as much as my propensity for sniffing out bent cops. Maras liked to hear about any hint of malfeasance in her command, and I usually found out before anyone else. Hence, the open invitation.

"What can I do for you, sir?" His tone was carefully measured and devoid of emotion. He didn't much like me, and in that, he did not differ from those toiling away on the building's first nine floors.

"If the DCC is available, I thought she might be interested in hearing about General Goresson's arrest."

His eyes widened slightly. "General Goresson, the Gendarmerie's number two? You arrested her?"

Maras sure could sit on whatever I told her about my investigations. If her aide wasn't aware of Goresson…

"Indeed. I left her with the provost marshal for a stay in the naval brig. It'll be on the news nets by now."

He kept staring at me with astonishment while his fingers danced on the screen embedded in his desk, telling Maras I was here. Instead of a reply, the door to her office opened, and Maras herself ushered me in with a sly smile on her face.

"I gather it went well?" She pointed at the settee group on one side, sparing me the long walk to her desk. The office had once served as the colonial governor's reception room and could comfortably accommodate a squadron of Marine gunships. "General Dubnikov just called to tell me you extracted Goresson from Gendarmerie HQ without raising a ruckus."

We sat facing each other, and I nodded.

"She blustered at first, like most of them, but once she realized she had no friends left in high places, Goresson came along quietly. The provost marshal is thrilled at hosting such a high-ranking officer in his cellblock. Though when I told him he couldn't put Goresson through the same penal discipline as the service detainees, he seemed somewhat disappointed."

"No doubt. Any chance of her getting bail?"

I shook my head.

"Considering who she is, no. Not after Louis Sorne slipped away from house arrest with the help of crooked gendarmes. And she has no hope of being acquitted at trial. Those charges are airtight, and since it's a federal case, thanks to the Cimmerians realizing they shouldn't touch it with an antimatter prod, she can't buy herself a slap on the wrist. The Director of Prosecutions was almost dancing with glee when he signed the arrest warrant."

"Do you think he'll give her a deal?"

"No. Goresson can't offer us anything we don't already know about."

"I suppose congratulations are in order. This was a touchy case. Still, by all appearances, you and your team carried it off with aplomb, and I'll be sure to tell Maximilian Hammett since you don't crow about your successes. I do read the case report copies you pass me on the sly."

Since I couldn't do anything else, I inclined my head by way of thanks. Maras was one of the good guys and understood my unit represented a necessary evil.

"Now that you've finished with Goresson, may I assume no other sensitive cases currently await your personal touch?"

"Not that I know. Do you have something for me?"

She nodded.

"You've been to Mission Colony, right?"

"Once, but that was many years ago. My senior team lead, Superintendent Ange Rowan, took care of the Kristy Bujold business."

Ex-Assistant Commissioner Bujold, the former Commanding Officer of the 24th Constabulary Regiment, Mission Colony's planetary police, had shown a poor taste in friends a while back. Her own people found her in a compromising position, next to the body of a woman executed by persons unknown. That woman had subsequently been linked to a now-defunct political group with violent tendencies.

"Her replacement seems to be in hot water with the governor. Jeanne Peet sent me a complaint alleging Assistant Commissioner Elden Braband is rude, disrespectful, and insubordinate. He apparently behaves with contempt toward the governor, which, as you may recall, is an offense under Section 85 of the Commonwealth Constabulary Act. Now, these incidents occurred in private, so it's a 'she said' at this point, and we can quibble about the matter of insubordination, since Braband reports to me, not Governor Peet, but still."

I felt my eyebrows creep up in surprise. After Bujold took early retirement for the good of the service instead of facing disciplinary action, DCC Maras asked me to vet Bujold's proposed successor by running him through an informal and hush-hush professional compliance review. Braband was as clean as could be, though he suffered from a roving eye.

"A colonial governor leveling accusations at the new chief of police, one who'd never set foot on Mission before? That's a first for me, sir. Does Peet offer any details?"

"She is rather vague, but I don't dare dismiss it out of hand since there's likely much more than meets the eye. The Colonial Office has received a copy, and I daresay I'll hear from the Chief Constable within days. Naturally, I'd like to tell him you're checking out the situation on Mission Colony in person. I'll even ship you and your team there aboard *Benton Fraser*, which will cut down on travel time."

I usually enjoyed the freedom to take or leave cases based on my judgment about whether the PCB should investigate them unless DCC Hammett overrode me. But if Maras felt I should take this one on, I'd be a fool to say no and wait for a rocket from DCC Hammett, wondering why I wasn't already on Mission Colony. Besides, it was a reasonably quick run aboard a Constabulary cutter, and the VIP quarters were comfortable.

"Give us a day to wrap up the Goresson paperwork and pack our bags."

"You're taking Inspector Galdi and Sergeant Bonta?"

"They're available and have become my personal sensitive investigations team. Assistant Commissioner Braband will figure out why we're there. We can't avoid it, unlike the Goresson matter where we kept out of sight while building the case against her."

"Understood. I was hoping you could make Braband aware of Governor Peet's complaint in person rather than my sending a subspace message."

"Certainly, sir." If Maras was offering one of her precious cutters as our personal faster-than-light yacht, I could hardly refuse.

"Thank you, Caelin. *Benton Fraser* will wait for you at the naval end of Howard Landing's spaceport in twenty-four hours."

Her tone told me our conversation was over, and I climbed to my feet.

"With your permission, sir?"

"Enjoy the trip."

When I reached the tenth floor, I found Arno and Sergeant Bonta in the break room, enjoying a celebratory cup of coffee while they waited for me. I served myself and sat with them.

"Do either of you have urgent business on Cimmeria in the next three or four weeks?"

"Are we traveling off-world, Chief?" Arno asked.

"Mission Colony. Governor Peet complained about the behavior of the 24th Constabulary Regiment's Commanding Officer, Assistant Commissioner Elden Braband."

"What? We vetted him thoroughly. He's as honest and professional as they come."

"How could he have annoyed the governor so quickly?" Sergeant Bonta asked in her deep, resonant voice. "It has to be a record."

"Maras didn't say it in so many words, but I suspect she thinks something is seriously amiss within the colonial administration if a solid, well-regarded assistant commissioner is at loggerheads with the governor so soon after his arrival. She used the word contempt, as in punishable under Section 85, Insubordinate Behavior."

"Ah." Arno's face lit up with understanding. "The DCC smells something rotten across the light-years. We're not headed there just for Braband, are we?"

"Unofficially, no. I'm sure when the brief from PCB HQ finally comes in, it'll give us leeway to investigate the governor as well. But for public consumption, we're there because of the complaint."

DCC Hammett, also known as the Constabulary's Conscience, was nobody's fool. He'd been in this business for a long time and put more corrupt colonial governors, administrators, and other high-ranking officials behind bars than anyone else in the service.

Arno rubbed his hands with glee.

"I'll stock up on my favorites to while away the trip. A bit of quiet contemplation each way bookending a nice little colonial investigation sounds like heaven after the grubbiness of Goresson's fall from grace."

"Will we see the actual complaint, sir?"

"A copy should be in my message queue by now."

— Three —

Arno was happy with a few days in hyperspace reading pre-diaspora novels, enjoying a glass of whiskey after the evening meal, and generally taking his ease. Meanwhile, Sergeant Bonta spent a lot of time in *Benton Fraser*'s gym, either exercising or sparring with all comers. But I suffered from a minor problem no one else knew about.

It wasn't an enormous deal in the grand scheme of things. But prolonged time in the upper hyperspace bands, such as those traveled by the Constabulary's fast cutters, triggered vivid dreams that stayed with me for a long time. And not just nonsensical ones either, but repressed memories surfacing while I was at my most vulnerable.

This trip, once again, I kept reliving that awful day the Pacifican State Security Police came for my family when I was nothing more than a gawky, seventeen-year-old girl with few prospects in life. My parents, university professors, had been deemed dissidents and stripped of jobs, honors, and civic rights for denouncing the Pacifican government's corrupt and heavy-handed so-called 'progressive' policies. I could still see it crystal clear with my mind's eye as if it were projected in three dimensions for my entertainment. And that's when I was awake. Sleeping while traveling at the upper edge of hyperspace put me right back there and then.

Just before the evening meal, my mother had sent me to buy a few items. When I returned to the street where we lived, I saw my parents and younger siblings dragged out of our apartment building by police goons and bundled into black skimmers. Dad had been dreading that it might eventually happen after watching so many of his friends in the opposition movement disappear when the Proggies tired of them.

The day I turned seventeen, he told me that if ever the cops came for him, I must head for the Commonwealth recruiting office and enlist on the spot in whichever service would take me. It was the only way off Pacifica for 'enemies of the people.'

When the skimmers peeled off, I'd ducked back into the doorway of the dilapidated flophouse at the far corner of the block of rundown apartment buildings. Some of them were so old, they dated back to the days of the first colonial settlement.

The street was empty, though I knew frightened citizens had been peeking through scarred, grimy windows, wondering which of the many unwanted, mostly destitute inhabitants of the slums had overstepped their bounds and attracted the cruel attentions of the government's enforcers.

Once the sound of skimmer fans faded in the distance, I uncurled my limbs and rose on shaky legs, tears streaming down my face. Those taken by Pacifican State Security were never seen again. That meant I was, for every intent and purpose, alone in the world, my parents and younger brothers now among the walking dead whose very names would be wiped from public registries.

I knew they would look for me as well. The secret police preferred keeping families together so that they could eradicate dissent, root and branch. Since my father qualified as a thorn in the government's side, they'd want to make sure an offshoot such as I couldn't continue rabble-rousing.

Panic wrapped its icy hand around my pounding heart, and I fought the impulse to run. Entering the apartment was obviously out of the question. They'd have left a sensor to alert them of my return. Besides, staying in the lower town was a bad idea because my face would be plastered across the news nets shortly. It meant half of the population would denounce me on sight while the other half would ignore me to the point of behaving as if I weren't there lest the police accuse them of helping a political criminal.

Seventeen years old and deemed a political criminal by a government that still preached the virtues of democracy and a free society. My father had been right to voice his concern with the regime. However, I wished it hadn't entailed dismissal from the university and our family's exile among the citizen masses, living on the dole, unemployed and unemployable — the first level of punishment for dissidents. There was no other level between that and vanishing into the Pacifican prison system from which few returned.

I carefully placed the shopping bag on the ground and pulled out the few items that fit in my pockets. Were it not for my mother finding herself short of ingredients for supper, I would have been at home when the State Security thugs came ringing. I emerged from the doorway's shadows and forced myself to walk with a lazy, unconcerned stride as I made my way toward downtown Hadley and the Commonwealth Services recruiting office. I had no idea what I should do for the night other than find somewhere I could hide until morning from people who might associate me with Professor Atticus Morrow.

Full dark had thrown its unhealthy cloak over the streets by the time I saw a mass of vegetation, like a curtain wall around a medieval fort, between buildings that were in better repair and cleaner than the ones around my now former neighborhood. It could only be the park near the recruiting office. Passers-by paid me no attention, and I silently blessed my mother for insisting that even though they'd fallen in the world, her children should always look and behave like taxpayers.

The air under the black canopy of native and Earth trees was cold and musty and reminded me of better times with such suddenness that the tears came once more. I found a secluded spot among the bushes far from the paths winding through the small, but dense nature reserve, incongruously planted on one side of a commercial plaza.

The night I spent shivering when I wasn't sobbing silently remained indelibly seared into my memory. When dawn broke over Hadley, I crawled out of my damp, uncomfortable lair and headed for the plaza where I would find my only chance at salvation. Moments after reaching the park's edge, I spotted a gray skimmer coming around the corner. It whizzed through open gates into a courtyard behind the recruiting office. I waited for a few minutes, until the lights came on inside, then left the cover of the trees, braving the chill rain that had started moments earlier.

The man inside must have noticed me because he unlatched the door and slid it aside. He studied me with his dark brown eyes for a few seconds.

"Come in, child."

Once I was inside, he locked the door again and led me through a waiting room with recruiting posters on the walls, above self-service terminals, and a few hard seats and into a short passageway with several doors on either side. One of them opened into a small office kitchen.

"Sit." He pointed at the clean table. "You look like you need nourishment and a warm tea."

The man's manner seemed strangely matter of fact as if he routinely offered prospective applicants a free meal. He was middle-aged, with graying, short hair, a craggy face that spoke of years on the frontier, and kind eyes. Though he still seemed fit, his body strained at the gray uniform tunic in a few spots.

"We'll talk after you've stopped shivering. You're perfectly safe here, child." With those words, he busied himself at an autochef and, moments later, placed a tray in front of me. As the aroma of eggs, meat, and tubers hit my nostrils, my stomach rumbled loudly, and I felt my cheeks redden with embarrassment. The man merely chuckled.

"I've heard it before. Now take your time." He poured himself a cup of coffee and sat across from me. "I'm Sergeant First Class Hank Beddows, of the Commonwealth

Constabulary. My Navy and Marine Corps colleagues will be here later. We each take our turn coming in at sunrise, in case someone like you shows up, needing a hot meal and a way out."

"You mean, you know who I am?"

"I can probably figure out what you are, child. Knowing who you are will depend on what you intend. We get folks trying to escape the Security Police in here regularly enough that we make sure we can do something for them — not necessarily out of the kindness of our hearts, mind you. None of us in the Commonwealth Armed Services like the government here, and we figure that folks they designate as political criminals are the good guys most of the time. Strictly speaking, if I find out you're wanted by the police, I'd have to call them and turn you in."

Sheer terror struck me. It must have shown in my face because he smiled gently.

"I said, strictly speaking. This office is legally part of the Pacifica Naval Station and thus out of bounds for local law enforcement. It's sovereign Commonwealth territory. Pacifican law doesn't apply here, so we don't recognize the concept of political crimes."

I nodded, my heart settling back into place.

"The way this works is that I check you out to make sure you're a true political fugitive and not wanted for something we recognize, such as murder, theft, fraud, etcetera. If you're clean enough for our purposes, we can discuss enlisting you. Once we swear you in, Security Police can't do a damned thing, though they might try to kidnap you. But that can't happen on the grounds of the naval station since we don't let them past the front gate. The trick is getting you there from here. Then, it's away with you on the next naval transport coming through this star system."

"Are you telling me the truth? It sounds too much like a miracle."

He held up his hand and placed it palm down over his heart.

"We consider it doing the Almighty's work, miss, and our officers back us up. Even if we can't save everyone, we save those who show up on our doorstep. You may not like uniformed service, or you may wash out of recruit training, but by then, you'll be away from here, and we won't send you back. Those who serve honorably, even if only for a single hitch, will have repaid what we do here many times over."

"Then, I'd like to enlist, sir."

Beddows chuckled.

"That sounded pretty determined. And it's sergeant, not sir. Let's check you out first, though. If you're wanted for something truly criminal, then I'd have to see."

"I'm not, sir — sorry, Sergeant. My name is Caelin Morrow, and I'm seventeen years old. My father is Atticus Morrow, my mother is Ines Morrow, and my brothers are Pietro and Paolo. The police took them last night."

"And what did your family do to attract the attention of the Security Police?"

"My father is a dissident. He taught history and political science at Pacifica University until he became too outspoken and was fired. We ended up on the dole in the lower town."

"Let me guess. Your dad didn't stop speaking out against the regime, and they finally got tired of hearing him."

"Yes, Sergeant."

"Follow me. I'll check up on you."

Without waiting for my response, he led me into a neighboring office where he sat at a neat desk and turned on a console.

"Sit." He waved at a padded chair, eyes on the screen. After a few minutes, a knowing smile spread on his face. "There's an all-points bulletin out on you, Miss Morrow. You're wanted for treason against the Pacifica government and for helping a well-known political criminal, your father, spread lies and dissent against the regime. Welcome to our recruiting office. Which service would you be interested in joining?"

"The one you belong to."

"The Commonwealth Constabulary? Why?"

"You're the one saving me, so I figure I owe a hitch in your branch."

He laughed softly.

"That's a better reason than many I've heard."

The frightened girl who'd enlisted in the Commonwealth Constabulary that day was now, decades later, a senior police officer enjoying the comforts of the VIP suite aboard a Constabulary cutter far from her birth planet.

I never saw Sergeant Beddows again nor did I ever set foot on Pacifica since the day I left aboard a Navy transport, wearing Constabulary gray as Constable (Recruit) Caelin Morrow. My personal file carries a notation that I cannot, under any circumstances, travel officially or unofficially to or through the Pacifica star system. My arrest warrant for political crimes has never been rescinded, and I never found out what happened to my family.

Looking back on that defining experience years after I became a seasoned investigator, I understood my joining the Professional Compliance Bureau hadn't been an accident. Rooting out evil among those sworn to serve and protect wasn't so much a job, but a calling.

— Four —

I felt nothing but relief when *Benton Fraser* dropped out of FTL at the Mission Colony hyperlimit. The cutter's crew was unfailingly polite. Yet because of what Arno, Sergeant Bonta, and I represented, they left us to our own devices. And traveling in a small starship with fellow Constabulary members who fell silent whenever I appeared got old fast.

Still, the cutter's skipper, a youngish superintendent, entertained me one evening and offered me bridge privileges, which I used only once or twice. I didn't know how my companions felt and wouldn't ask. We never discussed our status as the service's social pariahs.

A few hours later, we landed at the cargo end of the spaceport serving Mission Colony's capital, Ventano, where a gray Constabulary staff skimmer was waiting. *Benton Fraser* had called ahead, asking we be met by a car from the 24th and taken to regimental headquarters. At my request, the cutter's communications watchkeeper merely identified us as a staff assistance team from Rim Sector HQ, though even that would cause a minor storm.

Unannounced staff assistance visits usually either meant a snap inspection or HQ heard of problems which could range from rusty kitchen cutlery to heavy weapons going walkabout or worse. But it beat letting the 24th's Operations Center know ahead of time the Firing Squad was on its way. And not just any PCB team, but one led by the Lady High Executioner herself.

The skimmer's driver, a twenty-something corporal, snapped to attention as we approached and saluted. He seemed unsure which one of us was the most senior since, as usual, we wore civilian clothes, though we'd brought uniforms with us, just in case. I gave him a formal, officer-style nod.

"I'm Chief Superintendent Morrow. These are Inspector Galdi," I pointed at my colleagues in turn, "and Master Sergeant Bonta. We're from Rim Sector HQ."

"Yes, sir. Welcome to Mission Colony. My name is Caffrey. If you'll climb in, I'll have you at regimental headquarters in a few minutes. It's near the spaceport."

The Ventano landing strip was at the base of a long peninsula pointing eastward into the fifteen hundred kilometers wide Tyrellian Sea separating Mission's two equatorial continents, Nanshe and Ashima. The city itself covered most of that peninsula with seaports on either side, one for cargo, the other for leisure. Almost none of those ships sailed beyond the Tyrellian, and for excellent reasons. All of Mission's chief cities and towns were either on Nanshe's eastern shores or Ashima's west coast.

The planet-encircling oceans separating both from the polar icecaps were among the most savage across human-settled worlds. On Earth, the worst of the Antarctic Ocean latitudes were nicknamed the Screaming Sixties. On Mission, they called the equivalent the Godless Wastes. Those few settlements established on less hospitable littorals were mostly fly-in communities, though a handful of coastal tramps braved the frequent storms from time to time when conditions were right.

As human-settled worlds went, Mission didn't count among the worst, though its balmiest climate was within twenty degrees north and south of the equator, and that wasn't much warmer than Cimmeria's mid-latitudes. It meant cool summers and chilly winters thanks to an almost twenty-four-degree axial tilt.

Sun-tanning on the beach and skinny dipping in the middle sea weren't listed as attractions in the tourist brochures, never mind the pseudo-pliosaurs cruising offshore, looking for tasty surface swimmers. And yes, the local wildlife could digest human tissue.

Less than five minutes later, our car passed through an automated guard post with a large sign announcing we were entering the 24th Constabulary Regiment's Ventano Station, housing Regimental Headquarters and its 1st and Support Battalions.

We crossed an open parade square before pulling up in front of a three-story stone and glass building overlooking the end of the northern fjord separating Ventano from the Benden Peninsula. The latter reached out a thousand kilometers toward Ashima and protected the Tyrellian Sea from the worst of the globe-spanning arctic ocean.

As we climbed out of the car, leaving our bags behind for the moment, a slim, dark-haired woman in her late thirties wearing a chief inspector's three diamonds on her gray uniform collar came through the door.

I recognized her as Kalle Wuori, the regimental adjutant, from the personnel files I'd studied during our trip here. She, like the corporal, hesitated for a moment while trying to identify who of us was senior.

"Chief Inspector Wuori, I believe? I'm Chief Superintendent Caelin Morrow. With me are Inspector Arno Galdi and Master Sergeant Destine Bonta."

Unlike our driver, Wuori recognized my name, and I saw the shock in her brown eyes. Further proof came when, instead of welcoming us, she blurted out, "I was told you were a staff assistance team."

"We are." I gestured at the open doorway. "If you could tell us where we can drop our bags and then take us to see Assistant Commissioner Braband, I'd be grateful."

"I arranged for rooms in the senior staff quarters, sir. Unless you'd rather take hotel rooms in town."

"Staff quarters are perfectly fine, Chief Inspector."

"In that case, why don't I ask Corporal Caffrey to bring your luggage to your rooms?"

I gave her as friendly a smile as I could. "That would be lovely. Thank you."

She nodded at Caffrey, who snapped to attention, saluted, then climbed aboard his car.

"If you'll follow me." Wuori turned on her heels and re-entered the HQ building.

The lobby was nowhere near as ornate as Sector HQ's, but then the entire Mission Colony Constabulary base was purpose-built from scratch twenty or so years ago based on a utilitarian design like that used for permanent military installations. She led us up a wide staircase and along a carpeted second story corridor to the northern end where the view was presumably the best. A door beneath a simple sign that said 'Commanding Officer' stood open at the corridor's far end.

Wuori preceded us through the doorway, saying, "Sir, the staff assistance team announced by *Benton Fraser* this morning has arrived."

We followed her in, and I joined the adjutant a regulation three paces in front of Braband's desk while Arno and Sergeant Bonta kept back.

"Commissioner, I'm Chief Superintendent Morrow. I head the Rim Sector Professional Compliance Bureau."

"Good heavens, I wasn't expecting the Firing Squad!" Braband's pale eyebrows shot up, and he stared at me with light blue eyes set in a tanned face framed by blond hair and a narrow, graying beard. I knew from his file he was nearing fifty but looked at least ten years younger.

"No one ever expects us, sir." I kept a straight face, even though one of Arno's favorite comedy skits, dating back to pre-diaspora times, flashed before my eyes, and introduced my team. "Deputy Chief Constable Maras received a complaint and asked that we look into it. Perhaps we can talk in private."

Braband glanced at Wuori, who nodded and left, closing the door behind her. Then he stood, proving his height matched Bonta's, though his build was more muscular, and gestured at the oval conference table taking up one side of the room, near a bank of windows overlooking the North Fjord.

"It's probably best if we sit there." Braband took his accustomed chair at the head of the table and watched us settle in with curious eyes. "I'm listening, Chief Superintendent."

"Governor Peet submitted a complaint to DCC Maras, alleging your conduct toward her was rude, disrespectful, and insubordinate, which meets the definition of contempt as per Section 85 of the Commonwealth Constabulary Act."

Braband reared up.

"What? We've experienced disagreements and the odd harsh words in private, but I've always treated Peet with the respect a governor deserves."

His reaction struck me as genuine. He clearly didn't believe he behaved in a manner warranting PCB attention.

"After your predecessor so thoroughly screwed up, the DCC asked my office to vet you before your appointment. It wouldn't do the service much good if she sent two indiscreet commanding officers in a row. We found nothing in your past that might even hint at a hidden propensity for unacceptable behavior toward senior officials. Now, I know from long experience that cops, especially those with oak leaves around their diamonds, don't just wake up one day and decide they'll butt heads with governors. It takes time for Constabulary members to develop discreditable conduct patterns.

"By the time we're brought in, we always find warning signs in their professional and personal behavior patterns dating years back. This makes Governor Peet's accusations puzzling. I know we missed nothing when we vetted you. The DCC thinks something happened between you and the governor since you took command of the 24th Regiment. We're here to find out why she complained."

A look of relief crossed Braband's patrician features as he sat back. It, too, seemed unfeigned.

"May I say I'm glad you're not here guns blazing to arrest me like you did Joel Haylian. At the time, I was at Sector HQ, and the senior Financial Crimes officers couldn't stop talking about your grand entrance for weeks, even after Joel resigned in disgrace."

I gave him an amused smile. "You're lucky. I got my monthly taste of Firing Squad theater before leaving Cimmeria."

"Lieutenant General Goresson." He nodded. "I heard the PCB took her in on behalf of the Gendarmerie."

"I see the Constabulary gossip network still reaches the furthest corners of the Rim Sector. Since we've established we're not here to end your career, unless we uncover evidence of discreditable behavior you've hidden from us, perhaps we can discuss your relationship with Governor Peet."

"Chief Superintendent, I can assure you I'm as pure as the driven snow, although I'm less sure of the governor."

His statement didn't particularly surprise me. Peet's unexpected accusation stemmed from something out of the ordinary. Perhaps this was it.

"You've been looking into her conduct?"

He shook his head.

"Not exactly. I know enough to leave that sort of thing for the PCB and believe me, I've called on your branch a few times during my career when I found funny business in my unit."

"As we saw from reviewing your confidential record, another clue you're not the sort who would take a detour into darkness. So, what's the issue?"

He didn't immediately answer. Instead, he stared out at the fjord as if parsing his next words.

"I think the governor's unhappiness with me stems from my becoming intimate with a member of her staff."

Arno and I exchanged a glance. Roving eye, indeed.

— Five —

"Her name is Mayleen Allore, and she's the governor's social secretary, a locally engaged employee, not a member of the Colonial Office. We met during a reception to mark my arrival and hit it off right away." Braband kept staring out the window as if discussing his personal life with PCB officers was somehow embarrassing. It wasn't like we wanted a graphic depiction of his most intimate moments.

"Naturally, Mayleen and I engage in pillow talk, and she tells me about Government House goings-on. Gossip, you could call it. Nothing that would make me call your office. But things seem a little off — at least to a cop's suspicious mind. As a result, I've been poking around here and there, engaging in idle chitchat with Government House staffers, and hanging around with colony notables."

"Did you find anything?"

He glanced at me and shook his head.

"Nothing actionable. Peet has been here for a few years. She's reasonably well-liked by the local upper crust. I've not picked up much grumbling about her from the colonial administration, and the political commentators seem to think she's doing a decent job. Not stellar, mind you, but vanishingly few governors appointed by Earth are rising stars in my experience. She's a career bureaucrat who treads lightly and lets her chief administrator, another old Colonial Office functionary, manage the day-to-day business of governing Mission Colony."

His description sounded familiar.

"This place suffered from a little political radicalism problem a while back, didn't it? The Mission Colony Freedom Collective, I believe they called themselves?"

Yes, I was disingenuous. I knew perfectly well what occurred and who did it, though that was another thing Arno, Sergeant Bonta, and I never discussed.

Braband nodded. "I read the files when I took over. That problem evaporated days after a sniper shot and killed the Collective's leader. When his spouse died at the hands of an assassin soon after that, the entire movement fell apart. Or so our intelligence analysts believe. There were a few more deaths and one unexplained explosion on the Benden Peninsula that destroyed an old family villa, but no one's heard a peep from those radicals since. We never found the perpetrators and suspect they were off-worlders who left this star system undetected. Since it happened so fast, little if anything registered with the public at large and Peet didn't need to involve herself."

"I see." My friends in Naval Intelligence would be happy to find out they left no one the wiser on Mission Colony. "Sir, could I ask you for a favor?"

Braband let out an involuntary chortle. "The PCB wants a favor from me? I'd be mad to refuse."

"So far, only you and Chief Inspector Wuori are aware we're from the Firing Squad. I hope she's not put the word about after leaving this office."

"Kalle? Perish the thought. She's hardly talkative at the best of times, and she'll be waiting for my lead to announce your presence among us."

"Then please don't mention who we work for. Keep calling us a staff assistance team helping you deal with certain matters related to policing on Mission Colony. It's nothing less than the truth."

"Some of my senior officers will make the connection, unfortunately. You're not exactly anonymous in this sector, Chief Superintendent Morrow, nor is the rest of your team, I suspect."

Fame cut both ways, as I understood only too well. Most of the time, it helped. But when we wanted discretion, not so much.

"If someone figures out who we are, please tell them they'd be helping the 24th Regiment by going along with our cover. We're here so we can find out why Governor Peet complained about you, nothing more. I rarely handle straightforward discreditable conduct investigations myself, Commissioner."

"What the chief means," Arno Galdi spoke for the first time, "is that she only comes out for the most politically sensitive cases and lets us deal with ordinary corrupt cops."

Braband studied Arno for a few seconds as if he were a statue suddenly coming alive. Mere inspectors speaking out of turn to assistant commissioners on behalf of chief superintendents were unheard of in police regiments. But

Arno wasn't an ordinary inspector. He'd racked up more time as a PCB investigator than anyone else in my unit. If he judged it was time for an intervention, then intervene he would, and I rarely countermanded him.

"I suppose that's a relief, Inspector." Braband turned his attention on me again. "What now?"

"Considering it's late in the afternoon, I'd like to call it a day, unpack, and enjoy a drink in the regimental mess. Perhaps we could eat the evening meal together. Show the 24th we're on the same wavelength, protecting the honor of the service."

Braband tilted his head to one side as he decided if I was sincere or sarcastic. Sincerity won out because he gave me a determined nod.

"A splendid idea, Chief Superintendent. And the drinks will be on me."

We left a thoughtful Assistant Commissioner Braband and headed for the low-slung, two-story accommodations block across the parade square from regimental HQ. When we were well out of anyone's earshot, Arno gave me a sideways glance.

"Am I right in assuming your approach with the commissioner is a variation on giving him enough rope to hang himself, Chief? I certainly can't see you exonerating Braband without further inquiries."

Arno knew me about as well as I knew myself after working so many politically charged cases together. Yes, we'd vetted Braband before his appointment, but that didn't mean we wouldn't look at him again considering Mission Colony's environment and conditions.

"Pretty much. Let's hope Braband's not a paranoid who'll make the same conclusion."

"Judging by how relieved he looked when you told him he wasn't the focus of our inquiries, I'd say we're in the clear for now."

Our individual suites were on the second floor of the building, in the senior officers' wing, and lacked for nothing — bedroom, sitting room, kitchenette, and of course, full private bathroom. We were the only occupants in that section, which meant Sergeant Bonta could set up a secure working area for us.

I found my bag on one of the chairs and quickly unpacked, then locked my weapons in the suite's safe. There was a time when I rarely went around armed, but more recently, I've been a lot less cavalier with my personal safety. The Rim Sector's political stability was deteriorating more rapidly than ever, and those of us in the Commonwealth services were increasingly prime targets for radicals, malcontents, and organized criminals such as cartels flexing their muscles.

My friends in Naval Intelligence had warned me a while back this would happen, but my complacency wasn't shattered until the terrorism campaign on Cimmeria erupted. However, here on a Constabulary Regiment's base, I didn't need a blaster on the hip. My clothes were loose enough that I could do so without discomfort, but I still don't feel quite right with the extra bulk and weight. Arno and Sergeant Bonta didn't suffer from my adaptation problems and always carried their sidearms.

Half an hour later, we met in the lobby and headed for the all-ranks mess. Anyone wanting a commission in the Constabulary starts off in the ranks and must at least become a corporal before applying to the Academy. It meant we weren't quite as hung up about separate messing facilities for officers, senior non-coms, and junior enlisted members as the military.

Or at least the military outside the Special Forces community. I remembered the all-ranks Pegasus Club at Fort Arnhem on Caledonia with fondness. The fort was where I earned my Pathfinder wings and spent a busy two years as Constabulary liaison non-commissioned officer with one of the squadrons. But I mostly kept quiet about that time. Not by choice. The missions I was on will remain classified until the universe collapses into a black hole.

We made our way to the bar without problems thanks to Arno's nose for such things, but it was almost empty. A few off-duty non-coms were clustered around a table, talking in quiet tones. They gave us the once-over, but their stares didn't linger. By now, most people on base would know about the staff assistance team from Sector HQ. As a former sergeant, I understood just how well the non-com grapevine worked.

Braband hadn't shown up yet, so we took a table by the window and used its embedded screen to order and pay for our drinks. A human waiter in black trousers and a white shirt appeared a few minutes later with a laden tray. He bestowed a pleasant smile on us.

"Welcome to the Steele Club. You must be the snag hunters from Cimmeria."

Bonta, who sat with her back to the man, and I exchanged glances. Her lips formed the words 'Steele Club' and 'snag hunters' while she put on a puzzled expression. The waiter either didn't notice or chose not to. He served our drinks and withdrew.

"What was that?" Bonta asked.

"Snag hunter is probably a local colloquialism for staff assistance team," Arno replied, examining his foamy ale mug. "And I believe the gentleman in the portrait hanging over the fireplace is Major General Sir Samuel Benfield Steele, a famous pre-diaspora police officer."

"Trust you to fish such an obscure piece of knowledge from that capacious database you call a brain." I raised my gin and tonic in salute.

"Considering our beloved service adopted many of its traditions from old Earth constabularies, especially the Royal Canadian Mounted Police, I'm shocked neither of you is aware who Sam Steele was."

Bonta scoffed. "I bet you stumbled over the club's name during our passage from Cimmeria and looked it up. We know how much of an information ferret you are."

Arno placed his hand over his heart.

"You wound me deeply, my dear sergeant. But you'd be familiar with Sam Steele if you'd read the full info package on the 24th Constabulary Regiment, handily available from *Benton Fraser*'s library. This club has existed for several years."

Movement at the entrance caught my eye. Braband, thank the Almighty. When Arno and Sergeant Bonta started tossing good-natured barbs at each other, it never stopped.

"Here comes our host, so let's put the debate to rest, shall we? I wouldn't want a man who's probably quite proud of his unit to find out none of us were familiar with this club's patron saint."

"I was," Arno mumbled through his beard. "Can't help it if you two don't read."

When Braband neared our table, I made as if to stand, but he waved me down with a friendly smile and sat across from Arno.

"I trust you're settled in?"

"We are. Nice quarters."

"They were renovated two years ago. Most of my senior officers live in the town with their families, so we use that block of rooms for ranking visitors. And we don't see many of those." The waiter appeared as if by magic and put a tall glass of amber pilsner in front of Braband. "Ah, thank you, Emil."

"Always a pleasure, Commissioner." He bowed his head respectfully and left.

"Word of our arrival made the rounds pretty quickly, it seems. Emil called us the snag hunters from Cimmeria."

Braband let out a bark of laughter.

"That would be my regimental sergeant major. It's what he calls folks from higher headquarters who show up unannounced offering assistance."

I gave him a sardonic look.

"As in the most frightening words ever spoken are, we're from HQ, and we're here to help?"

"Precisely. Mission Colony is one of the sector's furthest backwaters. When Cimmeria pays attention to us, we worry."

I raised my glass.

"You shouldn't be this time. We are here to help. So, tell me — what's happening in Government House that doesn't smell quite right?"

— Six —

"Did you ever hear of a company called Aeternum?"

I shook my head. "No."

"I'm not surprised. It hasn't been operating on Mission Colony for long — less than two years, I believe. Aeternum is owned by something called Pure Breath Incorporated, which in turn belongs to the Honorable Commonwealth Corporation zaibatsu via several holding companies. The cut-outs and shells separating Aeternum from ComCorp are clearly designed to give the latter legal distancing. It took me weeks of research before I made the connections."

Arno and I glanced at each other. Our last investigation involving ComCorp, on Aquilonia Station, almost cost me my life.

"What does this Aeternum do?"

"Pharmaceutical research and development, which is all they'll tell anyone. Aeternum runs a laboratory complex about an hour's drive south of Ventano or twenty minutes by aircar. The lab's security arrangements make my base look like an amusement park. I'd need a warrant signed by a federal superior court judge, Earth Division, just to get past the guard post."

"Sounds very hush-hush."

"There's an obscene amount of money in legal pharmaceuticals, Chief, and a lot of intellectual property theft between companies."

Braband nodded. "There most certainly is, Inspector. And a lot of political influence. An obscene amount if you ask me."

"This is where Government House comes in, I presume?"

"It is. The man who runs Aeternum's operations on Mission is a Luca Derzin. He's an Arcadian by birth and a ComCorp creature by career choice. And he spends a lot of time socializing with Jeanne Peet, whose colonial administration regulates the private sector in this star system, including Aeternum's operations."

"Business lobbying is almost as old an occupation as prostitution," Arno said in a philosophical tone.

"Considering they're both pretty much the same thing…" Sergeant Bonta shrugged before taking a sip of her wine.

"No doubt," Braband said. "But the governor seems a lot chummier with Derzin than with any other corporate executive in town."

"Any signs of possible corruption?"

"No. But I can't help feel uneasy."

"Does anything else strike you as slightly off?"

He opened his mouth to reply, then raised a hand and fished his communicator from a tunic pocket.

"Braband."

"Operations, sir. There's been an incident at Government House. Amaris Tosh, the governor's chief of staff, was found dead in her office by the social secretary a few minutes ago. The regular guard detail is securing the scene. CSI is on the way."

"Any preliminary indication of how she died?"

"Unable to tell, but the guard sergeant thinks something isn't right, which is why he called it in. Based on the video feed, I concur and recommend we treat this as a suspicious death."

Braband stared at his communicator's screen for a few moments, then nodded.

"Agreed."

"That's it, sir."

"Braband, out." He glanced up at me. "Amaris is, or rather was the governor's chief of staff. She was another career Colonial Office bureaucrat, but her tenure predates Peet's arrival. The guard detail belongs to my HQ Battalion's security company."

"Who will investigate the incident?"

"Detectives from the Major Crimes Unit, also part of the HQ battalion."

"Could I make a suggestion, Commissioner?"

He nodded.

"Sure."

"Since Amaris Tosh died under suspicious circumstances inside Government House, your friend Mayleen is at the very least a witness. If Tosh's death isn't from natural causes, she might even become a person of interest. Because the governor has a beef with you, Peet could raise the conflict of interest flag. And you're the star system's chief of police, meaning there's no Constabulary investigator available who isn't under your command, except for the three of us."

"Meaning I should give you the case?"

"Why not? You'll stay a step ahead of Peet, and we can sleuth inside Government House without raising questions."

He kept his eyes on me as he mulled over my proposal.

"When is the last time any of you investigated a suspicious death?"

"It hasn't been that long. Homicides feature in some of our more complicated cases, and when the PCB is running the show, we become our own homicide squad if necessary. We'll need support from your people, of course." When he didn't immediately reply, I figured I should sweeten the pot. "Look at it this way. If we're working the Tosh case, are we really Firing Squad inquisitors sniffing around federal officials? It's a great deflection, and who says Tosh's death isn't in some way connected to your suspicions?"

"Very well. The case is yours, Chief Superintendent. I'll put out a notice you're the senior investigating officer."

"Then I suppose our meal will be delayed. Can we borrow a car to take us there?"

"I'll see you're assigned a permanent car and driver. Since the Operations Center has already alerted the forensics team, it'll likely be there before you. I'll personally make sure the team lead, Inspector Kosta, knows you're the SIO."

"In that case, we'll return to our quarters and fetch our gear. If the driver can pick us up there?"

"Done."

The gear in question was my personal weapon since Arno and Sergeant Bonta had no qualms about entering the Steele Club armed, despite tradition forbidding weapons in a Constabulary mess. We didn't bring murder kits with us, seeing as how we didn't expect a suspicious death to fall in our laps within hours of arrival. I stood, imitated by my companions.

"We'll be off then, sir. Where can I reach you once we finish at the scene?"

"You carry issue communicators?"

"Yes."

"Patch them into the operations net before leaving the base. When you're done, link in again, and they'll put you through."

"You live on the base?"

"The CO of the 24th has an official residence, but I prefer the townhouse I'm renting. The residence is for official functions only. I value my privacy, Chief Superintendent, and yes, I know, in a suspicious death investigation, there is no such thing as privacy. *If* this it is truly suspicious."

"Did Tosh have any reason to commit suicide or potentially fatal health issues?"

He shook his head. "I wouldn't know. She was always so grounded in the present and vivacious."

"Then we'll find out for you."

Mission Colony's Government House was a smaller but no less ornate version of the complex that now served as Rim Sector HQ. However, it was successfully holding Ventano's urban sprawl at bay thanks to an extensive, tree-lined property surrounded by a forged iron fence. A simple Constabulary checkpoint at the main gate kept the unwashed masses from invading Governor Peet's privacy.

The constable on duty waved our staff car, driven by Corporal Caffrey, through on the strength of our identification beacon. Once inside the enclosure, I couldn't help but compare it to the sprawling Howard's Landing estates owned by wealthy Cimmerians. Whatever damage the occupying Shrehari inflicted on the colony the previous century, no sign of it marked what was clearly a venerable structure and not a modern, quickly built stone and concrete monstrosity.

We didn't speak a word during the trip, aware Corporal Caffrey not only possessed two ears but presumably a functioning brain between them. Not that I suspected Braband would spy on us, but why take chances? In our line of business, the slightest ambiguous word could cause a stampede.

The main building, four stories of it, was clad in the same grayish pink granite one saw across Ventano, but its grim facade was liberally studded with balconies and topped with a verdigris copper roof. Several smaller one and two-story structures surrounded it at discrete intervals. The largest of them, hidden behind tall hedges, was the governor's official residence, Ventano Hall. Most of the colony's administrative functions were carried out in modern low-rise structures lining the streets outside Government House, but the entire star system was governed from this spot.

I couldn't remember the last time someone was murdered inside what should be an entire world's most secure building or at least one of them. Suicides, sure, but not murders. Nothing of the sort had happened since I took over the sector PCB, which would naturally be informed of such events if not necessarily involved in the investigation.

A uniformed Constabulary member pointed our car at a roped-off parking area reserved for the police. When we climbed out, a sergeant came up to us, and politely asked for our credentials. We produced them while I identified myself as the newly appointed SIO. Apparently, he'd already received word from the Operations Center. If nothing else, Braband ran a tight ship.

"Yes, sir. You and your team are expected. The forensics people are already on site." He gestured at a young constable standing by the open main door. "Lee will take you there."

"Thank you, Sergeant."

He raised his hand to his brow in salute, even though I was in civilian clothes. "Sir."

The constable led us through a grand, three stories high, marble-floored lobby lit by a chandelier that would have seemed ostentatious in the Versailles Palace on Earth — at least based on imagery I saw long ago. A grandiose, winding staircase ran up the far wall, and we took it to the second floor where a broad, wood-paneled, carpeted corridor ran past sumptuous offices assigned to the governor and her principal staff.

Two uniformed constables stood in front of an open door near the corridor's far end where, presumably, Governor Peet held court. A murmur of conversation reached our ears as we neared it. I held up my credentials again.

"Chief Superintendent Morrow. I'm the SIO."

The constables snapped to attention, and one of them said, "Please go ahead, sir."

Amaris Tosh sat in a high-backed executive chair behind a desk large enough to re-enact the Battle of Ventano. She wore a stunned expression on her face, eyes wide open, mouth agape. Based on the info pack the Operations Center sent us during our drive here, Tosh was fifty-one, unattached, with little by way of family, and was firmly married to her Colonial Office career. She'd been on Mission Colony for over a decade and would likely have retired here if she weren't merging with the Infinite Void right now.

One of the individuals wearing white crime scene coveralls stepped over to where I stood, just inside the doorway.

"Sir, I'm Inspector Basil Kosta. I head the forensics unit."

"Chief Superintendent Morrow. Did you find a cause of death?"

"No. Everything is as it was when the first responders arrived. Both are waiting in the guard room downstairs to give you their statements. We've not found any visible injuries or signs of trauma. It's as if she just gave up the ghost."

I already knew Braband's friend found the body, but I was interested in Kosta's reaction. "Who raised the alarm?"

"Mayleen Allore, the social secretary." I couldn't quite pin down the look in Kosta's eyes, but inevitably, Braband's relationship with Allore would be well known. "She's in her office, expecting you."

"Me as in Chief Superintendent Morrow, or me as in the SIO?"

"Madame Allore is rather well versed in police procedure, sir. She's expecting someone to take her statement." Kosta paused for a moment. "And Governor Peet asked that the lead investigator speaks with her as soon as possible. She's in the conference room downstairs, cooling her heels."

— Seven —

I glanced over my shoulder. "We will take a few minutes and examine the scene, then Inspector Galdi, please take Madame Allore's statement and Master Sergeant Bonta, those of the first responders. I'll speak with the governor."

"Yes, sir." They had long ago perfected the art of answering in unison. Judging by Kosta's expression, he probably figured they did it more as a comedy act than anything else.

I wasn't expecting us to find clues, of course. That was the forensic team's job. Their work and the autopsy would tell us more than we could ever see with our Mark One eyeballs, but I like to carry a visual record of a potential crime scene in my head for future reference. As expected, we noticed nothing that jumped out at us, but it was the absence of indicators that struck me the most, such as no sign of a struggle.

Tosh's desktop was neat and organized. Nothing seemed out of place. She sat with her hands resting on the chair's arms, feet firmly planted on the floor, perhaps getting ready to push away from the desk and stand when she died. The more I studied her face, the more I became convinced her last emotion in this life had been outrage rather than surprise or fear.

Arno studied the office, hands behind his back.

"I think something, or someone caught her off guard when she died, as if she couldn't believe what was happening."

Both of us independently coming to the same conclusion was always a good omen.

Sergeant Bonta nodded. "Concur."

"Inspector Kosta, do we know the approximate time of death?"

"No more than three hours ago. That's when Tosh was last seen alive by the guard detail as she came back in after a walk. The autopsy will narrow that down."

"Thank you. Inspector Galdi, Sergeant, go take your statements while I find Governor Peet."

I thought I heard Inspector Kosta mutter good luck as I left the room, but that might have been a figment of my imagination.

Back on the ground floor, I found a directory that pointed me to the conference room. Its door was ajar, and I saw an older woman in a quiet conversation with a man at least ten years her junior. Platinum gray hair framed a narrow, patrician face notable for a thin, almost lipless mouth and pale blue eyes, which reminded me of Mission Colony's ice caps. Jeanne Peet.

Even at a distance, I knew her business suit — high-collared charcoal tunic over loose, silky trousers — didn't come from a fabricator. The half-dozen understated pieces of jewelry she wore were no doubt equally pricey. The Colonial Office obviously paid its governors a handsome salary on top of the freebies that came with the job. We'd check her financial status in due course.

The man, who I immediately identified as Terrence Salak, Peet's personal secretary, from the Operation Center's data feed, wasn't as much of a fashion plate. However, his suit would put anything Arno wore to shame. Handsome in a slightly seedy way with wavy dark hair, a cleft chin, and an aquiline nose, he was at least half a head taller than Peet even though the governor wore elegant high-heeled boots. I cleared my throat as I reached the door, and their quiet conversation died away instantly. They watched me enter with wary eyes.

"Governor Peet, I'm Chief Superintendent Caelin Morrow of the Commonwealth Constabulary. At Assistant Commissioner Braband's request, I'm acting as the senior investigating officer in the matter of Amaris Tosh's death."

"I've never heard of you." A frown creased Peet's high forehead.

"That's because I'm from Rim Sector HQ on Cimmeria, Madame. I arrived on Mission Colony this afternoon, along with two of my people. We're on a staff assistance visit to help Commissioner Braband with a few matters. Since he's personally involved with your social secretary, Mayleen Allore, he felt it would be better if someone not in the 24th Constabulary Regiment's chain of command led the investigation into what we consider a suspicious death at the moment."

"Did you say you're on a staff assistance visit? Are you even qualified to investigate this sort of thing?" Her slightly nasal voice took on a querulous edge.

"Madame, my team and I are among the most experienced investigators in Sector HQ. Between the three of us, we've successfully closed hundreds of cases, including homicides, over the years."

"What exactly is it you do at Sector HQ?" Salak gave me a faintly supercilious look.

"I head a team that handles the Constabulary's most difficult criminal cases, Mister Salak. We operate throughout the sector."

It was the truth and nothing but. The fact we weren't part of the Rim Sector Group but reported to Constabulary HQ on Wyvern was a detail not worth mentioning now, or ever, if I could manage it.

"I gather you know who I am. Well done."

His statement didn't merit a reply, mostly because of his arched eyebrow, which seemed somewhat mocking.

"Governor, Inspector Kosta said you wished to speak with the SIO. I'm at your disposal."

"Well yes." She pursed her lips as she leaned against a polished wood table that could comfortably seat fifty. "Why does the Constabulary consider this a suspicious death?"

"Unless there's an obvious underlying cause, such as vehicular accident, history of health issues, or misadventure, we treat every death as suspicious until the evidence proves the contrary. Amaris Tosh died suddenly, sitting at her desk, without making a sound that might have attracted her colleagues' attention. As suspicious deaths go, this one counts."

"Tell me about your intentions."

I mentally rolled my eyes. Peet was one of those. No doubt once I'd laid out my strategy, she would pick it apart just because.

"Every investigation unfolds differently, Madame. I arrived less than thirty minutes ago, and we're still at the very start of the data collection stage. The forensics unit is doing its job right now, working the scene. Once they're finished, Amaris Tosh's body will be transported to the Ventano General Hospital morgue for an autopsy. My investigators are interviewing witnesses to establish a timeline and decide who else should be interviewed. What happens after that depends on the information we're collecting."

I could see my reply didn't satisfy her, but she couldn't find a dangling thread to pick at.

"If it was murder, what about my security and that of the other Government House staffers? Amaris was in excellent health. I can't believe she would simply expire at her desk like that."

"I'm sure Commissioner Braband is already planning to augment the guard detail."

It was a lame answer, but what else could I say? If Tosh didn't die of natural causes, her killer was likely someone with unrestricted access and working for Governor Peet's administration. I already knew without checking that a review of the access control records wouldn't show us an outsider entering and leaving the complex during the relevant time frame. My instincts told me that if it was murder, Tosh knew whoever faced her when she took her last breath.

"Then I'll ask him since you're obviously not concerned with protecting the living." Peet turned away from me.

Fortunately, I was used to her sort. "Madame, my job is determining why people die and, if necessary, hunt down those responsible for causing their deaths. Unless there's something else, I'll return to our investigation and make sure Amaris Tosh rests in peace."

Salak gave me a dirty look but didn't say a word. He, too, showed me his back as he fell into a murmured conversation with his boss. I've experienced ruder dismissals from lower-ranking officials, so their attitude didn't faze me, but my first impression of Peet and her private secretary wasn't flattering. Advantage Braband in the matter of Peet's complaint.

After returning to the second floor, I watched Inspector Kosta and his people finish their examination of the crime scene. I stepped aside as technicians from the Ventano General Hospital came through with a stretcher. Hopefully, the medical examiner would do the post-mortem first thing in the morning. Potential crime victims enjoyed priority service, and Ventano was one of the safer frontier cities in this part of the Commonwealth, which meant there shouldn't be a backup of stiffs who died from other than natural causes.

After about ten minutes, Arno came out of Allore's office. "So?"

"She needed to speak with Tosh about the governor's schedule next week and found the office door closed, which I understand is unusual. Peet apparently always prefers open doors unless people are discussing confidential matters. I think she believes in a few peculiar management theories based on what I picked up from Allore. In any case, Allore knocked. When she received no answer, she cracked the door open and immediately realized Tosh wasn't breathing anymore — the vacant stare apparently did it for her. Allore then ran back to her office and called the guard room. She stayed there until I showed up. Allore heard nothing around the relevant time. Nor did she notice anyone pass in front of her open office door, but states she routinely ignores people in the corridor."

"Bull or no bull?"

Arno shrugged.

"Can't say. Allore strikes me as self-aware and self-possessed. The forensic evidence won't do much because we'll find traces of her in just about every office on this floor, if not the entire building. You should speak with her yourself, Chief. She's an interesting subject. I can understand what Braband sees in her while I find myself unable to figure out why a police officer of his experience can't see through her."

"Meaning?"

"An impression, nothing more. There's a lot hidden behind seemingly innocent eyes. We need to examine her relationship with Tosh."

I trusted Arno's impressions. He, like most of us in the PCB, possessed a sixth sense when interviewing witnesses and suspects. Of course, there was always a tiny percentage who could fool my built-in detectors, notably a Navy commander of my acquaintance, and her late colleague who saved my life on Aquilonia. Sadly, he died in the line of duty not long afterward.

Sergeant Bonta came up the stairs a few minutes later.

"Nothing much from the duty constables. They came, they saw, they called the Operations Center. One of them scanned her for vitals, the other remained in the corridor. But I learned a few interesting facts. First, there are no surveillance pickups anywhere inside Government House. Peet ordered them removed when she arrived."

Arno shrugged. "Can't say I blame her. Bad for morale and redundant if you're keeping good perimeter security."

"But so useful when investigating a suspicious death. Anyway, no one entered or left the building between the time Tosh returned from her walk, and Allore found the body."

"Who else works in this section?"

Bonta produced her pad.

"I obtained a copy of the office assignment roster. There are six of them. Four are occupied — the governor, the victim, Terrence Salak, and Mayleen Allore. The chief administrator has an office next to the governor's, but he prefers working from the colonial government building across the street. The sixth office is unassigned." She gestured at the landing. "That's the only way into this section. I understand from the guard detail that the governor isn't what you might call approachable."

"No surprise," Arno said. "She's a functionary, not a politician."

"The rest of the gubernatorial staff have offices on the first, third, and fourth floors. Most of the administration now works in more modern buildings, where the governor can't pay them a surprise visit." When Arno cocked an eyebrow at her, Bonta nodded. "Chief Administrator Demetrius Rudel isn't the only senior official who keeps his distance. I have the names of those in the building during the relevant three hours."

"Is Mayleen Allore still in her office?"

"Yes. I figured you might want to chat with her." Arno gestured at a closed door. "I told her she couldn't contact anyone until we're done."

"Thanks." I knocked on the door and entered without waiting for an invitation. The knock was for form's sake only.

The elegantly dressed woman by the window turned to face me.

"Madame Allore? I'm Chief Superintendent Caelin Morrow, the senior investigating officer in the matter of Amaris Tosh's death. Inspector Galdi works for me."

— Eight —

Allore nodded politely as she studied me with intelligent brown eyes set in a delicately sculptured face. I now understood what Arno meant. She was tall, lithe, and wore her long black hair in an artistic bun at the nape of her slender neck. But something about her poise, the way she studied me, seemed unusual.

"What can I do for you, Chief Superintendent?" Her gentle, alto voice struck me as somewhat hypnotic.

"I understand you're in a relationship with Assistant Commissioner Braband."

A regal nod. "Yes. I gather you took this case because of it. Your inspector told me you arrived from Cimmeria only a few hours ago and aren't in Elden's chain of command."

"You finding Amaris Tosh's body puts the AC in a potential conflict of interest, should her death be from other than natural causes."

"Because I'm a potential suspect?" A finely arched eyebrow crept up her smooth forehead. She struck me as more self-possessed than anyone I'd met on Mission Colony so far.

"Until we determine the cause of death, there are no suspects. But if it wasn't natural, everyone in Government House between the time the security system recorded Madame Tosh returning from her break and you found her is a potential suspect."

"That's a lot of people."

"Perhaps. But I believe she knew the last person to see her alive rather well."

"Amaris knew everyone who works here."

"Did anyone in Government House dislike Madame Tosh enough to murder her?"

She shook her head. "No. Amaris was one of the longest-serving Colonial Office staffers in the administration. We considered her a bit like a favorite aunt, always there to listen, cheer us up, and share her wisdom."

"Did Amaris and the governor get along?" This time, I saw a brief air of hesitation in Allore's eyes. A fraction of a second, no more. Most people would miss it.

"Certainly."

"Her employment as chief of staff predates Governor Peet's arrival, right?"

"Yes."

"And does yours predate the governor's arrival?"

Allore shook her head again. "No. She hired me. Governor Harker didn't employ a social secretary."

"I would think governors picked their own chiefs of staff. Isn't that a perk of the job?"

She shrugged. "Sorry, I couldn't tell you, Chief Superintendent. When Governor Peet replaced Governor

Harker, she kept everyone on except for the private secretary who left with Harker."

"Terrence Salak arrived with Peet?"

"Yes. As I understand, he's worked for the governor in the same capacity for many years."

"Was Amaris on friendly terms with him?"

"Why do you ask?"

"Humor me."

"Terrence can be, I guess, overbearing is the best word for it. He considers himself one step above the governor's chief of staff."

"And several steps above her social secretary. Why do I suspect Mister Salak isn't a fan-favorite among the long-timers in this place?"

A faint smile played on her lips. "Because you possess a cop's instincts? Terrence cares about two people in his life — himself and the governor, in that order. The rest of us are merely a means to an end."

"Was Mister Salak's predecessor more of a team player?"

She nodded. "That's what the other staffers told me."

"Do any specific disagreements between Amaris and Terrence Salak come to mind?"

Allore bit her lower lip for a few seconds as she parsed her memory. "No. Terrence is careful to avoid open disputes. It's more his attitude that rubbed Amaris the wrong way. But I don't believe him capable of harming anyone."

"Why?"

"You know how some people act superior because they're basically cowards on the inside? Terrence is one of those."

"Back to Amaris' relationship with the governor. Did it become strained in recent times?"

Allore took on a guarded expression.

"I think the governor would have preferred naming her own chief of staff but couldn't replace Amaris without either her consent or proof she no longer did a satisfactory job. Amaris was quite good at what she did and didn't plan on leaving the Colonial Office or Mission. She was one of those people capable of working with anyone, and her relationship with the governor was always professional."

"Did they get along well?"

"My impression was they respected each other, but weren't friends, let alone confidantes. The governor kept her out of the loop on a lot of things that didn't directly concern a chief of staff."

"Unlike Peet's predecessor?"

"So I heard. I wouldn't be surprised if Amaris found the change difficult, but she adapted. Look, Chief Superintendent, if her death wasn't natural, I couldn't tell you who among the staff might commit such a horrible act. She had no enemies either here or out there." Allore gestured at the office window. "Amaris was, if not loved by all and sundry, then respected by everyone."

"But not Terrence Salak."

"He neither likes nor respects anyone around here. I secretly think Terrence is unhappy at being stuck on what he considers a backwater planet but knows he wouldn't enjoy a comfortable Colonial Office career if he resigns as the governor's private secretary. Now, if that's everything, could I please go home? I'm tired and hungry and would rather deal with my grief in private."

"You're free to go with my thanks. We'll no doubt speak again in the coming days."

I watched Allore shrug on an elegant, waist-length wool jacket and tie a silk scarf around her neck, then stood aside to let her leave. After she was gone, I spent a few minutes studying her office, so I could get a sense of the woman behind the carefully composed facade. But even though she'd occupied it for approximately two years, I picked up almost nothing about Allore's personality.

As we drove back to the base later, Arno gave me a knowing look.

"Why do I think you've already decided Amaris Tosh's death isn't natural?"

"Because healthy, happy people don't just sit at their desks like that and die. Let's wait for the autopsy before going any further."

"No visible injury, but dead as a doornail?" Sergeant Bonta grunted. "Better make sure the ME checks her exposed skin for puncture wounds."

Arno nodded.

"Needler. That could be an explanation. Someone stepped into her office, pointed a needler at her. She gets outraged, tries to stand, and plink, a poison dart in the neck. I'll bet the tox screen won't show anything."

"Heart failure — cause unknown. An assassin's weapon. CSI should secure the victim's residence now and search it in the morning." I called the Operations Center and told the watchkeeper to contact Kosta. As we passed the base's main gate, I received a message saying Kosta was headed for Tosh's home.

— Nine —

The next morning, we observed Tosh's autopsy in the basement of the Ventano General Hospital even though attendance in person wasn't required. Medical examiners usually provided video recordings of the procedure along with their reports. But I was curious. Mission's murder rate wasn't high enough to call for a law enforcement ME organization, which meant civilian pathologists who'd taken forensic pathology training carried out post-mortems.

We stood behind a glass wall separating us from the autopsy room itself and saw everything. The doctor, a gray-bearded man who could easily be old enough to remember the Shrehari occupation, looked up from Amaris Tosh's body halfway through.

"By now, at least one of your lot should be looking for the nearest garbage pail. Congratulations on keeping breakfast down." His tone was conversational, as it had been since he began recording his observations.

"We've been around long enough to develop immunity, Doctor."

"Seasoned homicide investigators, eh?" He winked at me. "Don't meet many around here. So far, I can tell you she was in perfect health. Her heart simply stopped. But I can't find anything explaining why."

"Is the tox screen in yet?"

"Hang on." He walked over to a display and queried it. "Yep. Nothing unusual in her blood. I'll analyze tissue samples from the various organs, but I doubt I'll find anything useful."

"What about puncture wounds on the face, neck, or hands?"

He looked up at me and frowned. "Needler marks?"

"The best way of killing someone without leaving more than a puncture is with highly illegal, dissolving darts covered in a fast-acting poison, one that breaks down soon after the victim dies."

"Give me a moment." He pulled a magnifying device from a drawer and slowly scanned the parts of Tosh's skin that were exposed at the time of death. A large display on one wall relayed what it picked up. Several minutes later, the device stopped moving and zeroed in on a tiny dot just beneath her chin. "What do you think, Chief Superintendent?"

I'd seen enough of those over the years and knew right away it didn't come from a bee sting.

"Looks like we found our cause of death."

"Probable cause of death. With nothing in the tox screen that proves someone poisoned her, we might never find out. But yeah, that's almost assuredly a needler puncture, made shortly before death."

We watched him until he finished removing the major organs. I knew what was coming next and didn't feel like sticking around.

"What about the time of death?"

"Approximately sixteen hundred hours yesterday, give or take thirty minutes."

Which was an hour after she came back in from her break and an hour before Allore found her. Plenty of time for the dart to dissolve and any toxin to break down. It would have been a fast-acting poison as well, something that took a human from everything is good to fatal heart failure in a matter of seconds, so she couldn't call for help. In other words, an assassin's tool. She was killed where she sat by someone she knew.

"Thank you, Doctor."

He waved at me.

"All part of the service. You can stick around until I zip her back up, but you've seen the important parts. She was healthy and could have expected at least another half-century among the living. You'll receive my report and the autopsy recording by the end of the day."

"In that case, we'll be off. Forgive me if I say I hope we never meet again in a professional capacity."

"Ditto, Chief Superintendent." He turned back toward Tosh and promptly forgot about us as we filed out.

"Where now?" Arno asked once we stepped out into the fresh air.

"Government House. This is officially a murder investigation, which means we establish a timeline and place the staff members in the building on it."

Corporal Caffrey drove us across town, and when we reached the Government House main gate, I was amused at seeing a visibly larger guard detail, whose members now wore battledress uniforms, tactical helmets, and harnesses, and carried carbines. The sergeant in charge checked our credentials, then saluted before waving us through.

"Weaponizing the hen house door when it's clear the fox is already inside, disguised as a chicken," Arno muttered, shaking his head. "It's kabuki all the way down."

"What did you expect from the AC?"

He shrugged. "Anything that would get the governor off his back, and I suppose this is the best option short of us arresting the doer."

Caffrey let us off by the front door where further armed constables in tactical gear stood guard. We showed our credentials again before running them through the automated security system, another innovation that didn't increase security by an iota.

At my request the previous evening, the Government House Constabulary guard unit had turned the empty executive office into my incident room. They'd equipped it with tables, chairs, secure terminals rated up to secret, and dedicated communications gear. I was curious how Governor Peet would react at my summarily taking residence three doors from her richly appointed domain.

The inspector in charge did an outstanding job. They plugged us into the 24th Regiment's Operations Center and its secure systems, as well as the Government House computer core. It meant once someone gave us access, we could read the staff's personal files and pretty much anything that wasn't classified top secret. Arno and I watched Sergeant Bonta run a quick scan to make sure no one planted surveillance devices overnight.

When she gave us the nod, I took the office desk while Arno chose one of the two additional workstations. First, the timeline, then look into the victim's private and professional lives and find out where people and events intersected.

I wandered out of our incident room and crossed the corridor to where Tosh's office was still marked as off-limits save for Constabulary personnel. It seemed eerily empty, with only the furniture remaining. Kosta's people had removed everything else and carted it off to the evidence lab. They should be going through Tosh's private residence this morning, looking for anything that might tell us why someone killed her.

The crime scene investigators wouldn't find anything useful from the trace evidence they collected. Every staff member would have, at one point or another, entered the room. I took a quick peek next door. No Mayleen Allore, nor any sign she'd come in this morning. Understandable.

The governor's office door opened, and I glanced over my shoulder, wondering whether I was about to get an earful from Peet, but a man came out. He noticed me, and an oily smile appeared.

"You must be Chief Superintendent Caelin Morrow."

"Why must I be?"

"Because the governor described you in some detail."

"And you are?"

"My apologies. I'm so well known in this building, I sometimes forget to introduce myself. Luca Derzin — I run Aeternum, a pharmaceutical research and development firm."

I should have guessed. Derzin looked like the poster boy for senior ComCorp executives. He wore an expensive, bespoke suit and had a sculpted face with a square jaw, aquiline nose, and hooded eyes beneath exquisitely coiffed gray hair.

Derzin oozed insincerity as he spoke, and there was no evidence of a soul behind those eyes. ComCorp — The Honorable Commonwealth Corporation — didn't become the biggest zaibatsu in human space by selecting its executives for a well-developed sense of empathy. Quite the contrary.

"I daresay you've been naughty, Chief Superintendent." His smile broadened, though it contained no humor. At least he didn't wag his finger at me. I might have snapped it off.

"In what way?"

"You didn't tell Jeanne you head the Rim Sector's internal affairs bureau."

"So?"

"Why would the PCB detachment commander arrive on Mission with her team hours before poor Amaris dies under mysterious circumstances and wind up as the senior investigating officer?"

"Assistant Commissioner Braband asked me to take over because of his relationship with Mayleen Allore."

Derzin shook his head.

"Come now, Chief Superintendent, you know that's not what I mean. Why are internal affairs on Mission?"

"How do you know who I am?"

"I checked my parent corporation's vast database and noticed there was only one Chief Superintendent Caelin Morrow assigned to the Rim Sector, and she was the Constabulary's local Lady High Executioner."

He seemed pleased at his wit and clearly expected a reaction.

"Good to see ComCorp's intelligence division is still up to snuff. They've been hit or miss in recent times."

He didn't react. "So is the Constabulary's."

"Aeternum being part of the ComCorp zaibatsu is hardly a secret."

"Perhaps, but we prefer not publicizing the affiliation."

"Why?"

He tut-tutted at me, and this time he waved his finger, though I restrained myself.

"You have reasons for not letting folks around here know you're from internal affairs, and I have my reasons for not publicizing Aeternum's corporate lineage. So what do you figure? Spontaneous death? Assassination? Act of God?"

"We found evidence a person or persons unknown murdered her."

"Ah! So, what was it? Lover's quarrel? One of the deadly sins is surely in play."

"It's still early days, Mister Derzin. But since you specifically mention lover's quarrel, is there anything about Amaris Tosh's private life we should discuss?"

"No." He gave me what he meant as a disarming look, but it seemed a little too reptilian for my taste. I found the more I investigated humans with twisted souls, the quicker I discovered their dark side. "It just seems that lovers' quarrels bring out the worst in members of our species."

"Not quite. Greed, for wealth and for power, brings out the worst in humans. Funny a senior ComCorp executive doesn't know that."

"Aeternum executive, Chief Superintendent. And I'll try not to take it as a veiled insult. On that note, I'll bid you goodbye. We'll probably talk again soon. I visit Government House regularly."

"That's what I've been told. Enjoy your day."

I returned to the incident room without giving him another look. Moments after I sat at what would be my desk for the duration, Terrence Salak stuck his head through the door.

"Chief Superintendent, apologies for intruding on your investigation, but the governor wonders whether you would give her a few moments of your precious time."

Salak's condescending tone and choice of words reminded me of Allore's comments the previous evening. I could well believe he had few friends in Government House. Why did Peet tolerate him?

"Now?"

"Preferably."

Arno, who sat with his back to the door, gave me a meaning-laden grimace. He and Bonta had, of course, overheard my conversation with Derzin. I repressed a sigh and stood.

"My time is the governor's time."

A lie, but I can play this game all day long and twice on Sundays. Make Peet and her factotum believe I'm subservient and who knows how much I'll learn. The arrogance of unearned superiority revealed a person's genuine character like nothing else.

— Ten —

Governor Peet didn't bother standing when I entered her office, which wasn't quite as expansive as the one occupied by Deputy Chief Constable Maras, but it came close. Salak followed me in and closed the door. Peet gestured at the chairs in front of her desk.

"Thank you for accepting my invitation so promptly, Chief Superintendent. Please sit."

"What can I do for you, Governor?" I dropped into one of the chairs, conscious of Salak staring at my back. It made me feel slightly greasy.

"I was reliably informed you've been less than candid about your status."

"In which way?"

"You did not tell me you were the head of the Rim Sector Professional Compliance Bureau." Her wholly theatrical air of disappointment would have been comical under any other circumstances.

"It isn't germane to this investigation. I accepted the job of senior investigating officer for Amaris Tosh's murder at Assistant Commissioner Braband's request."

"And you can do that? Take on a homicide case without reference to your superiors?"

"Yes." If Peet intended to read me the riot act, I'd make sure she worked for it.

"Why are you here on Mission Colony, Chief Superintendent?"

"To help Assistant Commissioner Braband with certain administrative matters."

"And they are?"

"Internal to the Constabulary, Governor."

"Meaning none of my business." Her disdainful expression took on a sourer note. "Perhaps I should ask that the Colonial Office speaks with your Chief Constable."

"Please do whatever you wish, Madame." And good luck with that.

"Then, I shall question your competence as a homicide investigator. This is hardly the same thing as collaring bent cops." She tilted her head to one side, like a quizzical bird.

"We collar more than just bent cops, Governor. Over the years, I've also investigated and arrested senior armed forces and planetary police officers as well as officials from most branches of the Commonwealth government. We are the federal government's internal affairs unit, not just the Constabulary's."

A light finally came on in her eyes.

"You're here because of my complaint against Assistant Commissioner Braband."

"I can neither confirm nor deny that, Governor, for obvious reasons."

She raised a hand and pointed at me with an extended finger.

"That's it. You're here because of Braband and are using Amaris' death as some sort of cover-up. The Thin Gray Line, is that it? Cops protecting each other? Not on my watch. I'm the governor of this star system."

"Don't let my lowly rank fool you. I answer to a deputy chief constable on Wyvern and nobody else, not Assistant Commissioner Braband, Deputy Chief Constable Maras who heads the Constabulary's Rim Sector Group, nor the Governor of Mission Colony."

"We'll see about that."

I stood. "Seeing about it is your prerogative. Braband and Maras will confirm what I just said."

My dismissive attitude must have stung because she glared at me and changed tack.

"Is the incident room a few doors down from my office necessary?"

"Yes. If there's nothing else, Governor, my investigation into Amaris Tosh's murder awaits."

"Murder?"

"The medical examiner discovered a puncture on her neck consistent with those left by needler darts. He figures it was made shortly before she died. Since he found no apparent cause of death, barring evidence to the contrary, I'm assuming Tosh was killed with a fast-acting poison, the sort that leaves no trace in the bloodstream. There's an assassin on your staff, and I will find him or her. If you'll excuse me."

"I don't like your attitude, Morrow."

"Most people don't, but I try not to take it personally. Internal affairs units became pariahs approximately two seconds after their invention in the pre-spaceflight era." I turned on my heels and headed for the door, glaring at Salak until he stepped aside and opened it.

Maybe Peet and company finding out we were the Firing Squad instead of the Flying Squad would generate dividends. Worried people made mistakes, and even though my focus was on Tosh, my primary task remained Peet's puzzling complaint against Braband.

Arno and Sergeant Bonta gave me quizzical looks when I re-entered the incident room and closed the door behind me.

"The governor has officially joined the legion of people who dislike me. Of course, my manners or lack thereof didn't help."

Arno nodded knowingly.

"You chose the angry people make mistakes option. Not as elegant as your usual approach, Chief. But if the jig is up anyway? She obviously sussed out our presence on Mission is related to her complaint."

"Obviously. Peet didn't like my no comment answer. It went downhill after that. While you two develop the timeline and figure out who was in the building, I'll dig into Mister Derzin's personal and professional life."

Police work, even in my specialty, was over eighty percent perspiration, along with a little luck. I had found little on Governor Peet's best buddy by the time a constable from the guard detail showed up shortly before thirteen hundred hours with three lunch boxes from the 24th Regiment's dining facility. After wolfing down my meal, proof I was hungrier than expected, I drafted a request for any information Sector HQ's intelligence section could dig up on Derzin and asked the Operations Center to bundle it with the 24th's daily subspace packet for Cimmeria. By now, Maras should know about the murder and my taking on the SIO job. She'd make sure anything I asked for became a top priority.

Not that the intelligence analysts routinely held out on me. Unlike so many. We enjoyed a mutually beneficial relationship. They received copies of everything we discovered during our investigations, including stuff that never showed up in our case files or reports. In return, they gave me priority service whenever I reached out.

Not long after, Arno stood and walked over to the display covering one wall. It lit up with a graphic representation of the crucial hours between Tosh re-entering Government House and Allore raising the alarm. Names and faces appeared, each with a pair of time notations — when they entered and when they left for the day.

"Twenty-three potential suspects, Chief. Including the governor, Luca Derzin, Terrence Salak, and Mayleen Allore, as well as Demetrius Rudel, the chief administrator who paid Brionne Milton, the facilities manager, a visit around sixteen hundred hours."

He led us through each of the possible suspects — name, function, time on Mission Colony, and so forth. None stood out. Other than Derzin, they were a mix of Colonial Office career bureaucrats and locally engaged employees. The most recent arrival among the former had worked here for a little over a year and the most senior just under ten, which made Tosh the longest-serving Colonial Office staffer before her death.

Those locally engaged were a mixed lot, though none besides Allore had less than five years of service. The chances of a local spontaneously murdering a co-worker in cold blood after years together were slim, absent unbearable provocation. Federal bureaucrats seemed equally unlikely candidates. They enjoyed secure careers, with plenty of benefits, and could look forward to a comfortable retirement in the star system of their choice. From memory, the ones who were convicted of murder killed their victims in crimes of passion, and my gut told me Tosh's slaying was cold and calculated. Only assassins carried needlers with fast-dissolving, poison-coated ammo.

"None of them jump out at me. How about you, Sergeant?"

"Nothing on my end, sir."

"Arno?"

"Same."

"We already have Mayleen Allore's statement, and I spoke with her afterward. I'll take the governor, Derzin, Rudel, Salak, and Brionne Milton. That leaves you with seventeen staffers and me with those most likely to know something about the conflict between Peet and AC Braband."

"I thought you might do so and parceled out the rest between the sergeant and myself." Arno touched a control surface, and the remaining names were outlined in either red or blue. He glanced at her. "You're blue. Are we good?"

"Yep."

"In that case," I stood, "let's get going."

I needed fresh air along with a bit of distance from Government House's stuffy atmosphere. A brief walk across the street to where Rudel worked would do wonders. It was early afternoon on a weekday, and the chances of catching him unawares were excellent. I preferred not giving witnesses, let alone potential suspects warning of my impending arrival. I wasn't a welcome visitor at the best of times, and when targets suffered from a guilty conscience, even if it was for personal peccadilloes rather than misconduct, they avoided me like the plague.

The automated security gate controlling access to the main colonial administration building accepted my credentials without so much as a hiccup, one advantage of working on a planet policed by the Commonwealth Constabulary. The moment the Operations Center added me to the all-access list, I could pretty much enter any government site without questions.

I scanned the directory displayed on the lobby's far wall, beneath a double winding staircase that seemed like a less ornate version of the one across the street. Rudel's office, not surprisingly, was on the third floor, a few meters higher than Governor Peet's, though I figured the height competition predated both their tenures.

Governors were, by and large, political appointees, even if they were career Colonial Office drones, while chief administrators were long-service bureaucrats chosen for their adherence to policies and procedures. The two species didn't necessarily get along that well. Rudel's choice of primary workspace spoke volumes.

I took the stairs at a leisurely pace, ignored by the few staffers who crossed my path. If I had no business here, security wouldn't have let me in. The third-floor executive corridor was a strange mirror image of the one across the street. Wide, decorated with landscapes and portraits proclaiming Mission Colony's greatness, it lacked its counterpart's opulence while projecting a more modern aura of power — tile and stucco versus marble and wood wainscoting. The architect who designed the Executive Building probably spent a lot of time studying Government House, which predated it by a good forty years.

A subdued metal sign hung over the door leading to Chief Administrator Rudel's suite at the corridor's far end. I didn't doubt his office overlooked the southern fjord framing the Ventano peninsula, but since the commercial port lay along its shores, the view wouldn't be nearly as pleasant as that from AC Braband's office. The woman sitting at a desk in the middle of the antechamber looked up with an air of displeasure when I entered.

"Chief Superintendent Caelin Morrow, Commonwealth Constabulary. I'd like a few minutes with Chief Administrator Rudel."

She stared at me as if in disbelief at my impudence, "Did you make an appointment?"

"I'm the senior investigating officer in the matter of Amaris Tosh's death. I don't need appointments. Is Mister Rudel in his office?"

"Let me check."

"Either he is, or he isn't. Which is it?" I gave her my best death stare, the sort that could sink a thousand ships with leaking hulls. Or annoy self-important executive assistants. "Unless Mister Rudel is an updated example of Schrödinger's cat."

Her face took on a charming shade of puce, though her eyes conveyed less than delicate thoughts. I was getting rather good at making friends on Mission Colony, though I was impressed she understood the reference. Or it might have been my less than respectful tone. Probably the latter. Few nowadays bothered with pre-diaspora thinkers.

"One moment, please." She tapped her screen while I admired the sparseness of Rudel's antechamber. The door behind her opened thirty seconds later. "You may enter."

— Eleven —

Rudel, a slender, dark-complexioned man with strong features, jet black hair, and beetling brows, didn't stand when I entered. He watched in silence as I took a chair in front of his desk without waiting for an invitation.

"Thank you for seeing me, Mister Rudel."

"The infamous Chief Superintendent Morrow, from the Rim Sector Firing Squad. I was wondering when you'd grace me with a visit. Jeanne didn't exaggerate when she said you showed no deference to rank or position."

"After years investigating and arresting some of the highest federal and star system officials for corruption or worse, rank and position are meaningless to those in our line of work."

A faint air of amusement lit up his deep-set brown eyes.

"No doubt. I'm sure you've met your share of Colonial Office executives who tossed their professional ethics out the nearest airlock."

"Colonial Office, Armed Services, Constabulary — I've seen the dark underside of pretty much every federal government branch in this sector."

"And now you're investigating the death of a high-ranking civil servant whom I counted among my closest friends on Mission."

"Murder, Mister Rudel."

He grimaced. "In that case, I'll do everything possible to help you, Chief Superintendent. Before you ask, I can't think of anyone who'd do such a dastardly deed. Amaris was beloved by everyone in the colonial administration and at Government House."

"There's at least one person who didn't love her."

"Granted. Any suspects?"

"Twenty-three people were in the building during the relevant time frame, all but one of them employees. The security system didn't record any visitors other than Mister Derzin."

"Most probably an inside job, then. Since you're here, I assume I'm one of those twenty-three."

"You are. As is the governor."

A sardonic smile appeared. "Jeanne will bust a vein when you tell her. Too bad I can't witness it."

"You assume I've not done so yet."

"I would have heard by now. Jeanne likes to vent whenever her blood pressure creeps up. Giving Terrence an earful rarely suffices, and I'm the only other official she can trust with her feelings on the issue of the moment."

"But you're telling me."

The smile broadened.

"I understand there's no such thing as privacy in a murder investigation, especially for potential suspects. Besides, someone will eventually tell you that Jeanne and I aren't bosom buddies."

"Which is why you work across the street and not across the hall."

He tapped the side of his nose with an extended index finger.

"Jeanne can be a little overbearing and enjoys sticking her nose into the minutiae of running a colonial administration."

"I heard Terrence Salak described with some of the same words."

"Birds of a feather, those two. Terrence takes his cues from her, and she lets him act above his station. I exchanged a few choice words with Salak shortly after they arrived on Mission. Fancied himself the deputy governor by virtue of traveling in Jeanne's pocket. If anyone over there didn't like Amaris, he's your man. But I don't believe he has the guts to murder anyone. Salak is the sort who'll sulk about every slight, imagined or real, for weeks until he comes up with a stinging retort. However, he's a coward at heart and a bully when he can get away with it."

I was beginning to like the chief administrator. Where I'd expected a bureaucrat's obfuscation and refusal to speak openly, I found unexpected candor. Interestingly his assessment of Salak matched Allore's.

"So, you don't think he's my murderer?"

Rudel shook his head. "Doubtful. I've never seen him worked up to the point of doing something out of character, and I've never known Amaris capable of provoking anyone."

"What were you doing in Government House yesterday afternoon?"

"Ah! The interrogation begins."

"I prefer the term interview at this point. Interrogation is for those I've arrested."

"Of course. I met with Brionne Milton, the Government House facilities manager, about Jeanne's latest renovation ideas. Usually, I let my finance and procurement directors deal with such matters, but Brionne felt pressured by Jeanne. Since she works for me and not the governor, I step in whenever Jeanne throws her weight around."

"What was the issue?"

"Jeanne has expensive tastes. This is her first appointment as a star system governor, and she's feeling entitled to indulgences above and beyond Colonial Office norms."

"Why go there instead of Milton coming here?"

"Discretion. Folks around here know if I want something, I'll visit my subordinates. Conversely, if they want something, they visit me. I'd rather not risk Terrence seeing her cross the street and wonder."

"Are relations between your office and hers strained?"

"On days when I don't give Jeanne what she wants, yes. Though her storms blow over quickly. As I said earlier, Terrence, on the other hand, can keep a grudge going well past its natural lifespan."

"Do these days happen often?"

Rudel shrugged. "Once or twice a month, maybe."

"Did you visit the second story yesterday?"

He shook his head.

"No. Brionne's office is on the ground floor, at the back of the building. I don't interact with Jeanne's personal staff and only see her by appointment, which happens as infrequently as we both can make it. Her fondness for me isn't any greater than mine for her."

"Why is that?"

Another shrug.

"Colonial Office politics. I came up through the administrative service ranks, she via the policy branch. Our views on what constitutes proper colonial governance differ. It's not uncommon."

"Was her predecessor a product of the policy stream?"

"Jim Harker? No. He came from the administrative services like me and understood there are limits to a governor's powers. If you ask me, policy wonks shouldn't run star systems. Unfortunately, those who spend most of their careers advising Colonial Secretaries, Deputy Secretaries, and Assistant Secretaries on Earth can talk themselves into an appointment as governor to round out their government careers. Those of us who spend their lives toiling on distant worlds and understand what does and doesn't work, not so much."

"How long were you with Brionne Milton?"

I knew from the security log but had to ask anyway.

"Thirty minutes, give or take. I'm sure she'll corroborate. Brionne is blessed with a good internal clock." Rudel hesitated for a few seconds. "If I may ask, Chief Superintendent, why are you on Mission? Surely you couldn't predict days in advance you'd be needed for a murder investigation. Did someone in the administration or the 24th Regiment screw up?"

It was my turn to hesitate. Should I give him a no comments or go with my gut and see if he can help me with the Braband situation? Option two won out.

"How are relations between Governor Peet and Assistant Commissioner Braband?"

He gave me a look I couldn't interpret.

"Did either of them lay a complaint against the other? Or should I not ask?" When I remained silent, he raised both hands. "Understood. Mum's the word. I figure Braband rubs Peet the wrong way and has from the day he showed up at Government House to make his manners. It's probably reciprocal, simply because Jeanne has a knack, although Braband is better at keeping his feelings hidden. I know they kept their disagreements private."

"Because of Mayleen Allore?"

He thought about it for a moment.

"In part. Mayleen is privy to details about Jeanne's private life our esteemed governor doesn't want in a Constabulary dossier. So was Amaris, by the way."

"Misconduct?"

"Not that I'm aware. Otherwise, I'm sure Amaris would have told me. Jeanne is a tad paranoid, although she could be doing things behind closed doors that might not impress our superiors on Earth. She'd hardly be the first colonial governor who indulges her appetites. Running an entire star system can become a little too heady at times."

"Are you speaking from experience?"

"Vicariously. I'm not among the anointed few who'll ever be tapped for the honor. This is likely the highest I'll ever go, and something tells me Mission Colony is my last posting before I'm shown the door."

Did I detect a hint of bitterness in his tone? If so, he wouldn't be the first official disillusioned after a lengthy career of exemplary service and precious little by way of official recognition.

"What about Luca Derzin?"

Rudel's expression lost its whimsical edge.

"Aha! It was Jeanne you were after before someone murdered Amaris."

This time, I didn't hesitate. "I can neither confirm nor deny."

"Too oily by half, that one. I don't know what going on in that sprawling laboratory complex of his because he doesn't allow my people in. Legally, he shouldn't be able to stop occupational health or other inspections. Hell, he didn't even let us in during construction. But he has certificates issued by the Commonwealth government, and Jeanne considers them sufficient. So far, I haven't found a way of overriding her." Rudel tapped his desktop, clearly irritated. "Something about Derzin and Jeanne huddling together in her office at least once a week bothers me. And she spends an inordinate amount of time at Derzin's estate in the hills out west. He bought the former Kerlin place, a nice piece of land. You might remember Gustav Kerlin, one of our leading rabble-rousers before a sniper blew his head off at that same estate."

"I do." And I was personally acquainted with the sniper. He and his partner were among my few genuine friends outside the PCB. "Did he also buy the Kerlin townhouse?"

"That's what I understand. Derzin conducted the transaction off-world, so I couldn't say how it happened. I suppose when you run a ComCorp subsidiary, no matter how well hidden behind shell companies, the universe is your oyster."

Naval Intelligence likely kept a dossier on Derzin, but it wouldn't hurt if I send Captain Talyn a quick message. She always figured ComCorp or its allies were behind the terrorist campaign that shook both Mission and Cimmeria, along with half a dozen other Rim Sector worlds. But how did Rudel figure Derzin was a ComCorp drone?

"ComCorp subsidiary?"

A low, throaty chuckle escaped Rudel.

"I have my contacts, Chief Superintendent. The Colonial Office might have handed its intelligence service to the Fleet during Grand Admiral Kowalski's reforms, but that doesn't mean we stopped looking and listening. I like to be aware of what's happening on my patch, especially when the happenings aren't cooperative. Or congenial."

"Are you saying Governor Peet's friendship with Luca Derzin is suspect?"

"You believe so, Chief Superintendent. Otherwise, you wouldn't ask. Industrialists making nice with senior government officials is hardly unusual."

"Did Derzin try making nice with you?"

"I'm not his type."

"Meaning?"

"I'm immune to flattery, cocktail parties, and country estate weekends."

"Those are the warning signs of potential corruption."

"I realize that which is why I stay far away. Too bad Jeanne doesn't share my caution. Not that I've seen her do anything improper, but it is a slippery slope, and Derzin strikes me as both persistent and persuasive." He made a brief grimace of distaste. "And wealthy."

"You certainly are being candid, Mister Rudel."

"It'll eventually come out, anyway. Better I get my say earlier rather than later, lest you decide I'm hiding something and tear my life apart."

"I wish more people shared that view. Just out of curiosity. Did Governor Peet enjoy good relations with former Assistant Commissioner Kristy Bujold?"

A vague look of amusement pulled at his lips.

"A little too good if you ask me. Of course, that ended when Bujold was found unconscious beside the body of Eva Cortez."

"Do you mean they were intimate?"

He raised both hands, palms facing outward, in surrender.

"No idea. I just thought Jeanne and Bujold sometimes behaved as if they were scheming behind closed doors. That Bujold took early retirement after your people investigated her involvement with Kerlin and Cortez, surprised no one around here. Her replacement is a breath of fresh air." Rudel frowned. "I don't know if this is useful, but I often got the impression Terrence Salak didn't like Bujold."

"In what way?"

"He struck me as being jealous of her relationship with Jeanne. And that's about all I can think of."

"If something else comes to mind, please call the Operations Center. They'll patch you through. One last thing. Who controls access to the colonial administration's personnel database?"

"My people do. I suppose you want the unfettered ability to call up everything we have on Government House employees."

"If you wouldn't mind."

"I'll make the arrangements."

— Twelve —

I took my time returning to Government House. The afternoon was mild and pleasant, the sun shining brightly overhead in a sky so blue it could break your heart. I didn't recall seeing anything about a relationship between Peet and Bujold in the investigation report my team submitted. Either they didn't consider it germane to the case, as in Peet wasn't involved with Cortez and Kerlin, or Rudel imagined things.

The colony's chief administrator was an interesting man. I didn't know what I'd expected, but now I was left wondering whether his surprising openness stemmed from unshakable integrity and a deep personal sense of honor or whether it was an attempt at deflection. Speak someone else's truth to hide one's own. I've seen it before. My gut told me it was most probably the former, but until I discover every secret about a human, I remained mildly suspicious of their motivations.

That comes from dealing with the best liars and dissemblers our species can produce. And he made that comment about his career winding down. Did he sound just a tad disillusioned? Many bureaucrats who went down the wrong path did so because they believed themselves taken for granted by their employer, perhaps even exploited, their hard work unrecognized. No, on second thought, I wouldn't put Rudel in the clear just yet. Not without more examination. But he wasn't part of my brief. Absent fresh evidence of misconduct, only Braband and Peet were.

I found Brionne Milton in her office on the first floor. She was obviously expecting one of us if not necessarily me. Perhaps Rudel called after I left. He struck me as the sort who took care of his people. The office, while almost the same size as those upstairs, lacked most of the opulent trappings that screamed senior bureaucrat. Its decor seemed as unprepossessing as the plump, middle-aged woman who peered at me with bright blue eyes set in a round, grandmotherly face framed by curly brown hair.

"Good afternoon. I'm Chief Superintendent Caelin Morrow of the Constabulary."

"Please come in." She gave me a gentle if somewhat sad smile as she indicated the chairs in front of her desk. "Everyone in the colonial administration knows who you are by now. I'm afraid we're frightful gossips around here."

"Thank you." I made myself comfortable while studying her.

"In what way can I be helpful? Amaris was a dear friend, and her murder is a terrible shock."

"We're tracing the movements of everyone inside Government House during the relevant time frame."

"Of course. I was in my office when Mayleen raised the alarm, working on the governor's most recent renovation ideas."

"Did you leave your office between fifteen hundred and seventeen hundred hours yesterday?"

Milton shook her head. "No."

"Can anyone attest to that?"

"Demetrius Rudel was here from about quarter to four until quarter after."

It matched the access control logs within a few minutes. "Why?"

"We discussed those renovation ideas."

"Because they're problematic?"

She nodded.

"A bit. I needed his advice. Governor Peet can be rather insistent. She's quite a force of nature when she wants."

"Like most governors, I suppose."

Milton's face took on a pained expression.

"Governor Harker and Governor Appleby weren't quite so determined, if I may say so, Chief Superintendent."

"What about their private secretaries?"

Her pained look deepened.

"Lovely people. It's a shame that private secretaries move with their principals. But what can you do?"

Chalk her up as another fan of Terrence Salak. Though what it meant in the grand scheme of this investigation, I couldn't say.

"Any idea who might have wanted Amaris Tosh dead?"

"No. I can't even conceive of working alongside someone capable of such a despicable act."

"What makes you believe it was a colleague?"

Milton hesitated.

"The killer has to be one of us. Otherwise, you'd be looking for outsiders. I oversaw the security system's upgrade, Chief Superintendent. You know precisely who was inside Government House when Amaris was murdered."

"Luca Derzin was on the premises during the relevant time frame."

She gave me a startled glance.

"Oh. I didn't know that."

"No reason you should. I understand he and Governor Peet see each other often."

I watched Milton mentally test several replies as the seconds of silence between us multiplied.

"Mister Derzin is a favored guest, Chief Superintendent, as well as one of the star system's leading industrialist and head of the Mission Colony Chamber of Commerce."

She sounded uneasy to my trained ears. And that meant the Derzin-Peet nexus was becoming ever worthier of examination, but not necessarily in relation to Amaris Tosh's death. Or could the complaint against AC Braband be related? Colonies on the outer edge of human space were, by and large, small, incestuous societies where secrets died under the weight of gossip, and nothing happened in a vacuum.

"If you remember something that could help our inquiries, please don't hesitate to call on me."

"I will."

"Thank you." I stood. "Enjoy the rest of your day."

On my way up to our second-floor incident room, I came face-to-face with Terrence Salak.

"Just the man I wanted to see."

"Why?"

"Everyone inside Government House between fifteen hundred and seventeen hundred hours yesterday is a potential suspect."

A faint sneer turned his slightly seedy air into a mask of barely disguised contempt.

"Surely you're not implying the governor, or I were involved with Amaris's death."

"I'm not implying anything."

"Well, you can cross the governor, Luca Derzin, and me off your list. We were together behind closed doors in the governor's office from around fifteen-thirty until Mayleen raised the alarm."

"What were you doing?"

"That's none of the Constabulary's business."

"Everything is our business in a murder investigation."

Salak made a sweeping arm gesture at the staircase.

"Then I suggest you tell the governor in person. She'll set you straight on what is or isn't your business."

How this man made it into his early fifties without getting punched into the next century, let alone end up serving as a colonial governor's personal secretary, was beyond me. Surely Peet saw something in Salak if she'd let him ride her coattails for so long. But I couldn't figure out what.

"By the way, I understand we share something in common, Chief Superintendent."

"Oh?"

"We were both born on Pacifica, though I understand you didn't leave voluntarily to pursue a career in the Constabulary. Quite the opposite. There may still be an active warrant for your arrest in the Security Police database."

"Let me guess. Luca Derzin told you."

The sarcastic smile he gave me did little to improve his looks.

"You certainly are quite the detective. Yes, Luca has information sources we can only dream of."

"I still need formal statements from you, the governor, and Mister Derzin."

"Consider this conversation my statement. I'll see what the governor says, and you can do as you please with Luca."

"Thank you for your courtesy and cooperation, Mister Salak."

I kept my tone so neutral he gave me a searching glare as if I'd just mocked him. As I climbed the stairs, he left via the main entrance, perhaps done for the day.

As I entered the executive corridor, I heard voices wafting through an open door. Peet and Derzin enjoying a grand old time, by the sounds of it. I suddenly felt the urge to become a killjoy, and instead of stopping at the incident room, I headed for the governor's office. What could I say? Keep your door closed if you don't want police intrusion.

"Governor Peet, Mister Derzin. Glad I caught you together."

They turned and stared at me with almost comical looks of surprise. Whether it was because of my unannounced arrival or choice of words, I couldn't tell.

After a few seconds, Peet's right eyebrow arched up in question. "Chief Superintendent. What is the meaning of this?"

"We're interviewing everyone who was in this building between fifteen and seventeen hundred yesterday, and that includes you."

She raised her hand and wiggled the fingers dismissively.

"Neither Mister Derzin nor I have any connection to Amaris' death."

"Can you account for your whereabouts during the time frame I just mentioned?"

"I most certainly can, and I don't like your attitude."

Derzin laid a restraining hand on her arm.

"Humor the unfriendly police officer, Jeanne. Her type is remarkably persistent, and someone like Chief Superintendent Morrow is unimpressed by your importance as this star system's head of government."

Peet glared at me for a few heartbeats, as if hoping I might vanish in a puff of smoke.

"Luca, Terrence, and I were discussing confidential business matters from shortly after fifteen hundred until Mayleen lost her composure if you must know."

The governor's choice of words struck me as strange. Mayleen lost her composure rather than found her colleague dead?

"And those matters were?"

Her glare hardened.

"None of your business, as in not germane to the investigation."

As much as I enjoyed sparring with Peet, I let her reply pass and turned my attention on Derzin.

"You were here with the governor and Mister Salak between fifteen-thirty and seventeen hundred yesterday?"

"I was, and I can confirm neither of us heard anything until Madame Allore screamed."

Since I wouldn't get anything more from either of them, I inclined my head.

"Thank you for your cooperation."

Arno and Sergeant Bonta were in the incident room when I entered. I closed the door behind me and let out a soft sigh.

"Tell me you got something from the staffers because this seems more and more like a locked door mystery. Milton and Rudel vouch for each other, while Peet, Salak, and Derzin were scheming in the governor's office, meaning they also vouch for each other. Although what value that has depends on whether we believe them capable of conspiring to murder Tosh, which seems unlikely."

Arno grimaced.

"Bupkis. No one heard or saw anything, and most of them can give each other alibis. Locked door mystery indeed."

I took my chair and leaned back.

"We may not be any further ahead on the murder, but I'm forming a picture of the colonial administration's upper echelons, and it's not pretty."

After I related the gist of my interviews, Arno said, "AC Braband might be onto something. This wouldn't be the first time a zaibatsu compromised senior planetary officials, and they don't play nice with anyone who interferes, ComCorp least of all. Luca Derzin strikes me as a snake of the first order."

"Oh, he's probably that, if not worse, and he's been digging into my background, no doubt in case I decide there's a stench of corruption wafting through Government House, and he hasn't been shy about letting me know. I fully expect he's obtained a copy of the old arrest warrant against me from Pacifica and will spread the word I'm a wanted criminal."

"Taunting you, is he? Either Derzin is confident he can weather any storm or foolish enough to believe so. Neither bodes well, Chief." Arno stood and cracked his back. "Unless new evidence surfaces or a killer with a guilty conscience confesses, I think this murder will become a cold case. We know someone in this building did it, but bugger if I can figure out who's lying."

Bonta snorted.

"I'd start with the corner office, sir. The governor is clearly in cahoots with Derzin, and Tosh didn't like it. There's your motive. Based on what we know about the victim, Tosh wouldn't put up with anything that might harm her adopted homeworld."

"In that case, why not Allore as well?"

She smiled at me.

"I didn't forget her, Chief. Four people were in this wing at the time of the murder, as far as our witness statements go. Allore is the only suspect without someone vouching for her whereabouts."

Arno scratched his majestic beard.

"Makes for a perfect patsy. *If* we accept a scenario where the governor, her personal secretary, and one of the planet's leading industrialists are part of a secret plot to commit murder."

"Truth being stranger than fiction, why not? With what's happening in the Rim Sector lately, I wouldn't place anyone above suspicion. Remember how many in the Cimmerian government were playing footsie with terrorist backers. You know, backers who were likely connected in some way with the largest zaibatsus, such as ComCorp, Derzin's ultimate employer."

"You smell a conspiracy, Chief?"

"Always. It's a professional hazard. But there's nothing more we can do here today." As I stood, Bonta called Corporal Caffrey on her communicator. "After supper, we can convene in my suite's sitting room, enjoy a drink, and brainstorm both of our cases. Buying a needler isn't difficult, especially on a world like Mission where most folks own weapons thanks to memories of the Shrehari occupation. Dissolving darts covered with a deadly poison that can't be detected by a tox screen on the other hand… It's the only angle we can attack right now."

"Let's hope the ME's organ tissue tests give us a clue."

"And the background checks on Peet's staff. Which we will start in the morning."

As it turned out, the ME found nothing.

— Thirteen —

The rumble of a starship's thrusters at full power yanked me out of a pleasant dream, and I woke to find the world shaking uncontrollably. It took a few seconds before I realized it was an earthquake. Ventano experienced them regularly. Mission's very own version of the ring of fire ran along the shores of the Tyrellian Sea, and everything was built so it could withstand even the worst tremors. They subsided just as quickly as they'd come on, but before I could fall asleep once more, a siren startled me. It had to be the tsunami warning I read about in the information package I found on my sitting-room table the day before.

Most of Ventano was well above the shoreline, and the 24th Regiment's base was even higher, so we weren't in danger of being swept away. I turned on my bedroom's primary display and called up the local news net. An underwater volcano had blown its top, triggering the quake. The Mission Colony Geological Service had been monitoring it for weeks, so the eruption didn't come as a total surprise. Still, since it was almost oh-four-hundred, I climbed out of bed and slipped on my exercise clothes for an early morning run, hoping I could catch sight of the tsunami as it barreled up the North Fjord.

I wasn't the only one with the same idea. Sergeant Bonta came out of her suite moments after I left mine. We exchanged nods and made our way to the lobby. It was a given Arno wouldn't join us. His idea of exercise didn't involve jogging.

Once outside, we saw a fair number of Constabulary members, both in civilian or exercise gear and in uniform. Bonta and I joined others assembling at a spot overlooking the fjord. There, we stretched, eyes on the black waters reflecting both the stars and the city lights.

Almost half an hour later, we watched in awe as the water receded as if someone pulled a plug at the bottom of the sea. A few minutes later, a wall of water barreled up the fjord, growing in height as the fjord narrowed and became shallower. It crashed ashore at the base of the Ventano peninsula, where the government had deliberately left the low-lying ground vacant.

"Wow." Bonta shook her head. "That's impressive. I'd hate to be on the receiving end."

"It's just the first of several waves," a woman from the 24th wearing an inspector's twin diamonds on the collar said. "Sometimes, the second is even bigger. When they sound the all-clear, you should visit the impact area. Many of our more enterprising criminals bury unwanted things, bodies included, in shallow pits there, hoping a tsunami will suck them out to sea."

I glanced at her.

"You see a lot of tsunamis?"

"Maybe half a dozen a year."

The water receded again, signaling a second crest would come in a few minutes. We kept watching, mesmerized, as it sped up the fjord, growing more massive than the first wave before scouring the base of the peninsula.

"I can well believe that sort of thing might unearth a shallow grave and suck out its contents. What happens to the docks and boats in both the north and south fjords?"

"The docks are drowned, which is why no one ever leaves anything on them. As for the boats, when the warning siren sounds, their mooring lines are automatically lengthened so they can ride the crests. Not all survive a bad tsunami, but we don't see many casualties, and most of those come from folks being stupid. My name is Lestrade, by the way, Chief Superintendent Morrow. Operations watchkeeper."

"You know who I am?"

"Everyone knows about the Sector HQ snag hunters turned homicide investigators. Besides, I've been monitoring your case. Kind of hard not to, since it's the most interesting game in town at the moment." She drew herself to attention. "I'd better return. The calls go up after a tsunami. There are always people who find themselves in trouble because they're foolhardy or missed the alert."

Lestrade turned on her heels and headed back for the HQ building just as I spotted a private car coming through the main gate. It crossed the parade square and parked in the slot with the sign 'Commanding Officer.' Braband getting an early start to the day as well. Everyone in Ventano and around the Tyrellian Sea must be doing the same. The eastern horizon took on a delicate shade of pink, announcing imminent dawn, and I nudged Bonta.

"Want to stay around and watch the next few waves, or go for a run?"

She glanced over my shoulder.

"Since AC Braband is heading in our direction, I think I'll go for a run by myself, sir. He looks like he wants a word with you."

Bonta stepped off without further comment, leaving me wondering whether Braband was coming to discuss the investigation. That would be unwise, considering his position. I gave him a polite nod.

"Good morning, sir." Everyone within earshot moved away, giving Braband and me a broad circle of privacy.

"Good morning, Chief Superintendent. Your first tsunami?"

"Yes."

"Awesome force of nature, aren't they?" He seemed and sounded preoccupied.

"Indeed. Can I do something for you?"

"When did you last see Mayleen Allore?"

"The night of the murder."

"So, it was a homicide."

"The ME found a needler puncture on Tosh's neck, made shortly before death. The tox screen didn't pick up any poison, but there are several substances I'm aware of which degrade rapidly after killing the victim. Why are you asking me about Allore?"

"I haven't seen or spoken to her since the day before yesterday. We normally see each other, at least via video link, every evening. I stopped by her townhouse on my way in this morning, and it was dark when others around it were brightly lit, thanks to the alarm. Mayleen wouldn't sleep through a tsunami, and she would open the door to me without hesitation."

"Perhaps she's staying with friends. Finding Amaris Tosh like that could have been traumatic."

A dubious look crossed his face.

"I don't know of any friends who'd bring her more comfort than I can. In fact, I'm not sure she has many friends. I certainly never met any that weren't colonial administration people."

"Isn't she a Mission Colony native?"

He shook his head.

"No. Mayleen immigrated here a few years ago. She worked as head of marketing for the local branch of a large retail chain before Peet hired her."

"What chain?"

"Roso."

I didn't need the Constabulary's intelligence database because I knew about Roso thanks to several investigations involving Louis Sorne and his Deep Space Foundation. Roso was yet another subsidiary of ComCorp, one allied with the late Louis Sorne's miniature zaibatsu.

"Let me get this straight, Assistant Commissioner. Your friend Mayleen Allore used to work in an executive capacity, minor as it was, for a company that belongs to the same consortium as Luca Derzin's Aeternum. The same Derzin you think spends too much time with Governor

Peet and evades the sort of government oversight applicable to normal businesses."

He answered in a vaguely sheepish tone after a long moment of silence.

"When you say it like that, Chief Superintendent, then I suppose I might have placed myself in a compromising position."

"There's no suppose about it, sir. I'm not attributing blame, but something led to Amaris Tosh's death, just as something triggered Governor Peet's accusation that you acted in a contemptuous manner toward her. And now, Mayleen Allore isn't answering her calls or opening her door. Do you see what I'm getting at?"

"In exquisite detail, Chief Superintendent. What can I do to assist your inquiries?"

"Did you run a trace on her activities since she left Government House the day before yesterday?"

"That wouldn't be ethical. No one has reported her missing."

"You just reported to the SIO that one of the witnesses and potential suspects in her homicide case is incommunicado. That makes a trace not only ethical but mandatory. Could you ask your people to run it and report back directly to me?"

"Certainly."

"And what about her residence? Do you have access?"

He nodded. "Yes."

"You didn't go in to check when you passed by earlier this morning?"

"No. We gave each other access to our respective homes, but never entered uninvited. We're lovers, not partners. Intruding doesn't seem right unless I've exhausted other possibilities."

This was the man we vetted last year. Scrupulous to a fault. But with a blind spot. Mayleen Allore found Amaris Tosh's body, then she went dark. There were no coincidences in either a homicide or a professional compliance investigation, and I was running both simultaneously.

"If the trace doesn't tell us anything, I will intrude, so please keep your access code handy, sir."

"Of course. Thank you for your time and attention, Chief Superintendent. I feel relieved that you'll check on Mayleen."

I didn't have the heart to tell him that unless we found her within the next few hours, she would become the number one on my list of suspects. Although something in his eyes told me he already knew and hoped against hope I'd find her before lunch.

"She's part of my investigation, sir."

"I'll see that my intelligence team does the trace. Enjoy your run."

Suddenly, with dawn breaking and the tsunami show over, I didn't feel quite so keen on a run. I'd rather discuss this new development with Arno and Sergeant Bonta over a cup of coffee and a breakfast sandwich. But I forced myself into a ground-eating trot, nonetheless, looking for Bonta. Her dedication to fitness was one of my few motivators, even though I knew achieving something like her sculpted physique was beyond my reach. The Morrow genes simply couldn't match hers.

— Fourteen —

"You think she scarpered, Chief?" Arno looked up from his breakfast plate after I finished telling him and Sergeant Bonta about my conversation with AC Braband.

"Right now, I don't know what to think. But Allore is smart and will surely know going dark a few hours after Tosh's murder puts her at the head of our suspects list."

Bonta shrugged. "Or it could be something perfectly innocent. She took off for a secluded cabin in the woods so she could process finding the body."

"You know what the Chief says about coincidences."

"Sure. There's no such thing."

My communicator buzzed softly. One glance at its screen told me all I needed. Intelligence couldn't pick up a single trace of Mayleen Allore. The last record of her in any system on Mission Colony was when she left Government House the night of the murder. Her personal communicator vanished from the net shortly afterward.

When he saw my expression, Arno asked, "They drew a blank?"

"Ironically, if she did a runner, then I was one of the last people to see her, besides the guards at the main entrance. We're visiting her townhouse after breakfast." As if on cue, my device buzzed again. This time it was from AC Braband. The code for Mayleen Allore's residence. He likely read the trace report at the same time I did. "And we're set."

The townhouse was ordinary, a middle-class two-story in an unremarkable middle-class neighborhood west of downtown Ventano. Sergeant Bonta had borrowed a handheld police sensor from the 24th Regiment's quartermaster stores and scanned the building from inside our car. I didn't want us to enter unannounced and scare the living daylights out of Allore, although my instincts told me she wasn't home.

"No life signs, sir."

"Let's go."

We climbed out under the curious gaze of morning walkers a few dozen meters up the street. Our car, though unmarked, was nonetheless an identifiable police model. And to civilian eyes, the trio of watchful, business-suited people who emerged from it could only be plainclothes cops — especially tough-looking Bonta with the noticeable bulge of her sidearm beneath a waist-length jacket.

We walked up a short flight of stairs to the front door, which opened with a soft sigh when I broadcast the code Braband sent me. I stepped aside and let Bonta enter first. She had an annoyingly effective way of scolding me without sounding insubordinate whenever I went into an unknown space ahead of her.

Empty houses gave off a unique vibe, a feeling of loneliness, and this one sent the right signals. The lights were off in the foyer and in the rooms opening onto it, and the silence was deafening. Moreover, the air seemed exceedingly pure, thanks to the environmental system scrubbing out any remnant trace of human occupation, such as carbon dioxide and the simple scents of life.

I waited in the foyer while Arno and Sergeant Bonta cleared each room on the ground floor before doing the same upstairs. The sensor might not detect life signs, but there were ways of foiling it.

"No one's here, sir, and everything is tidy."

I wandered through the house, trying to get a sense of Mayleen Allore and why she went dark the night of the murder. Yet try as I might, I couldn't form a picture of the private woman and her inner self. Everything seemed picture-perfect, the decor designed by a professional. Her furniture was elegant, and the artwork struck me as reproductions whose sole purpose was subtly pleasing the eye.

But it felt soulless. Even the bedroom didn't seem like the private sanctuary most of us create. It was overly neat, unlike most bedrooms I've seen in my time as an investigator, and I've seen plenty. My own back home wasn't this perfectly arranged, and I can be a little obsessive about neatness.

"Let's see if we can figure whether she packed her bags." I nodded at the two chests of drawers. "Arno, Sergeant, those are yours. I'll do what looks like a walk-in closet."

Ten minutes later, we regrouped on the second-floor landing.

"No obvious empty spaces anywhere, though I'll say she has excellent taste in clothing."

"Better than yours from what I saw, sir." Bonta gave me a knowing look. When she wore her own suits, rather than the bulletproof issue, Bonta was as much of a fashion plate as she was a recruiting poster in uniform.

"Didn't seem like overly expensive stuff, though. What I saw came from fabricators, not bespoke tailors." Arno shrugged. "The jewelry wasn't much to write home about either."

We searched every room, opening closets, cupboards, and drawers, but we found little that hinted at the occupant's character.

"Where are the messy bits everyone hides away? This place is a model house, not a home." I pulled out my communicator and linked it with the Operations Center.

"What can we do for you, Chief Superintendent?" A cheerful voice asked moments later.

"Can you find out when Mayleen Allore moved into her current place of residence."

"Give us a few minutes. That shouldn't be difficult to track down."

"Morrow, out." I pointed at the kitchen. "Let's do an inventory of the foodstuffs and find her booze stash."

We found pre-prepared meals in the freezer and little else, along with a few wine bottles and a liter of Glen Arcturus, which I suspected was for AC Braband. Allore didn't strike me as a single malt connoisseur.

"Either she ate out a lot, or she—" My communicator buzzed. "Hang on. Morrow here."

"Sir, Mayleen Allore moved into her current residence in December of last year. The lease on record has her starting on the fifteen of the month."

"Thank you. Morrow out." My wingers and I exchanged glances. "She rented this place shortly before AC Braband's arrival on Mission."

"But after his appointment became public knowledge." Trust Arno to store obscure bits of data in his capacious brain. "As I said the other day, I can understand what Braband sees in her, but I can't figure out why he doesn't see through her. Something about Allore struck me as off-center from the beginning."

"Could she have another residence elsewhere in the city and kept this one strictly for Braband's sake?" Bonta asked.

"Possibly."

"Time for a little theorizing, Chief."

I held up my hand.

"Sergeant, let's make sure Inspector Galdi's theorizing won't be overheard."

"Sir." She pulled out her bug detector and let it scan the immediate area. "Clear."

"Go ahead, Arno."

He scratched his beard as his eyes lost focus.

"Just spit balling here, but I figure something unlawful is happening on Mission Colony, and it involves Governor Peet and Luca Derzin. Peet hires Allore shortly after her arrival, except Allore isn't a Mission native. She's an immigrant who worked for a ComCorp subsidiary. Could be her taking the job was engineered by someone. Then, AC Kristy Bujold steps on a rake with Eva Cortez and a new police chief lands, one with a roving eye. That eye lands on Allore, who seems good at pillow talk. With me so far?"

"Yes, and I can tell you the rest of that theory. Allore's job is controlling or influencing Braband, but when that doesn't work, and he starts snooping, Peet lodges a complaint against him with DCC Maras. In the meantime, our victim finds out about things Peet wants to keep quiet, and she's poisoned. Either the ME doesn't notice the puncture mark and calls it cardiac arrest, cause unknown, or he finds the puncture mark and calls it suspicious. But Braband's people running the investigation raises the conflict of interest issue, especially if Allore's a suspect. That could lead to a standoff, and compromise Braband, which is second best after not finding ways of controlling him."

"Then we show up unannounced, and you take over as SIO. Oops, there goes a cunning plan." Arno chortled. "No one ever expects us. That's a big part of our charm."

"As theories go," Sergeant Bonta said, "it's rather good except for one thing. The pillow talk that made Braband suspicious."

"Perhaps Allore didn't think Government House gossip would lead to him snooping. After all, anything she shared would be public knowledge, at least where the staff was concerned."

"True. Do we assume Allore is still among the living and in the wind?"

"We do." I retrieved my communicator once more and pinged the Operations Center. We had no choice but to put an all-points bulletin on Mayleen Allore, Assistant Commissioner Braband's pride be damned.

"Chief Superintendent?"

"I am registering Mayleen Allore as a person of interest in the death of Amaris Tosh. Please disseminate her biometric data throughout the colony. She should be detained on sight and barred from leaving the planet. When is the next scheduled starship?"

A momentary silence, then, "The regular Cimmeria-Mission run, a transport by the name *Thebes* is due in forty hours."

"Make sure anyone who bears the slightest resemblance to Mayleen Allore doesn't board *Thebes*."

"Understood, Chief Superintendent."

"Morrow, out."

"Crime scene investigation, Chief?" Arno asked.

I gave the question a few seconds of thought. If we were dealing with a broader conspiracy, they wouldn't find anything useful. This place screamed professional cleaning.

"Sergeant, did you bring surveillance limpets?"

"Of course."

"Then we're done here. Set limpets on both front and back doors and link them to the Operations Center. I don't think any persons of interest will show up, let alone Mayleen Allore, but better safe than face an annoyed federal prosecutor."

"Consider it done." She crossed the foyer and re-entered the living room, where a glass door gave onto a small garden.

Arno cocked an eyebrow at me. "What's next, Chief? No point in returning to Government House."

"I should speak with AC Braband and let him know he might have been sleeping with the enemy."

"He'll be thrilled, no doubt."

"Even more so when I tell him that his liaison with Allore, innocent as it may have seemed, could require a professional compliance investigation."

"Only if you decide so, Chief."

Arno was right. I might as well simply roll Braband's relationship into the original investigation. That way, he wouldn't spend the rest of his career branded with a question mark concerning his personal judgment. We watched Bonta set the front door limpet, then left the townhouse and its eerily artificial atmosphere.

— Fifteen —

Braband slumped back in his chair after I finished describing our search of Allore's townhouse and laid out the conclusions we drew from it, although I didn't share our working theory.

"I've been a damned fool."

"Possibly, and you wouldn't be the first, but it's circumstantial for the moment. I've put out an APB on Allore. Vanishing like that makes her a person of interest."

"I suppose I can kiss my chances at a commissioner's star goodbye. Senior officers who fall for honey pots don't become flag officers."

"If you did nothing wrong, then the honey pot failed. Your career shouldn't be affected because of it."

A wry smile appeared as he snorted.

"It's entirely possible you saved my bacon by showing up on Mission without warning and taking over the murder investigation, Chief Superintendent. Rescued by the Firing Squad's Lady High Executioner — the irony is simply out of this world. I shudder at thinking how events would be unfolding without you." He sat up, put his elbows on the desktop, and steepled his fingers. "What the hell is happening in this star system?"

"That's what I plan on finding out."

"And Amaris Tosh's murder?"

"Mayleen Allore is our sole suspect, and only because she vanished shortly after finding her body."

"I can't believe she's a cold-blooded killer. Surely I would have noticed something."

"Did you ever work homicide or major crimes?" I already knew the answer but asked anyway.

He shook his head. "No. I've been a uniformed member my entire career."

"One thing I discovered when I was a detective in the Rim Sector Major Crimes Division, is that the people who can kill in cold blood are extremely good at fooling others, including experienced investigators. I've met my share of psychopaths who were plausible beyond belief. The only way we caught them was waiting for the one inevitable mistake."

"It hurts my police officer's pride to think I might have misjudged Mayleen so badly." The wounded expression in his eyes was borderline comical.

"We don't know if she's our killer, sir."

"True, but if you're right, then I most certainly misjudged her."

"Again, supposition based on circumstantial evidence."

"Good circumstantial evidence. Considering my predecessor was thoroughly compromised, someone on Mission wants the CO of the 24th Constabulary Regiment under their thumb."

"The trick will be finding that someone."

"The regiment's resources are at your disposal, Chief Superintendent. I'll make sure the Operations Center knows."

I found Arno and Sergeant Bonta leaning against our car in the HQ parking lot, but no sign of the driver.

"Where's Corporal Caffrey?"

"Since we'll be delving into AC Braband's personal life, I thought it best if the young fellow weren't around to overhear us. Sergeant Bonta took charge of our metal steed and will steer us around town. I have Allore's previous address." He nodded at Bonta, and the car doors opened. She slid in behind the controls while Arno and I took the rear seats. "How did the AC react?"

"About as you'd expect. He's embarrassed and a bit angry at himself for not noticing that things were amiss with Allore. And afraid his career will derail once Maras finds out he fell victim to a calculated seduction."

"But he didn't fall victim. At least not that we know of. The honey pot, if there was one, misfired."

"He thinks it might still have worked if we hadn't shown up out of the blue on the day of Amaris Tosh's murder."

"An honest man."

"Where are we headed?" Bonta asked over her shoulder.

"Government House. We're speaking with everyone there again, this time about Mayleen Allore."

Arno nodded. "That's what I thought."

I let Arno and Sergeant Bonta scan the incident room when we arrived, just in case someone planted surveillance gear overnight, and stuck my head into Terrence Salak's office.

"Is the governor available?"

He gave me his usual glare.

"Why?"

"I need a few minutes of her time."

"Concerning?"

"My recommendation she hires a new private secretary, Mister Salak. Your attitude and lack of manners are becoming tiresome." He gave me a stunned glare as if I were the first to call him on his manners. Considering how bureaucracies worked at the best of times, I probably was. "Perhaps we should delve into your private financial affairs and see if you've been naughty. Remember, we don't just investigate Constabulary members. All federal employees are subject to investigation for misconduct by the Professional Compliance Bureau."

His stunned expression turned into one of fear, and I briefly wondered whether Salak felt guilty about a personal peccadillo. But he scrambled to his feet and slipped through the connecting door between his and Peet's office. He reappeared a few moments later.

"Governor Peet will see you now, Chief Superintendent."

"Thank you." Before he could say or do anything else, I turned on my heels and left his office so I could let myself into the holy of holies from the hallway.

Peet glared at me from behind her desk as I crossed the room and dropped into one of the upholstered chairs facing her without waiting for an invitation.

"You seem rather careless with your personal staff, Governor."

"What do you mean?"

"First, someone murders your chief of staff next door to where we sit, then your social secretary, who found her body, vanishes not long after. Did you not notice Mayleen Allore hasn't shown up for work since the day before yesterday?"

"She's entitled to vacation time after the trauma of Amaris's death."

"Has she asked for a few days off?"

"No. I've not seen or spoken with her since she found Amaris. Neither, as far as I know, has Terrence."

"And you're not worried about her welfare?"

An air of impatience pinched Peet's face.

"Of course, I am. But Mayleen is a competent adult, and Ventano is one of the safest cities in the Rim Sector."

Her claim was debatable, but I didn't feel like a protracted discussion.

"You hired her soon after taking up your appointment."

"Yes. You already knew that."

"How did she come to your attention?"

"Must we do this?" When I didn't reply, she raised her hand in a gesture of surrender while irritation replaced her earlier air of impatience. "Very well. In the early days after my arrival, I attended an extensive list of social functions, to meet and greet the colony's notables and not so notables. It was quite exhausting, as you can imagine. Terrence, despite his many other qualities, isn't discerning enough to manage my social calendar. I mentioned my need for a social secretary in passing at the Mission Colony Chamber of Commerce reception, and Roso's local general manager mentioned his head of marketing, Mayleen Allore, was looking for a step up. I interviewed her. We meshed, and I hired her a few days later."

And just like that, another thread appeared. Coincidence or an opportunistic plant? Allore was looking more and more like the principal actor in this tragedy. If neither Peet nor Braband saw through her, she was a person of interest indeed. However, I didn't think the former was a particularly skilled judge of character, considering she kept Salak at her side and socialized with Derzin. But Braband was a thirty-year veteran of the service.

"Did anything in Allore's behavior during her time with you seem strange or questionable?"

"No. Nothing. Mayleen is a splendid social secretary and has made my life immeasurably easier."

"Any idea where she might be right now? A hideaway or friends where she could take a breather?"

"Can't think of anything, Chief Superintendent, but then I pay little attention to my staffers' personal lives. They're entitled to privacy outside the colonial administration's fishbowl."

Somehow, I couldn't see concern for privacy motivating Peet. She didn't strike me as the sort who cared about others beyond how they could help further her career. Did she even know the real Mayleen Allore or the real Amaris Tosh for that matter? Probably not.

"I'm sure she'll turn up when she's ready. Now was there anything else? I am rather busy, seeing as how I no longer have a chief of staff to help me."

Peet was all heart.

"Thank you for your time, Governor." I stood and left her office without another word, conscious of her eyes burning holes in my back.

The incident room was empty, proof my wingers were already re-interviewing staff. I logged on and found a brief message from Rudel telling me we had full access to the employee files. I pulled up Mayleen Allore's personal details and drafted a message for Sector HQ intelligence, asking they run a background check on her. It would take several days, but I wondered what else about Allore didn't fit the carefully composed image she projected. Fortunately, the Constabulary policed her homeworld of New Tasman, which meant no need to involve local police.

The Mission Colony file on Allore was rather thin, however. Only one previous employer listed — Roso, whose local head was her sole reference. I searched for his name in the police database and saw he'd left Mission shortly after the Bujold matter last year, destination unknown.

I passed her banking information to the Operations Center and asked that they have the financial institution watch it for any activity. Then, I checked her earlier address, an apartment now occupied by a family whose name didn't trigger any results. A few minutes later, I received a message from Operations confirming no one accessed Allore's financial accounts since early on the day of Tosh's murder and that they held healthy balances.

"What did you do, Mayleen? And where are you?"

I touched the desk's embedded screen and called Rudel's office. His assistant put me through right away.

"What can I do for you, Chief Superintendent?"

"How well do you know Mayleen Allore?"

"Why? Did she become your primary suspect overnight?" Before I could reply, he raised a hand. "Never mind. I shouldn't ask. I don't know her beyond the odd Government House function and hallway greeting. She always struck me as self-possessed, someone who lives behind a facade."

"What would you say if I told you Mayleen hasn't shown up for work the last two days? She's not answering queries and hasn't been home since the night of the murder."

"That you have your killer."

"There could be many good reasons for Allore's absence. Were you involved in her hiring?"

He shook his head. "Jeanne just called up one day and told me she was taking Mayleen Allore on as her social secretary under the locally engaged employee rules, and that was it."

"No vetting, no background checks, no civil services rules involved?"

"The governor can hire locals without following the normal process if she justifies her actions and has room in her budget for added Government House staff. I didn't think it was worth my time opposing Allore's appointment as the social secretary, and I simply countersigned the job offer. If it turns out she killed Amaris, I'll blame myself for the rest of my days."

He probably meant it too.

"Thank you, Mister Rudel."

"Any time, Chief Superintendent."

"Enjoy the rest of your day."

"You as well."

I cut the link and sat back. Did someone slip Mayleen Allore into Government House when Peet took over? And if so, why? Sparking a relationship with AC Braband was nothing more than seizing the opportunity as it presented. When Peet hired Allore, AC Bujold was still in command, and so far, we'd found no evidence of any connection between them.

I spent an hour combing through the remaining personal files, including Peet's but found nothing of interest. As I closed the last of them, I heard voices in the corridor. Arno and Luca Derzin. The latter seemed to spend as much time here as any staff member.

"Mister Derzin. A moment of your time, please."

Seconds later, Arno ushered him into the incident room. By the expression on Derzin's face, Arno had probably crowded him in my direction.

— Sixteen —

"What can I do for you, Chief Superintendent?"

I gestured at one of the chairs in front of my desk. "Please sit."

"If you only want a moment of my time, then thanks, but I'll remain standing."

"Best do as the chief asks, Mister Derzin. She's not in a good mood today."

He gave Arno a hard stare but complied. "Let me guess, Chief Superintendent — he plays good cop, and you play bad cop?"

"I leave the bad cop part to Sergeant Bonta. She's more intimidating. How well do you know Mayleen Allore?"

"Why? Is she your prime suspect?"

"She hasn't been seen since the night of the murder."

"That's what I heard." When I cocked a questioning eyebrow at him, he said, "Jeanne — Governor Peet called and told me before I arrived just now. Why do you believe I might know Allore enough to help you find her?"

"She worked for the same zaibatsu as you before joining the governor's staff."

"Are you aware of how many people are employed by ComCorp and its subsidiaries and their subsidiaries? Literally millions."

"But there aren't that many ComCorp people on Mission, and you regularly socialize with the governor."

"You understand Mayleen left Roso before I arrived. She was no longer part of the great ComCorp family at the time."

"Yet you're aware of her past employment."

A faint smirk appeared. "You should understand that I know a lot about many people, Chief Superintendent, including those who are still wanted by the Pacifican State Security Police."

"Only because no one ever canceled the warrant. Even political crimes have a statute of limitations on Pacifica."

"Oh, the star system government can reissue it at any time. But you were asking about Mayleen. I couldn't tell you where she is or why she might have killed Amaris. We were acquainted with each other in the same way I was acquainted with Amaris — because both work for Jeanne. That being said, I can't see her as a murderer, especially not a cold-blooded one. She's not the type. But if it turns out she killed Amaris, I wonder what that says about Assistant Commissioner Braband's judgment as a senior Constabulary officer."

"Let me worry about that, Mister Derzin. It's what I do for a living. When you say she's not the type, what do you mean?"

He gave me a languid shrug. "Just an impression. Mayleen didn't seem passionate about anything."

"Passion isn't a requirement to kill. Professional assassins are as unemotional as it gets."

"Oh! So now you consider her an assassin. That's quite the leap."

He was trying to goad me. But you didn't survive for long in the Professional Compliance Bureau without becoming inured.

"Is there anything besides her lack of passion that makes you believe she can't be responsible for Amaris Tosh's death?"

Another shrug.

"Call it my feel for people. For example, I can tell that you possess a killer instinct, unlike Assistant Commissioner Braband."

"Don't let the persona I project during an investigation fool you. I don't go around the Rim Sector executing corrupt officials. At best, I terminate their careers and comfortable lifestyles."

"But you have killed." His tone made it a statement, so there was no point in me responding.

"If you or any of your business acquaintances hear from or about Mayleen Allore, I'd appreciate a quick call. Thank you for your courtesy, Mister Derzin. You're free to go."

He stood, keeping his eyes on me as if wondering why I neither confirmed nor denied his assertion.

"Chief Superintendent."

Once he was gone, Arno closed the office door and grunted.

"Now that man could easily get under anyone's skin if he so desired. A dangerous customer."

"Most of the top-level ComCorp executives are. Do you figure he knows more about Allore than he lets on?"

"Without a doubt, Chief. ComCorp doesn't differ much from organized crime groups like the Confederacy of the Howling Stars or the cartels. Not only is the code of silence paramount, once a manager reaches a certain level, leaving the gang becomes impossible. Allore being hired as Peet's private secretary predates Derzin's arrival on Mission, however that doesn't mean he wasn't keeping tabs on her, or even that she wasn't still connected somehow with ComCorp."

"Perhaps he was using her to keep tabs on Peet and Braband. Did the re-interviews do any good?"

"Negative. Turns out Mayleen Allore is more of a cipher than we thought. Yours?"

"Same. I asked Sector HQ for a background check on her, but that'll take a few days. We have access to the personnel files, by the way. I already looked at those of the staffers present at the time of the murder and found nothing useful. But you and the sergeant should go through them as well."

"Will do, Chief. I wonder what Derzin and the governor are talking about right now."

"I've wondered what they discuss since day one."

"You know, our good sergeant can turn Peet's computer terminal into a listening device with no one the wiser."

"If we want evidence admissible in court, we'll need a warrant from a federal judge, and we don't have sufficient cause. Besides, this star system strikes me as incestuous enough, we might end up petitioning a judge who also enjoys Derzin's hospitality."

"True. We've nabbed a few indiscreet ones over the years." Before Arno could reminisce, Sergeant Bonta returned from her re-interviews and dropped into a chair.

"Nothing. Everyone thinks highly of Allore, but no one knows much about her, let alone her personal life. AC Braband is probably the closest, and even he doesn't have a clue. She's a blank slate on which everyone drew their own impression of Mayleen, the model social secretary." Bonta grimaced. "Truth be told, sir, Allore strikes me as the sort who might be in the same line of business as your Naval Intelligence friends. Although perhaps working for the other side."

"Not unsurprisingly, I agree with the sergeant, Chief. Can I suggest we turn our attention to Luca Derzin? Since we have no obvious suspect and Allore is in the wind, I figure he's next in line."

"I already put through a background check request, but that too will take a few days. While you add the latest interviews to the case file, I'll see what we can dig up on our over-friendly executive."

Like a typical ComCorp executive, Derzin's public record was scanty, and his local police record non-existent. We learned no more about the man by delving through Mission Colony's governmental and open source databases.

"We're pretty much dead in the water until the background checks on Allore and Derzin come back, Chief. Or until someone finds a needler of the right caliber with a staff member's fingerprints or trace DNA on it, which is unlikely in the extreme."

Sergeant Bonta let out a humorless chuckle. "Maybe the needler was washed out to sea by this morning's tsunami."

Arno gave her a questioning glance, and she related Inspector Lestrade's comments about the local criminals using tsunamis to dispose of unwanted objects.

"Then I suppose it's too late for a search of the area."

"The way those waves came in. Without a doubt."

I shut off my terminal and stretched. "How about a pleasant excursion into the countryside tomorrow? Somewhere south of here?"

"Aeternum's facility, Chief?"

"Yes. We won't knock on the front door, though. I just want a peek at it and be seen looking by Derzin's people."

"Aha!" Arno raised an extended index finger. "A little provocation to advance our professional compliance case. I like it."

"Aircar, sir?"

"No. I don't want any questions about our trip. We'll take the scenic route."

Arno's forehead creased into a frown. "You're not trusting the 24th anymore?"

"Too many strange things around here. I'd rather we keep our own counsel, especially since I'm beginning to believe the murder and our professional compliance matter may be connected."

"Ditto."

— Seventeen —

Mission Colony's mostly unspoiled native vegetation outside the major settlements and agricultural areas was worth a lengthy drive by ground car. Impossibly green, lush, and even a bit eerie under a reddish sun, it held me rapt for most of the trip. When we crested the last hill before the Aeternum site, which occupied a broad valley a dozen kilometers inland, safe from any tsunamis, I asked Bonta to stop and park by the side of the road. Since it ended at the facility's main gate, traffic was no worry. We climbed out and stretched our limbs.

The place looked more like a spaceport than a pharmaceuticals research and development facility. A sprawling, warehouse-like building sat next to a landing strip big enough for standard faster-than-light commercial sloops. Both were surrounded by a double layer of fencing at least three meters high, topped with razor wire. The ten-meter expanse between the inner and outer fences was grassy, except where the single access road cut through, but I thought I saw suspicious bumps at regular intervals. Hidden sensor arrays, or even remote weapon stations, although privately owned RWS systems were strictly regulated. Us cops and our Fleet cousins didn't like that kind of weaponry in just anyone's hands.

I didn't doubt we were under observation by their security already. Our car likely triggered an alarm well before it came into view. We studied the facility in silence with the service-issue sensors we'd borrowed before leaving the base but saw no signs of life, not even ground vehicles. It could have been an automated warehouse or factory for all we knew.

"Sergeant, please check if that landing strip is a recognized private spaceport."

"One moment, please." Bonta pulled out her communicator and linked it with the Operations Center. A few moments later, she said, "The strip is registered and certified. Ventano Spaceport controls traffic to and from it below ten kilometers altitude."

Private companies operating their own terminals weren't unusual, especially on less populated worlds, and a vertically integrated zaibatsu like ComCorp owned a fleet of starships, most notably under the Black Nova Shipping flag. Mission Colony operated under federal customs rules, which in practice meant unrestricted import and export of legal, Commonwealth-produced items. Customs officials would not be required to clear incoming ships if their captains showed provenance.

It meant Aeternum could bring in and ship out whatever it wanted, and no one the wiser. Since this star system was within easy reach of the Shrehari Empire as well as the Protectorate and its lawless worlds, my cop's instincts told me we were looking at more than a simple pharmaceutical

R&D laboratory. ComCorp, like every major zaibatsu, wasn't exactly shy about maximizing profits by means both fair and foul. It would explain the secrecy. The bribes Aeternum probably paid to build this monstrosity without oversight must have been stunning. Were members of the local administration beneficiaries, or did Colonial Office bureaucrats on Earth enjoy the largess?

I repressed an unexpected urge to wave at unseen watchers, but that would tell a perceptive individual such as Derzin I was goading him in turn. No, I needed a natural reaction from this mostly futile expedition, not another round of gamesmanship.

"When we return, let's find out who's been landing here since the place opened for business, and who's scheduled in the coming weeks."

"You think this might double as a smuggler's way station, Chief?"

"It's convenient as hell. They bring forbidden items in from the Protectorate aboard free traders, process or repackage them, then ship into the Commonwealth in ComCorp hulls. It would fit with Derzin keeping the governor sweet and barring Rudel's people from doing the normal inspections."

"Imagine the profit margin if you're right. And that's above the hefty bribes they would have paid to high-ranking Colonial Office executives for their certificates and exemptions. Bureaucrats with generous salaries and benefits and a pension plan most can only dream of don't come cheap."

"My thoughts exactly, but remember, we also enjoy generous salaries, benefits, and good pensions, and we don't sell out at any price."

"True, Chief. But we prefer being inquisitors. Some would call it a moral failing. I prefer thinking of it as a specialized kind of virtue."

Bonta snorted loudly. "Don't get too full of yourself, Inspector."

"Worldly delights can never fill the hole in my soul, Sergeant."

We were headed for the usual banter rabbit hole — one I didn't feel like moderating.

"Does either of you want more time staring at the lifeless Aeternum monolith?"

Arno shook his head.

"I recall a charming roadside inn near where a private road leaves the main highway, headed for what is now Derzin's country estate. Lunch anyone?"

The inn wasn't what I would have called charming, but it had a lovely patio where we could talk without being overheard, not that it was full of diners this early on a weekday. Armed with sandwiches and steaming coffee cups, we took the table furthest from the back door, beneath a towering native tree.

"So, what did we learn?"

Arno let out a soft grunt.

"It'll take a company from the 1st Special Forces Regiment to find out what's really going on. Can you dial one up via your buddies in Naval Intelligence? Otherwise, I figure we're facing another dead end."

Bonta snapped her fingers and pointed at Arno.

"That's what was bugging me about the Aeternum compound. It looks very much like a military installation and not an R&D lab. I've seen Marine forward operating bases with less airtight defenses. What the hell *are* they doing?"

Arno took a sip of coffee, then said, "Smuggling? Drug running under cover of pharmaceutical R&D? The possibilities are endless."

They were indeed, and I didn't quite know what we could do next. On the way back, we drove up to the gates of Derzin's country estate and studied it from a distance, knowing his security system would pick up our presence.

Even though it was mid-afternoon by the time we reached Ventano, we headed for Government House. If Luca Derzin was visiting the governor, he might poke his head into the incident room and ask about our interest in his facility and mansion. Stillness reigned over the executive corridor. Allore was still among the missing, and Salak wasn't behind his desk, though the door to Peet's office was closed.

I checked for updates from forensics while Sergeant Bonta and Arno called up the list of ships that touched down on the Aeternum landing strip. Inspector Kosta had sent no messages, meaning they'd found nothing new. So far, we didn't know why Tosh died, who did it, and where Allore went after I released her the day of the murder. With nothing else to go on, I composed a message for Captain Talyn, telling her about the situation on Mission Colony and our suspicions, both in the matter of official misconduct and Tosh's murder.

Shortly after firing off the encrypted missive, my ears picked up the soft sound of Peet's office door opening, followed by the voices of Derzin and the governor. Both Arno and Sergeant Bonta glanced at me. Would it be another round of verbal sparring with the ComCorp executive? I was sure he knew about our expeditions by now, but would he let on?

When Derzin's head poked through the open incident room door, I knew he was letting on.

"Are you perchance angling for a guided tour of Aeternum's plant and my mansion, Chief Superintendent?"

I gave him a languid smile. "Whatever do you mean, Mister Derzin?"

"Come now, my security folks spotted the three of you ogling the plant and the estate. I can't help wonder why."

"Would you show us around if I asked nicely?"

An icy smile appeared. "No."

"What if I obtain a warrant?"

"On what grounds? Because you're annoyed with me won't wash, especially not with Justice Bisso. He and I break bread regularly."

Derzin had me there. Pierce Bisso was the chief federal judge in this star system and not known for suffering fools gladly. The other judges on the Mission Colony Bench would naturally take their cues from him.

"But if you'd like to visit the estate on Saturday, I'm hosting a small get-together of like-minded businesspeople over the noon hour."

His smile changed from cold to predatory. He well knew I couldn't be seen socializing with anyone on this planet other than my team.

"Pass."

"Pity. But I can assure you Mayleen Allore isn't hiding in either place." He gave me an ironic wave and vanished.

Arno made a face.

"Lovely man, our Mister Derzin. Always ready to poke the bear. He must feel sure of his position."

"This bear doesn't mind getting poked if it means results, but I think it might be for naught. Any luck with the ships landing at the Aeternum facility?"

"Yes, Chief." Bonta pointed at the incident room's primary display where a list of names and dates appeared. "Regular as clockwork, a free trader, seemingly unaffiliated with any of the big shipping conglomerates, lands around oh-one-hundred every second Monday, sits on the ground for approximately four hours, then lifts off. The crew never leaves the facility. There are six unique names and registration numbers listed, and they seem to arrive in the same order every twelve weeks. None of them provide a point of origin or a destination, meaning traffic control either doesn't care or is paid not to care."

"I vote paid," Arno said.

A new list of names and dates replaced the first one.

"Again, regular as clockwork, those Black Nova Shipping Line freighters land one week after a free trader, also in the middle of the night and lift off before dawn. As with the free traders, the crews don't leave the facility, and their captains don't offer points of origin or destination. And I'm with the inspector. Traffic control probably takes backhanders in exchange for not asking questions."

Arno shrugged. "It could be perfectly innocent. Raw materials from Protectorate star systems, finished pharmaceutical products into the Commonwealth. They wouldn't be the only ones importing exotic stuff for processing."

"How about illegal drugs from Protectorate star systems, repackaged as pharmaceuticals and distributed via Black Nova's network, Inspector? I mean, who likes to work in the middle of the night? Other than those with something worth hiding. Honest ships land in daylight when normal people work the docks."

"An excellent point. The facility does look like a giant warehouse."

I agreed with Arno. "And since the head honcho is best friends with the governor, he enjoys top cover in case overly suspicious cops start nosing around."

"Hence the complaint against Braband. I guess Peet and Derzin didn't consider the fact we might have vetted Bujold's successor to prevent a repeat and would consider unexpected accusations highly suspicious. Do you think they planted Allore on Braband, Chief?"

"ComCorp certainly planted Allore on Peet's staff. Why not add the AC to her brief?"

"And now their plans are unraveling since we're paying them more attention than we're giving Braband. You know what that means, right?"

"We'll soon come under enemy fire ourselves."

Arno nodded, his imposing beard bobbing against his chest. "How do you figure they'll do it?"

"Not with guns blazing. Someone making us vanish or murdering us after Amaris Tosh's death and Mayleen Allore's disappearance would guarantee a full-fledged investigation by the Flying Squad. And the investigators would most certainly be armed with warrants to search the Aeternum facility, warrants signed by someone in the office of the Rim Sector's chief federal judge. No, it'll be something more subtle and twisted."

— Eighteen —

We got an answer of sorts the next morning, shortly after settling into the incident room. I barely finished my coffee before a supercilious clerk from the Mission Colony Court Administration summoned me to Chief Justice Pierce Bisso's office forthwith. Yes, he used that word.

Justice Bisso and I shared something in common. Neither of us was answerable to anyone in this star system. But federal judges outranked Constabulary officers, even those who headed the sector's Professional Compliance Bureau, unless they did something that attracted the PCB's attention. I've run my share of investigations on judges who decided they were above the law.

The colony's main courthouse stood just down the road from Government House, so I opted for a pleasant walk under a clear blue sky, now that the early morning fog, so frequent in these parts, was gone. I showed my credentials to the man at the reception desk in the modern steel and glass, three-story building's lobby, but he made me cool my heels until the clerk with the elaborate vocabulary showed up.

"Chief Superintendent Morrow? Justice Bisso expected you at least ten minutes ago."

"I walked from Government House." And spent fifteen minutes waiting in the lobby, but I didn't think it was worth mentioning.

The clerk, a painfully thin man with a receding hairline and prominent Adam's apple, gave me a hard look, then gestured at the corridor behind reception.

"If you'll follow me."

Chief Justice Bisso's office was on the ground floor, at the back of the courthouse, where it gave onto a miniature private park reserved for him, his fellow judges, and their employees. The office itself rivaled that of Governor Peet for size and opulence.

Bisso, a heavyset, gray-haired man in his early seventies, didn't stand when his clerk ushered me in. He merely stared at me through deep-set brown eyes as I approached his desk while the clerk closed the door behind him, leaving us alone.

"I'm Chief Superintendent Caelin Morrow, Your Honor. You wished to see me?"

He didn't immediately answer, nor did he invite me to sit in one of the chairs facing him. It was part of the game, and since he was pretty much the only person in this star system with the power to cause me genuine grief, I didn't take a seat unbidden.

"I understand you're investigating Amaris Tosh's murder."

"And the disappearance of Mayleen Allore, my prime suspect."

"Yet you're the Rim Sector Professional Compliance Bureau's Commanding Officer. Why are you the SIO charged with this case?"

"Because of AC Braband's relationship with Allore."

"Then shouldn't the Rim Sector Major Crimes Division be tasked with the inquiry?"

"We were here on an unrelated matter, and I volunteered. As you're aware, sir, the first forty-eight hours in a homicide investigation are vital."

"And it's now been what, over four days. Did you solve the case?"

"No, sir. As I mentioned, my prime suspect vanished in the hours following the Tosh's death."

"I see." His fingers tapped an impatient tattoo on the polished desktop. "So, you have nothing to show for your efforts. Now tell me. Why did you come here in the first place?"

"With respect, Your Honor, you know I can't answer that question, not even if it's coming from a star system chief justice."

A scowl replaced his faint air of irritation. "I can see why so many people consider you vexatious, Chief Superintendent."

"It comes with the job, Your Honor."

"Does harassing one of the colony's leading citizens also come with the job?"

And there it was. Bisso would read me the riot act at Derzin's behest.

"I don't understand what you mean. Harassment isn't an approved investigative technique. I treat everyone with respect, even those I arrest." Butter wouldn't melt in my mouth.

"Luca Derzin claims otherwise, and he's hardly the sort who complains needlessly."

"Mister Derzin can lodge a complaint with my superior, Deputy Chief Constable Hammett, like any citizen."

"If you don't desist, that could still happen."

"Desist from doing what, Your Honor? My job? Mister Derzin was in Governor Peet's office at the time of the murder, which places him on the list of potential suspects. I can hardly carry out a proper investigation if I don't interview him as necessary."

"Take care with your tone, Chief Superintendent. You may be answerable to Constabulary HQ on Wyvern, but I can still hold you in contempt here, in my jurisdiction."

There was nothing wrong with my tone, but he held the ultimate ace card. Forcing him to play it could jeopardize both investigations, something DCC Hammett would not forgive despite letting me get away with all sorts of things. I bowed my head in contrition.

"My sincere apologies, Your Honor. Could you tell me what, specifically, I did that Mister Derzin considers harassment?"

"Let's start with unauthorized surveillance of his business premises and residence. I'm not aware my bench issued a warrant."

"Surveillance, sir? We took a drive in the countryside and looked at both sites from a distance. Considering the secrecy surrounding the Aeternum facility, and the former Kerlin estate's notoriety…"

I let my words hang between us. He knew we had breached none of the various regulations restricting police conduct. This was an attempt at intimidation, pure and simple. Did Justice Bisso not understand what he was doing opened him to a PCB investigation? At this rate, I would need my entire unit here, examining every part of the colonial government for signs of corruption.

"Don't become argumentative with me. Stay away from Luca Derzin. He's not involved in your case."

"If Your Honor is attempting to interfere in an ongoing investigation, I will inform the Rim Sector's Chief of Prosecutions any trial stemming from this case cannot be heard by the Mission Colony Bench. Your current behavior is tainting its impartiality."

He sat up, eyes widening in astonishment at my gall. But he knew I was one hundred percent right.

"How dare you? I'm within a micron of holding you in contempt and calling the bailiff."

"Your Honor's forgets the PCB also investigates federal judges for misconduct and your threats against an officer of the law carrying out her duties qualify."

I caught a flash of fear in his eyes and wondered what Derzin held over Bisso that made him cross the line. Star system chief judges, even colonial ones, were chosen from among the most experienced jurists. He surely realized this entire conversation could turn into a career killer. Or was he that imbued with his own sense of importance he didn't think twice about putting pressure on a mere chief superintendent? Perhaps he never presided over an official corruption case, let alone met one of us.

"I think we should end this conversation now and pretend it never happened, Your Honor. I also suggest you erase the recording you're making."

"How—"

"Please give me some credit, sir. You were hoping I'd say something to compromise myself as lead investigator and likely asked one of your colleagues to sign the required warrant. It's what I would do, and you're an intelligent man. Don't compound your earlier mistakes with one that will entail serious consequences." He visibly paled as he blinked his eyes, thunderstruck at unexpectedly losing the upper hand. "No one can bully or intimidate PCB investigators, not even star system chief judges. Otherwise, we'd be useless as the last line of defense against official misconduct."

With that, I turned on my heels and left his office, heedless of the clerk in the antechamber staring at me with curious eyes. What the hell was going on?

Arno scratched his beard after I finished relating my conversation with Justice Bisso.

"I don't think we've run across a judge that crass before, Chief. Could he have been making sure you'd become annoyed and push back enough to give him credible deniability?"

"As in preserving a shred of integrity while seemingly doing Derzin's dirty work? Perhaps." It was an intriguing thought. "I think we'll back off a bit and make it seem as if we're wary of annoying Derzin. On the other hand, I've suddenly developed an appetite for a minor surveillance operation. Derzin is holding a party at his country residence tomorrow. How about we see who attends? It might give us an idea of how extensively this colony could be corrupted."

"Could, Chief? I don't think there's any doubt. We three can smell an odor of rot by now."

Bonta nodded. "What the inspector said, sir."

— Nineteen —

Saturday morning blossomed as if it were on ComCorp's marketing department payroll. The rosy dawn told us it would be a splendid garden party at Derzin's country estate. We'd drawn tactical gear and clothing along with a surveillance pack from the quartermaster store the day before and headed out into the countryside immediately after breakfast.

I knew the approximate location used by the sniper who killed Gustav Kerlin as he stood on his patio, surrounded by some of the same people we expected to see. But Derzin was a smart man. He would make sure no one used that spot without being noticed by the security perimeter sensors. Besides, asking for the quartermaster for ghillie suits capable of foiling detection by both human and electronic eyes would have raised awkward questions.

A map reconnaissance of the area showed us a promising elevation to the southwest, approximately two kilometers from the estate, close enough to make out faces using the optical sensors that came with the surveillance pack. When we arrived, it took us a fair amount of time and effort before we found a spot that provided cover from curious eyes as well as a direct line of sight to the estate. I was pleased both Sergeant Bonta and I remembered the rules for setting up a proper field observation post from our time as Constabulary liaison officers with the Special Forces, years ago. We set up two of the high-powered optical sensors on their tripods and ranged in while Arno stood watch.

Memories of running surveillance while the deadliest Marines in existence prepared for a strike flooded back. Those were wild days.

"Are you getting a sense of déja vu, sir?" Bonta asked in a low whisper.

"Yep."

"Me as well."

For the next hour, one of us monitored the estate while the other two kept an eye and both ears on our immediate surroundings, switching every twenty minutes. Shortly before midday, while I was on the sensor, three figures came through the mansion's patio door.

"Contact."

Bonta slithered in beside me and glued her eyes to the second sensor.

"Derzin and two tough guys who look like close protection, sir."

"Concur."

They walked around the patio as if inspecting it in preparation for the guests. But something about their movements and gestures bothered me.

"Sergeant, am I seeing things, or are they frequently glancing at the far end of the glen?"

"Now that you mention it, sir, yes. Isn't that the area where Gustav Kerlin's killer set up his hide?"

"It is."

"Maybe they're expecting us," Arno said. "Or at least hoping we might watch Derzin's garden party?"

"And catch us carrying out unauthorized surveillance on law-abiding citizens? Perhaps. There's a movement afoot to discredit us and therefore discredit anything we find during the murder investigation. But why believe we would use the known sniper's hide?"

"Because it's known? Derzin is smart, but I bet he's the sort who underestimates the intelligence and cunning of police officers. Justice Bisso's dumb attempt at intimidating you on Derzin's behalf clearly shows he doesn't hold you in high regard, Chief. And that's a colossal mistake."

"The inspector is probably onto something, sir. Derzin is an arrogant sod who believes he's always the smartest man in the room. That invitation wasn't just a throwaway, knowing you couldn't possibly accept. He was baiting you. I wouldn't be surprised if he placed a few of his goons near the hide to wait for us and create an incident in front of Mission Colony's most notable citizens."

Both Arno and Sergeant Bonta were probably right, which meant Mission Colony faced more issues than a governor with questionable friends. Never mind she lost two of her closest staff members under suspicious circumstances in the space of a few hours. The problems hiding beneath the surface might well exceed our capacity. Although I could legitimately call on the 24th Regiment for help, at this point, we had no choice but to assume some of the senior members might also be compromised. If cops were incorruptible, I wouldn't have a job.

Shortly after midday, the first guests arrived. As expected, Governor Peet and Terrence Salak were among them, as was Justice Bisso and half the Mission Colony Bench, along with the CEOs of the star system's major corporations. More interesting were the faces we didn't see. There was no sign of Demetrius Rudel or any of the colonial administration's senior executives. No Braband either, thankfully. His predecessor had been on that same patio when Captain Talyn's partner shot Gustav Kerlin.

"Oops."

"What?"

"Look at the latest arrival, sir. Chief Superintendent Cyndee Sorem."

The 24th Regiment's Deputy Commanding Officer. So much for senior Constabulary members staying away.

"Didn't the Bujold investigation clear Sorem, Chief?"

"They found nothing that might indicate misconduct. But that was then, and this is now — different actors, different motivations. But perhaps she's here at Braband's behest, as his ear to the ground. I'll check when we're back in town."

We watched for almost two hours as Derzin's guests enjoyed the sun, the buffet, and each other's company. I saw familiarity and ease as if they socialized regularly as part of a small, select circle. Even Sorem seemed in her element, though at this distance, battlefield-grade optical sensors notwithstanding, reading someone's face remained challenging.

Derzin's protection detail kept well beyond the patio's intimate circle, though at least two of them monitored the glen's far end at any time. I was tempted to head there once the party broke up but feared walking into a trap. Sergeant Bonta and I might remember the basics of setting up an observation post. However, I doubted our patrolling skills would pass muster and that glen was enemy territory.

By mid-afternoon, the guest drifted away until none remained. Shortly after the last car left the estate, a pair of ghillie-suited men emerged from the dense brush at the glen's far end. They carried short, civilian-pattern carbines, though the way they walked, I was convinced the men wore military-grade armor under the ghillie suits.

"And that confirms our suspicions. Derzin had men waiting for someone. Whether it was us will probably stay unanswered. It might just be normal security precautions, considering the number of VIPs among the guests. Let's extract and head home." I flicked off my sensor and collapsed its tripod, then backed out of our observation post and over a small crest before climbing to my feet. Bonta followed suit with the second sensor.

"What now, Chief?" Arno asked over his shoulder as we made our way back to where our car was hidden from casual passers-by.

"We enjoy the rest of our weekend. With any luck, replies on Derzin and Allore's background checks will come in by Monday, and I might hear from Captain Talyn. As things stand right now, we're dead in the water."

"You think we need reinforcements?"

"Who? It'll take at least five days to ship another of our teams over from Cimmeria if DCC Maras sends them aboard one of her cutters. We can't trust anyone in the 24th, not if Derzin corrupted the system's chief justice."

"Are you saying we can't even trust AC Braband, sir?"

"At this point? No."

"I guess we'll be soldiering on alone, then, Chief. Fortunately, we do it well."

Our car appeared undisturbed when we reached it, but I asked Sergeant Bonta to run a scan anyway in case someone left us a present. The vehicle was clean, and we crossed the base's main gate two hours later, after taking a circuitous route from our aerie, to avoid inadvertently running across a partygoer, or worse yet, one of Derzin's men.

After showering and changing into regular clothes, I called AC Braband, who, to my surprise, was in his office.

"What can I do for you, Chief Superintendent?"

"Did you know your second in command attended a garden party at Luca Derzin's country estate earlier today?"

"Sure. Community outreach is part of her mandate, and it includes showing the flag when the colony's elite get together. I'm aware of all her forays ahead of time, including today's."

"That's what I thought."

"How did you find out? Or is it none of my business?" When I didn't answer, he raised his hands in surrender. "I withdraw both questions. Was there anything else?"

"No, sir."

"Then enjoy the rest of your weekend. Braband out."

A smart man, our assistant commissioner, letting his second in command hobnob with the local grandees while he maintained an Olympian aloofness, so everyone understood he wasn't Kristy Bujold. That Sorem visibly enjoyed herself might be entirely innocent. Some folks are more socially gifted than others, and friendly relationships with a star system's various communities were a vital part of effective policing. Still, I was a bit chagrined. Had Sorem attended Derzin's garden party without Braband's knowledge, she would become another thread to pull on.

Everyone knew by now who we were and kept their distance, which meant we could discuss the case around a drink or a meal in the Steele Club without curious ears listening in. Though from what little I gleaned, the members of the 24th Constabulary Regiment figured we were after someone in the colonial administration and not misconduct in their own unit, which proved once again the collective wisdom of the professional Constabulary rank and file.

"Are we sightseeing tomorrow, Chief?" Arno asked, pushing away his empty plate. "The folks around here take their Sunday stand-downs seriously, which means we won't make any headway with a case that has us stumped."

Arno had a way with words. Stumped. That's what we were.

"Sightseeing it is."

— Twenty —

"Why do I feel a pair of eyes drilling through my back, Chief?"

We were leaning against a metal railing that kept gawkers from falling into the massive flats at the base of the North Fjord, where tsunami waves came to die.

"Probably because a pair of eyes are drilling through your back, Arno. I'm getting the same itch. We picked up a tail somewhere along the way."

"And we're conveniently close to where the local mobsters dispose of incriminating evidence."

"Then we should head back, just in case the opposition gets ideas."

"Want to split up and give our tail a hard time, sir?" Bonta pushed herself away from the railing.

I shook my head. "No. Strength in numbers is the proper game plan right now. Let's head for the main plaza and see if we can casually spot whoever owns that pair of eyes."

"One of Derzin's men, I suppose," Arno said as we walked away from the flats.

"I can't think of anyone else with a goon squad we've annoyed in recent days."

"Unless the AC or one of the senior officers is curious about us."

Arno let out a bark of laughter.

"No one in the Constabulary is curious enough to pin a tail on the Firing Squad, Sergeant. That's a career-ending move."

"Only if we find out, and I've met enough Constabulary members who think they're the Almighty's gift to undercover operations. I'm sure the 24th has its share of blowhards."

After a leisurely forty-five-minute stroll, Ventano's central plaza, celebrating the colony's founders, hove into sight. On a Sunday, it teemed with citizens enjoying the sunshine and balmy weather, unburdened by the demands of work or school. The sensation we were being watched never left us. Yet the means of spotting a tail without looking back were scarce. That would change once we wandered around the plaza, window-shopping.

However, after twenty minutes ambling by storefronts, studying statues, and watching people walk by, we were no wiser even though the impression of being watched never wavered. A true professional was trailing us. We enjoyed a leisurely lunch in one of the few commercial establishments open on a Sunday, a downtown Ventano pub, and when we returned to the streets, the sensation of being watched was gone. Either our tail had enough or was taking greater precautions.

As if Arno was reading my thoughts, he muttered, "Odds are we picked up a fresh one, Chief. It usually takes me a bit before I can feel those eyes, and if they tailed us a good part of the morning, they won't give up now."

"Let's visit the Ventano Museum. If nothing else, we might learn something new about this place while we bore our new watcher to death."

The Museum, recounting Mission Colony's history from the first robotic probe's landing to the inaugural settlement, through the Shrehari occupation and their withdrawal after the armistice, was as bland as I feared. But since we were among the few who braved the not particularly exciting displays, keeping an eye out for covert surveillance was easy. And futile.

Our long walk back up the Ventano peninsula's spine toward the 24th Constabulary Regiment's base proceeded in silence, and with no sixth sense warnings we were being watched. It was as if we'd imagined the entire thing. But my instincts rarely did me wrong, and I knew both Arno and Sergeant Bonta's were just as keen as mine.

A subdued evening meal in the Steele Club didn't ease our somber mood. The opposition, whoever it was, held the upper hand. We rarely faced a dead end so quickly, but Mission Colony was threatening to give us our first loss in years. Yet, I could feel it in my bones. Something was terribly wrong here. Amaris Tosh's murder wasn't a spur-of-the-moment act. Nor was Governor Peet's slow seduction by Luca Derzin, let alone Mayleen Allore's disappearance after a convenient relationship with AC Braband.

"I could use a bent cop right now, Chief." Arno drained his ale and sighed. "This strikes me too much of the Aquilonia Station mess jumbled with that terrorism threat your Naval Intelligence friends neutralized, as in beyond an honest cop's purview."

"Yet here we are." I polished off my wine. "And after a day of idleness, a leisurely evening with my book and an early bedtime beckon."

Monday morning saw us back in our Government House incident room with no concrete idea of what came next. All we had were suspicions and precious little evidence. At this point, a homicide investigator would declare Mayleen Allore the primary suspect, file a report, and place the case in suspended animation until something new turned up.

Absent proof of the contrary, Braband's relationship with Allore was a misstep, not misconduct. Though once I filed my homicide report, a promotion to commissioner might be delayed, if not outright off the table for good.

Which left us with our professional compliance investigation. Peet obviously didn't expect the PCB to show up at DCC Maras' behest. Odds were she simply wanted Braband to stop snooping around. Maras yanking on Braband's leash would have sufficed. This certainly wasn't the first time a colonial governor and the commanding officer of the local Constabulary unit clashed since the latter was independent of the former.

Governors calling on the sector deputy chief constable to rein in the unit CO happened regularly. If we hadn't so thoroughly vetted Bujold's replacement before Maras appointed him, she would have sent a sharply worded missive reminding Braband he should stay away from colonial politics, and that would have been that. Instead, she listened to her instincts and asked for my help. Perhaps it was time I came clean with Peet and confirmed her suspicion we were here because of her complaint. Then we could watch the fur fly. Once I voiced my thoughts, both Arno and the sergeant nodded in agreement.

"We can't find anything else on the murder, Chief. Might as well air the complaint. If both are related, we could solve the Tosh case in a roundabout way."

At that moment, my terminal chimed softly, announcing receipt of a message from the Operations Center. I glanced at the display and saw it was a subspace message from Cimmeria, titled 'Preliminary Background Checks.'

"Good news, Chief?"

"A reply from sector intelligence about Derzin and Allore." I projected the message on the office's primary screen so the three of us could read it together.

First Derzin. Born and raised on Arcadia, one of the Commonwealth's core worlds settled during the first colonization wave, he came from an upper-middle-class family involved in star system politics and linked to various zaibatsus, ComCorp included. Recruited by the latter straight out of university, Derzin quickly rose through the ranks and became an executive at a relatively young age, moving from star system to star system and subsidiary to subsidiary. No known criminal links, no red flags in the Constabulary database. He was Mister Clean, although I didn't believe it. No one rose to his level without dabbling in corrupt practices and dealing with organized crime in some fashion. Maybe the in-depth check would turn up a few interesting tidbits. The Constabulary's criminal intelligence units routinely reached out to their Fleet counterparts, and I knew the latter kept a close eye on ComCorp.

Mayleen Allore's dossier was nowhere near as comprehensive. Born and raised on New Tasman, which we already knew, she left home after graduation and basically vanished from the records for almost five years. She reappeared when she entered the employ of a ComCorp subsidiary on Mykonos, then moved from job to job and star system to star system almost yearly until landing on Mission Colony a little over two years ago. Again, no known criminal links and no red flags in the database.

"Slim pickings, Chief. Let's hope the full reports give us more."

"True, but Allore's career path gives us a hint. Someone shifting jobs and star systems at that rate would be understandable if each move stemmed from a promotion, but they've mostly been laterals between ComCorp subsidiaries. It's as if she was doing things for the zaibatsu that weren't necessarily connected with her official functions."

Arno let out a disconsolate grunt.

"Of course. Shame on me for not seeing it right away. If you're correct, considering Allore's been on Mission longer than anywhere else since starting work as a ComCorp drone, does that mean she actually left the zaibatsu when she joined Peet's staff?"

"An interesting question. We know the big conglomerates run their own secret intelligence services, complete with direct action personnel, and they're not shy of infiltrating competitors or government agencies. Could be Mayleen Allore is one of them, and her job was getting on the Mission Colony governor's personal staff for reasons we can only guess."

"But they're likely related to that massive complex with the private spaceport, sir."

"Which means they, whoever that may be, are playing a long game."

"Or a longer one than Allore played in the past. It's time I spoke openly with the governor." I let myself out of the incident room and poked my head into the office next door. "Mister Salak, I need about fifteen minutes of the governor's time."

His face twisted into a silent sneer. "Now? She's rather busy."

"No doubt. I suppose following up on the promises the governor made at Derzin's garden party can't be easy."

Astonishment replaced his earlier disdain.

"I don't know what you mean. And how are you aware of the party?"

"I'm a detective, Mister Salak. I find things out. The governor will surely give me fifteen minutes once she hears it concerns the complaint she lodged with Deputy Chief Constable Maras concerning AC Braband's behavior toward her. Sooner rather than later would be nice."

I left before he could reply, and once back behind my borrowed desk, I re-read the preliminary background checks, trying to form a picture of the real Mayleen Allore and her loyalties. Salak appeared in the open doorway before I could formulate any fresh ideas.

"The governor will see you now."

All three of us stood, surprising Salak. "I meant Chief Superintendent Morrow."

"Since this concerns a professional compliance matter, my team accompanies me. That way, there can be no misunderstandings."

He gave me a hard look for a few heartbeats, then stepped back into the corridor, clearing the way.

— Twenty-One —

I opened the door to Peet's office without so much as a knock and entered, Arno and Sergeant Bonta on my heels. Peet stared at us wordlessly as we took the chairs facing her desk.

"Thank you for seeing us, Governor."

"I trust you're not wasting my time. Terrence said something about the complaint I sent to Deputy Chief Constable Maras."

"Indeed, Madame. We originally came here at her behest intending to investigate your allegations that Assistant Commissioner Braband behaved in a contemptuous manner toward you, an offense under Section 85 of the Commonwealth Constabulary Act. That we arrived in time to take over the investigation into Amaris Tosh's murder was coincidental."

She gave me a displeased look.

"I did not ask for a professional compliance investigation, nor did I lodge a complaint of misconduct. I merely wanted DCC Maras to rein in Braband, so he stops sticking his nose into my governance of this star system. When I asked him directly, he became insufferably rude. Surely governors unhappy with Constabulary overreach is a frequent occurrence."

Did I detect a hint of worry in her tone? Was she sufficiently self-aware to realize we might be here not just because of Braband but because of what he might have uncovered in the colonial administration?

"It occurs frequently. But sector commanders can ask for a professional compliance investigation at any time, just as I can start one or expand one requested by a senior officer. A member of the Constabulary behaving inappropriately toward a senior official is a serious offense under the Commonwealth Constabulary Act, one which merits more than just a sharp word by DCC Maras."

Peet let out a sniff of displeasure and turned sideways in her chair, a defensive gesture if I've ever seen one.

"And why are you telling me now, a week after your arrival?"

"Because we were busy with the murder investigation. Now that we hit a dead end, we can turn our attention back on your complaint."

"Dead end?"

"Unfortunately, barring the discovery of further evidence, I'm putting the case in suspended animation. A person or persons unknown murdered Amaris Tosh using a needler and a self-dissolving poisoned dart coated in a rapidly dissipating substance. Said substance left no traces in her bloodstream, making it the sort of weapon and ammunition favored by contract killers. Since Mayleen Allore found Tosh's body, then vanished without a trace shortly after that, we consider her a person of interest and issued a be on the lookout notification to law enforcement agencies in the Rim Sector. You will receive a copy of my formal report in due course."

"I see. How disappointing."

"Considering Tosh's death bears the hallmarks of a premeditated murder carried out by a professional, it's not surprising. Police only solve around sixty-five percent of homicides on average. That drops to well under five percent for contract killings, and they're usually solved by someone talking out of turn rather than forensic evidence."

"Those rates aren't particularly impressive, are they? It gives a whole new meaning to the expression getting away with murder."

"They've been steady since before the diaspora, Madame. The means for committing murder evolve in lockstep with the tools available to investigators."

Another sniff.

"I suppose I'll eventually make my peace with Amaris' murder being unavenged. Now, what about the matter of Assistant Commissioner Braband?"

"What about it? You alleged AC Braband behaved in a contemptuous manner toward you, was rude, insulting even, but didn't offer much by way of details. How about we start with that?"

Peet gestured at Arno and Sergeant Bonta. "Must they listen in on this?"

"Protocol requires at least two officers be present for professional compliance interviews." I retrieved my official recording device and placed it on her desk. "And we record them, so there is no doubt about what was said. You'd be amazed at the number of federal officials who give us a statement only to retract it later."

She put on a pinched expression as if she'd just bitten into something overly sour. "As I said before, I do not consider this a professional compliance matter."

"Unfortunately, that's not your call anymore. DCC Maras thought your complaint worthy of a look by the PCB, and after a week here, I agree."

"What do you mean after a week here, you agree?"

"A dead gubernatorial chief of staff, a missing social secretary, a star system chief justice with questionable discernment — the list of irregularities goes on long enough that I can't simply write them off as coincidence."

Peet sat up as an angry frown creased her forehead.

"Are you questioning my governance of this star system? If so, take care. Your Chief Constable wouldn't look kindly upon you after receiving a blistering subspace message from the Colonial Secretary."

"The Chief Constable generally goes along with what my boss, Deputy Chief Constable Hammett says, and DCC Hammett considers blistering subspace messages complaining about his officers a sign we're doing our jobs. You understand those of us assigned to the Professional Compliance Bureau cannot be threatened with career consequences. Our careers as regular Constabulary members end the moment we join the PCB. Those who cannot be threatened cannot be corrupted through coercion. And they pay us well enough that we can't be bought either."

"Very admirable, I'm sure." Her serial sniffs were getting a tad irksome.

"Let's get back to the matter at hand." I tapped my recorder and heard its little beep. "This is the interview of Governor Jeanne Peet in the matter of her complaint against Assistant Commissioner Elden Braband, Commanding Officer, 24th Constabulary Regiment. Present are Chief Superintendent Caelin Morrow of the Rim Sector Professional Compliance Bureau."

I nodded at my wingers.

"Inspector Arno Galdi, Rim Sector Professional Compliance Bureau."

"Master Sergeant Destine Bonta, Rim Sector Professional Compliance Bureau."

I gestured at Peet and pointed at my device. She gave me an exasperated look.

"Governor Jeanne Peet, Mission Colony."

"Thank you. Governor Peet, you sent Deputy Chief Constable Maras, Commanding Officer, Rim Sector Constabulary Group, a complaint about Assistant Commissioner Braband's behavior toward you, is that correct."

"It is."

"Please explain the nature of his behavior."

Peet's hesitation told me there was probably both more and less than met the eye.

"Braband was taking an inordinate interest in the way my administration interacts with the star system's business community, and I told him his behavior was inappropriate on several occasions. Each time he responded in an unacceptably rude manner, questioning my integrity and my fitness as governor. He even dared raise his voice in my presence."

"Why did he do that?"

An irritated shrug. "How should I know? Ask him."

"At the moment, I'm asking you. Did AC Braband's interest focus on one or more particular segments of the business community?"

Another moment of hesitation.

"He has a fixation on Aeternum in particular, but not exclusively."

"Do you know why?"

"Of course not. Really, Chief Superintendent, do I strike you as an omniscient being?"

"You strike me as the ruler of this star system, which means you bear the ultimate responsibility for everything that happens here."

"Except when it comes to policing. Do you know how frustrating that is?"

"There are good reasons for keeping the police separate from the colonial administration, as recent events on New Oberon proved once again."

Her face took on a sour expression at hearing the colony's name. The Colonial Office had replaced its administration wholesale, and the police force was placed under Constabulary control after an anti-slavery raid proved many senior New Oberon officials were in the pay of a particularly nasty criminal cartel.

New Oberon was not one of the Colonial Office's success stories, though in fairness, Arcadia settled and ruled it until the Commonwealth government took over. And on Arcadia, graft and corruption were common currency.

"Back to your concerns with AC Braband's behavior. Can you give me a concrete example of what you call his inordinate interest?"

"He often badgered Amaris Tosh with questions on the relation between my office, Aeternum, and other large businesses."

"Did Tosh complain about it?"

"No. But Terrence overheard them on several occasions."

"In her office?"

"Mainly at social events."

"And you didn't think it might be simple curiosity about the colonial administration's inner workings? As a newcomer, he would naturally try to learn as much as possible about the colony he polices. The big commercial ventures in this star system have a distinct impact on the economic, social, and political environment."

"If you say so." Her irritation was becoming more evident. "Terrence also told me Braband pressured Mayleen into gossiping about Government House goings-on."

"Did Mayleen Allore complain?"

"No."

"So, this is based on Terrence Salak's hearsay, which we can't verify because Amaris Tosh was murdered, and Mayleen Allore vanished. Do you have something more concrete, or are we merely talking about AC Braband losing his temper with you in private because you questioned his motives?"

Peet tapped the desktop with her fingertips, eyes raised to the ceiling.

"Perhaps I was too hasty in writing Deputy Chief Constable Maras." She looked at me again. "Tell you what, Chief Superintendent. Consider my complaint withdrawn. Your professional compliance investigation is, therefore, unnecessary. And since you're putting the matter of Amaris's murder into suspended animation, I'd say your work here on Mission Colony is done. You may leave with my thanks."

"That's not the way it works, Madame."

She arched a perfectly sculpted eyebrow. "Oh?"

"Once a professional compliance investigation is launched, it can only be ended by the sector commanding officer, meaning me, or DCC Hammett, who heads the entire PCB. Considering Mission Colony's recent history and the shadow an unresolved complaint casts over AC Braband's reputation, I consider it necessary to continue. I'm sure DCC Maras will be supportive since she appointed AC Braband."

"That is rather unfortunate."

"I hope we can count on your continuing cooperation and that of your staff."

She waved her hand in a dismissive gesture.

"Of course. But I trust you'll vacate the office down the hall now that the murder investigation is over."

"Over the next day or two, yes."

"Was there anything else?"

"No. Thank you for your cooperation. We'll see ourselves out."

Once back behind closed doors in the incident room, Sergeant Bonta ran another scan at my orders.

"Still clear, sir."

"I bet we'll find surveillance the next time we leave this place unattended."

"Which is why we're moving out. This area is now enemy territory."

"That's what I figured when Peet tried to weasel out once she realized we would be looking at her administration with Firing Squad intensity. How do you plan on proceeding?"

"Sergeant, can you hack into Peet's terminal and make it a listening device?"

"Give me about thirty minutes, sir. Since we're moving out, I'll see that periodic dumps are made to our encrypted server slice on the 24th Regiment's node."

We took our seats and looked at each other for a few moments.

"Impressions?"

"She's uneasy, Chief. The plan to rein Braband in failed, and now she has the Lady High Executioner sniffing around. Something is horribly rotten in this star system, and I think part of the reason sits in isolated splendor at the end of the corridor, even though she probably doesn't know it yet. I think the AC's suspicions are on the money. Derzin is seducing Peet so he can exert control over Mission Colony through her. Tosh figured it out, and either threatened her boss or let something slip. Allore, a ComCorp operative working from the inside, murders Tosh. They didn't count on us showing up. So instead of passing Tosh's death off as natural causes, or at the very least putting Braband in an untenable situation, Allore does a runner because she knows we'll figure things out. Or Derzin pulls her off the game board. Same result."

"A solid theory. The problem is proving it. And that means finding out what Derzin's doing, which won't be easy with just the three of us."

"Sir, if they murdered a senior, highly respected Colonial Office employee like Tosh and tried sidelining a Constabulary AC, we are now in danger as well."

"Which is why we're moving out today. Right after you rig your listening device."

— Twenty-Two —

On our way out just before midday, I left orders with the Government House watch commander to tear down the incident room. I felt a small but unmistakable wave of relief wash over me as we passed through the base's main gate. My laying things bare in front of Peet would inevitably accelerate things — if our working theory was correct — and that's what I wanted. But people who panic can become fatally dangerous in the blink of an eye. Tosh had likely been murdered by a professional using assassin-grade ammunition who then vanished into thin air. We weren't dealing with ordinary corruption here.

Bonta parked our car by the senior officers' quarters, and we headed for the mess, along with seemingly half the base. However, we found a private table in the far corner without difficulties after filling our trays at the buffet. Our status as PCB investigators bought us at least that small advantage. We ate in silence, lost in our thoughts. Finally, Arno wiped the corners of his mouth and sat back.

"I hate to say this, Chief, but we might be in over our heads. Sure, we can investigate Peet for misconduct should we find evidence Derzin corrupted her. The same goes for Justice Bisso and every government official who attended the garden party, including Chief Superintendent Sorem, for good measure. But first, we need to find out what Derzin is doing and whether it's illegal. If it is, the matter becomes a case for Major Crimes. Should Major Crimes uncover a link between Derzin's activities and various government officials, then we can pounce."

Arno was right, as always. But we couldn't simply walk away. My cop's instincts screamed criminal conspiracy involving federal employees.

"While I agree with you, I'm not sure Major Crimes would take this case based on our gut feel. The cartels are giving them plenty of work already. We need evidence, and whoever is behind Tosh's murder, Allore's disappearance and the attempt to muzzle Braband has Mission Colony wrapped up in a neat ball."

"Your Naval Intelligence friends, sir? They cleaned up the terrorists on Cimmeria despite the corruption in high places and the Constabulary's inability to intervene until afterward."

"I sent Captain Talyn everything we had a few days ago. If she thinks events on Mission Colony threaten Commonwealth security, she'll step in. But last I looked, her people don't deal with straight-up criminality."

Arno raised a finger.

"Beg to differ, Chief. No one's admitting the Fleet struck New Oberon, but they didn't deny it either. That hit taking out the Saqqa Cartel reeked of Special Ops, and Saqqa was in the money-making business, not regime change. They owned the regime. Ergo…"

"Perhaps. In any case, it's not over yet. This afternoon, I'll send a report on our findings and observations to DCC Maras and DCC Hammett. Maras can decide whether she wants Major Crimes here, and our boss can tell us whether we're done with this investigation. In the meantime, it's data drudgery for us. We'll investigate the personal and financial affairs of the federal employees at that garden party. Perhaps we'll get lucky, and one of them isn't as prudent as the others. I doubt we'll find much. They're senior people with what one presumes are above average smarts, not crooked beat cops or middle-grade bureaucrats with a penchant for larceny and a love of flashy toys. But we owe the case due diligence."

"Should I find us an office on the base, sir?"

"No. We'll work in our quarters — easy enough to set up secure links with the Operations Center from there. The less we're seen now that I'm turning the Tosh murder over to the 24th's cold case section, the better. Let everyone guess what we're doing while we dig through the data and wait for orders from above. I'll speak with AC Braband this afternoon on the Tosh matter."

"What'll you tell him about the other thing?"

"That Peet withdrew her complaint, and we're expecting direction from HQ about the next steps, which is nothing but the truth."

Arno grinned.

"But not the full truth, Chief. And we have the sergeant's listening device. Inadmissible in court, but oh so useful in determining whether Peet is bent. Which reminds me, what about warrants if we encounter stumbling blocks during the data dig? We can't trust any of the local judges."

"At least not those who were at Derzin's place, but since they probably gossip, word will reach Bisso's ears, and if I'm right, Derzin's. In my report to the DCCs, I'll ask for warrants from the Rim Sector chief justice, should our betters decide we keep investigating."

"Isn't working in enemy territory fun?"

Bonta let out an indelicate snort.

"Your definition of fun isn't the same as mine, Inspector."

"Don't I know it. Jumping out of perfectly good shuttles from low orbit makes me shudder just thinking about it."

"Youthful indiscretions. I wouldn't try it nowadays. How about you, sir?"

I was never much of a jumper. Each one terrified me, but I volunteered for the assignment, and Special Forces weren't shipping me home until my tour was over. I still had dreams about jumping every so often, the sort that left me a bit disoriented when I woke up.

"Perish the thought. My wings retired long ago." I spotted Chief Inspector Wuori, AC Braband's adjutant, out of the corner of my eye and waved at her. Since she was looking directly at us, she couldn't ignore me like everyone else. Wuori dutifully changed course for our table.

"What can I do for you, Chief Superintendent."

"I need ten minutes of the AC's time this afternoon to discuss the Tosh investigation."

She searched her mind for a few seconds, then asked, "Would fourteen hundred hours suit?"

"Perfect. Thank you, Chief Inspector."

"My pleasure. Enjoy the rest of your meal." She hurried off as if fearful of guilt by association with the Firing Squad.

At fourteen hundred precisely, I stopped on the threshold of Braband's open office door.

"Sir, thank you for seeing me."

He stood and waved at the conference table. "We'll be more comfortable here. So, what about the Tosh case?"

I sat across from him and leaned forward, elbows on the tabletop.

"You'll receive my report this afternoon, sir, the same report I'm sending DCC Maras. It will say Amaris Tosh was murdered by person or persons unknown, most likely using a dissolving needler dart covered in a rapidly dissipating poison that induces cardiac arrest. The ME's findings support this conclusion. I have no suspect but consider the murder akin to a contract killing. The suspected weapon and ammunition hint at a professional. Since Mayleen Allore vanished in the hours following the murder, she is a person of interest. I've issued a BOLO for her arrest." A pained look crossed his face. "Sorry, sir, but there's no way around it."

"I can't believe Mayleen is an assassin."

"We've not yet established that she is. Someone else could have killed Amaris Tosh and caused Allore's disappearance. Until we find a trace of her, we won't know."

"Did you at least figure out why someone murdered Tosh?"

I grimaced.

"It probably wasn't a crime of passion. Those rarely involve a professional killer's arsenal. I suspect Tosh discovered something that the killer or the killer's employer wanted hidden, but we found no evidence."

"Corruption in the colonial administration." Braband's tone made it a statement, not a question.

"That is a viable theory, sir."

"Yet you can't discuss it. I know. I suppose I'll be an AC until retirement after falling into a honey pot with an assassin as bait."

"Again, sir, we found no proof Mayleen Allore is guilty of anything. At this point, the case is in suspended animation until new evidence surfaces. Since I will probably be needed elsewhere soon, I'm hereby turning the case file over to the 24th Regiment. Your Operations Center will receive the data momentarily."

"And what will you do?"

"Wait for orders from my superior, Deputy Chief Constable Hammett."

"I see." He studied me for a few heartbeats. "Do you think there is corruption in the colonial administration? That my nosing around caused Governor Peet's complaint?"

"Possibly on both counts."

"Will you stick around and investigate?"

"That depends on what DCC Hammett decides. He is the ultimate arbiter. But if I may, sir, leave the nosing around to us. Next time you suspect things aren't right, contact me. It's easier for everyone and generally produces results. We know better than anyone else what the signs of official corruption are and can investigate without the subject's knowledge."

He inclined his head.

"Noted, Chief Superintendent. If there's anything else I can do to help, please call me, day or night."

"Thank you, sir. A last piece of advice if I may. Don't knock yourself over the head because of Mayleen Allore. You're not the first senior officer who was taken in, and you won't be the last. It happens. Only those who compound their mistake with indiscretions that harm the service, or the Commonwealth pay the price. I daresay DCC Maras might counsel you, but it shouldn't put a permanent black mark on your record."

"Kind of you to say so. But I'm a grownup. If I face consequences because of Mayleen, then so be it."

— Twenty-Three —

Both Arno and Sergeant Bonta's doors were open when I returned to the senior officers' quarters. Since none of the adjacent suites were occupied — the three of us owned the entire corridor — it was probably the closest we could come to our regular offices back home.

"How did he take it?" Arno asked as he spied me looking in on him.

"As you'd expect. Rueful for the relationship and curious about what comes next."

"Still think he's on the up and up, Chief?"

"Braband was with us when the call came in. Considering the timelines, he couldn't be responsible for Tosh. And we experienced that old gut feel about Peet heading for the slippery slope, pushed by Derzin who behaves like every predator we've seen."

"Concur," Bonta said from her suite. "Now that you're here, I'll put up the curtain of silence, cutting this corridor off from the rest of the floor. We can talk with no one overhearing."

"Excellent."

"We started the data dig, Chief. It'll be a while in case you're thinking about the reports."

Arno had a knack for ensuring I took care of the least appealing parts of my job. Thankfully, the reports weren't a big chore. I merely stitched my daily summaries together as a single narrative and appended the raw data, then wrote a covering note for each of the deputy chief constables. After encrypting and firing those off via the 24th Regiment's subspace node, I completed the Tosh homicide report for AC Braband. By the time I hit send, I had realized it was almost eighteen-hundred hours.

A quick shower and change of clothes and we headed back to the mess for a drink and a meal. As always, we were inside our own bubble, courtesy of Constabulary members who saw us as the enemy rather than the ones who ensured everyone wearing the gray uniform lived up to their oath.

Arno settled back in his seat with a foaming mug of ale and an air of contentment. "We didn't download today's recordings from Peet's office, Chief. Since there's not much else, maybe we can entertain ourselves by listening after supper."

"A splendid idea." I wasn't putting much hope in Sergeant Bonta's little trick. Surely Peet wouldn't discuss incriminating matters in her own office. The first rule of official misconduct was never to talk about anything compromising within earshot of the flagpole. You never knew who might overhear. "Anything from the data dig?"

"We combed through the public records and found no warning flags, though the social pages tell quite a story about Derzin's whirlwind conquest of the colony's senior officials and upper crust. He's everywhere, at every event, gala, charity auction, winter ball, you name it, he's at the center of things. I found pictures of Kristy Bujold, in mess uniform, chatting amiably with Derzin at the annual governor's ball last year. Based on what we saw so far, none of the folks at last Saturday's garden party seem to live above their means. We'll be sifting through the government records tomorrow. Then it'll be the financial institutions. Hopefully, DCC Maras will arm us with the necessary warrants by then."

"I'm sure the Sector Chief Justice won't balk at signing when he sees half of his judges on Mission Colony named in the warrant applications. After the last judicial graft scandal, we've become his favorite attack dogs."

We took our meal at the usual table, far from everyone else, and lingered over coffee until we were the last diners left. I didn't see Braband and figured he was at his townhouse, dealing with my revelations in a more private space. Upon returning to our quarters, Arno graciously offered us a postprandial whiskey from his travel stash while Sergeant Bonta called up the day's audio record.

"I set it to record only when someone spoke, so there won't be any empty space. Ready?"

"Go for it."

Governor Peet's high, nasal voice came through the speakers almost immediately.

"Luca! How are you? Did you notice those irritating Constabulary people are gone? They gave up on Amaris' murder and Mayleen's disappearance, thank the Almighty."

"Jeanne. A good day to you. Yes, I saw the empty office just now."

"The Morrow creature was more insufferable than ever if you can believe that."

Both Arno and Sergeant Bonta grinned at me. The former raised his glass of Glen Arcturus in a silent salute.

"Insufferable, but dangerous. What are her intentions?"

"She pressured me for evidence Braband's behavior constituted misconduct worthy of a professional compliance investigation. When my answers seemed unsatisfactory, I told her I was withdrawing my complaint and that she and her people should go home. Morrow told me she could continue an investigation at her own discretion even if a complaint was withdrawn and that only her superior on Wyvern could end this nonsense, a Deputy Chief Constable Hammer, or some such name."

"Hammett, the Conscience of the Constabulary. One of the most dangerous individuals to wear the gray uniform."

Arno cocked a surprised eyebrow. "Well informed, our Mister Derzin."

"Tell you what, Jeanne, they may no longer be down the hall from us, but I'm betting they left something behind. Give me a moment."

Bonta touched her device's screen, pausing the playback. "There's a gap of several minutes at this point, sir. I bet Derzin scanned for listening devices, which he didn't find."

"Nothing. But that doesn't signify. Everything Morrow has done since arriving tells me she came here to look at you, not Braband. Taking over the murder case gave her an excuse for interviewing staff and observing you. I'll bet she watched the *garden party from a spot my people couldn't identify beforehand."*

"You got that right, buster," Arno muttered.

"So, what if she did?"

"Think about it, Jeanne. If Braband is setting you up by using Morrow... In any case, we should avoid discussing business in your office until Morrow leaves Mission just in case she has a way of listening that my sensor can't pick up. My townhouse should serve, as should your residence. It means no more discussions during office hours. From now on, it'll be purely in social settings. And on that note, enjoy the rest of your day."

"You're leaving already?"

"The pressure of events is driving me, my dear, and Morrow's sudden change of tactics is a new event. Cheerio."

Bonta looked at her device. "There's a gap of five minutes."

"Mister Derzin didn't stay long, Madame. Is there a problem?"

"The charming Mister Salak."

"Nothing you need to worry about. But be a dear and see if you can find out what those irritating police people are doing."

"Yes, Madame."

Bonta touched her device's screen again.

"And that's it for today, sir. A shame I couldn't arrange for video as well without leaving traces. Seeing the governor's face after Derzin left would have been instructive."

Arno nodded. "It would indeed, but at least now we know without a doubt something is rotten on Mission Colony. Will you report this to the DCCs, Chief?"

"No. Our boss is a stickler for procedure, and he'd be displeased at my potentially risking a clean prosecution with unauthorized surveillance. Besides, what I sent today is enough for a command decision by either of them."

"A pity, though. If anything will rouse an old cop's hunting instincts, that conversation is it."

"I don't make the rules, Arno, and that's just as well. Who knows how many federal prosecutors I might piss off by doing as I please?"

"Considering you're an insufferable creature in the eyes of at least one colonial governor, I can understand your reticence. We could have made it two out of two if New Oberon belonged to the Rim Sector."

"Not a monumental success, that one. The Colonial Office didn't cover itself in glory. Thanks for the drinks, Arno. I'm done for the evening. Tomorrow, we continue digging and waiting. Good night to you both."

"Good night, Chief."

Sleep came with little effort, once I set aside my book, but my mind spent the night navigating Luca Derzin's nebulous schemes. The morning saw me no better rested than the evening before. Captain Talyn's encrypted message, waiting in my queue, was equally cheerless. Brief and to the point, it said stay away from Luca Derzin and Aeternum and forget about ever finding Mayleen Allore. The situation on Mission Colony was beyond the PCB's capabilities for now.

"I suppose that answers a few of our questions," Arno said after I let him and Sergeant Bonta read it. "Do you think Captain Talyn might send someone who can deal with matters? Her use of the words, for now, seems ominous."

"Who knows? She's a law unto herself. Until we receive orders from DCC Hammett, we'll continue with the data dig. After the New Oberon business, no one will fault us for looking into potential cases of official misconduct. But we won't leave the base, just in case."

"Sir, what did Captain Talyn mean about Allore?"

"It could be her way of telling us Allore is a known player who'll have changed her appearance, biometrics, and identity by now."

"A corporate spook, Chief, as we figured, which means someone has been playing the long game on Mission Colony, independent of the revolutionary wannabes."

"It certainly seems so."

"And then we showed up instead of Maras telling Braband to back off. Talk about stepping on your own toes. Isn't karma a wonderful thing?"

"Only if we can figure out what's really happening, otherwise it'll be business as usual around here after we leave."

— Twenty-Four —

We finished combing through the open and police data sources by late afternoon, without finding anything concrete on the federal officials we saw at Derzin's estate. I didn't want to approach financial and telecom institutions without both a warrant and my superior's backing in case their senior managers were also in Derzin's pocket. At least with a warrant, they faced criminal liabilities if they divulged our inquiries.

I stuck my head into the corridor.

"Let's call it a day and head for the mess."

"An excellent plan, Chief."

My communicator chose that moment to chime merrily. The Operations Center was passing on a subspace message from DCC Maras, along with our search warrants.

"Good news?"

"I hope you're not sick and tired of data digging. We have the warrants. But we'll start tomorrow. I'm getting slightly cross-eyed."

"You and me both. Come on, Sergeant, it's time we called it quits for the day."

"Just one more minute. I found a yacht registered to Justice Bisso in the Mission Colony Transport Department's database. I'm looking it up now."

Arno and I looked at each other. "Did the justice strike you as a yachtsman, Chief?"

"Not in the least. But appearances can be deceiving."

"Never mind," Bonta called out. "It doesn't appear too rich for a star system chief justice's pay. He probably uses it for private parties instead of cruising along the fjords."

"Did DCC Maras say anything in her message, beyond here are the warrants, enjoy?"

"Other than acknowledging my report, no. She, like us, is waiting for DCC Hammett's decision on whether we continue or back off until fresh evidence of corruption surfaces. Considering the political implications, he'll likely brief the Chief Constable first. The Colonial Office is a bit twitchy these days."

"Understandably—" My communicator gave off a new chime, silencing Arno. He waited until I read the other message passed along by the Operations Center, then cocked a questioning eyebrow.

"Captain Talyn again. Two words — stand by."

"Now *that* sounds worse than ominous. Your friend in secret places has a way of solving problems most explosively. The Locarno Wilderness Preserve won't recover in our lifetimes."

"Needs must, Arno. Just be glad it was a few square kilometers of forest, not the entire Rim Sector political leadership."

"Do you think we might witness an encore performance, but in Derzin's little valley?"

"With Captain Talyn, everything is possible. And I'm ready for a pre-dinner drink. Shall we?"

After an uneventful evening and night, I found DCC Hammett's reply in my message queue. Arno and Sergeant Bonta wouldn't be happy. Our orders were to continue investigating quietly but avoid interviews or arrests. Commissioner Taneli Sorjonen, who headed the Political Anti-Corruption Unit, one of the central PCB organizations operating out of Constabulary HQ on Wyvern, would be on his way with a large team and take over from me upon arrival. After handing him and his people everything we accumulated, the ship bringing out Sorjonen would take us home. That left us a week, perhaps a bit longer, before our involvement ended.

Sorjonen was a legend in the PCB and widely seen as becoming its head one day. Equally important, he wore a star on his collar and, upon arrival, would be the most senior uniformed federal official in the star system, with the power of issuing orders to Braband and the 24th Regiment. No doubt, Sorjonen would be armed with a series of warrants allowing him to access anything, anytime, including Derzin's domain, Colonial Office exemptions notwithstanding.

Hammett's decision made sense, even though we were disappointed we wouldn't be making any arrests. My job was not investigating the entire colonial government; it was checking up on DCC Maras' gut instinct that the complaint against Braband could cover something more serious. With that done and the simple fact three of us against what might be widespread corruption was utterly insufficient, there would be no point taking unneeded risks when Wyvern could field half a battalion's worth of investigators. Besides, Peet and Derzin had seen too much of me and my ways. Facing Sorjonen would be a totally different game.

Arno sighed theatrically when I broke the news over breakfast.

"A shame we can't stick around and help Taneli the Grand Inquisitor. Watching an artist at work is always so educational."

"You served with him before?"

"I most certainly did, Chief. Long ago, when Sorjonen was a superintendent. He can only have improved over the years, especially considering the cases he's been handling since taking over Political Anti-Corruption. I think he would terrify Tomás de Torquemada, were that worthy personage still alive. Governor Peet and Justice Bisso won't know what hit them."

Bonta made a face. "Which leaves Derzin, Inspector."

"No worries. I'm sure once Commissioner Sorjonen extinguishes the suspected viper's nest at the heart of Mission Colony's government, he will clear the way for an investigation into Aeternum and Derzin that even ComCorp can't stop, right Chief?"

"We can only hope."

That morning, we each took a warrant and reached out to the legal heads of financial institutions and telecoms, starting with the lowest ranking officials who attended

Derzin's garden party. I wanted to test the waters in case anyone broke confidentiality and warned the target of our inquiries. The big names — Peet, Bisso, and yes, AC Braband, would come last. I had no choice but to check the latter along with the others. Since I suspected widespread rot, doing my due diligence meant including him. My first target was Terrence Salak. Arno took Chief Superintendent Sorem, and Sergeant Bonta took the Mission Colony Superior Court's chief clerk.

The legal head of the local InterStar Financial branch took one look at the warrant and sent me the bank's records on Salak. She also confirmed without prompting, she understood her duty to keep my inquiry confidential. I liked lawyers who knew their obligations. It was surprising how many either didn't or played dumb with us. The Mission Telco legal rep wasn't quite as forthcoming, but cooperated, nonetheless.

By the time late afternoon rolled around, the three of us were getting cross-eyed again, and I called a halt. If we managed three or four subjects a day, we'd be done by the time Commissioner Sorjonen landed, and that's what mattered the most. I wanted as complete a dossier on the situation as possible for his people and not just because of Sorjonen's fierce reputation. I had my pride, and this was my turf.

"Anything on Mister Salak, Chief?" Arno asked as we settled around our regular table in the Steele Club, far from indiscreet ears.

"Nada. If he's receiving extracurricular payments, it's not through financial accounts we know about. Nor did he make any suspicious calls with his personal communicator. Doesn't mean he's not been corrupted. He could have a numbered account waiting for him back home on Pacifica, a private retirement fund of sorts. What about Sorem?"

"Clean as a whistle based on her bank and telco records, but she could also have a numbered account waiting on her homeworld."

"Which is?"

"Mykonos."

"A planet where a little extra money goes a long way. And the court's chief clerk, Sergeant?"

A sly smile crossed her face. "I may have a hit. He spends pretty much every cred that comes in, and his comms records show a lot of late-night calls."

"Gambling?"

"Possibly. Or recreational drugs. Or entertainers. I flagged his file for further review by Commissioner Sorjonen's team since the boss doesn't want us talking to people. On the balance of probabilities, my gut tells me it's run of the mill low self-control rather than corruption. Still, we know how quickly an official can become compromised via perfectly legal extracurricular activities."

"Round two tomorrow. The next level up."

"Aye. And mightily bored we'll be." Arno raised his ale in salute.

The next morning, as we entered the lobby of the senior officers' quarters after a quiet breakfast, a tall, lean black-haired woman in her early forties wearing civilian clothes intercepted us.

"Chief Superintendent Morrow, I'm Warrant Officer Aleksa Kine. Is there a secure place where we can talk?"

I studied Kine for a few moments. Her presence on the base meant she carried the right credentials.

"You're Constabulary?"

"Yes, sir." Kine produced her identification. It appeared genuine to my practiced eyes.

Arno snapped his fingers. "Aren't you the Kine from the Shield Sector Undercover and Surveillance Division who was rescued by Special Forces at the beginning of this year?"

She turned a deadpan stare on him. "Yes, Inspector, but my rescuers were mercenaries. The Fleet was not involved in the Saqqa Cartel slavery business."

He snorted. "And I'm the next Chief Constable. Give over, Warrant."

Before the conversation could deteriorate, I pointed at the staircase. "Our suites upstairs are about as secure as it gets. We've taken over a side corridor and placed it behind an electronic curtain."

Once in my sitting room, Kine pulled out a handheld sensor and scanned her surroundings, presumably for listening devices. She pointed at my computer.

"You're sure that machine is clean, Chief Superintendent? There's a way of turning them remotely into listening devices."

"I know. We've been eavesdropping on Governor Peet's office since Monday. Sergeant Bonta is rather skilled at making electronics do things they shouldn't."

She gave me a satisfied nod. "I'm assigned as Constabulary liaison officer with Ghost Squadron, 1st Special Forces Regiment, and here for a task that will, not coincidentally, help you with your problem."

— Twenty-Five —

"Captain Talyn sent you?"

"Yes, sir. I've been out on an operation with the squadron's Erinye Company. We were on our way back when a message from the captain caught up with us. Our ship diverted at once and entered orbit two hours ago."

"We, meaning Erinye Company?"

"All one hundred and twenty of them, under the command of Captain Curtis Delgado, Commonwealth Marine Corps. I understand you've worked with Captain Talyn and Colonel Decker before."

"Yes. We've been helping each other out for the last few years."

"Then you know what sort of work we do. Luca Derzin and his operation are under Naval Intelligence scrutiny, and Captain Talyn simply decided she would move up her timetable and help you with your investigation."

Arno let out a chortle of pleasure. "You mean we now have over a hundred of the deadliest Special Forces troopers on tap?"

"Tell me what kind of outcome you prefer, and we'll make it happen, then vanish without a trace. We are called Ghost Squadron for a reason."

I could hear quiet pride in her voice and decided Zack Decker recruited Kine as his Constabulary liaison right after he and his troopers brought her home. Or perhaps even during the return trip.

"There is just one problem, Warrant. I won't be the senior PCB officer in this star system by late next week. A large team under Commissioner Sorjonen, who commands the PCB's Political Anti-Corruption Unit, is on its way from Wyvern with an army of investigators. Upon their arrival, we're turning everything over to them and going home. In the interim, our orders are to keep a low profile."

"We're not here for a lengthy stay, sir. Our operational tempo is rising at an exponential rate. The goal is sorting out Derzin and his corporation within the next few days. With him gone, you'll enjoy a freer hand. He and his lot are highly dangerous."

"So Derzin's activities are illegal."

"Let's just say there's more than pharmaceutical research happening at the Aeternum facility."

"Such as?"

"The laundering of illegal items imported from the Protectorate and the Shrehari Empire."

Bonta let out a snort of disbelief. "The richest and most powerful zaibatsu in the Commonwealth engages in grubby smuggling?"

"Powerful, yes. ComCorp still owns half the senate and a good chunk of the Commonwealth executive. But they've been hemorrhaging wealth for years, largely because of overreach and the Fleet's hidden war against those who would turn the Commonwealth into a corporatist empire. Captain Talyn said you'd understand."

"I do." Talyn, a commander at the time, told me about it after I wrapped up the Aquilonia business and set her free.

"Aeternum isn't the only subsidiary they set up as a cover for illegal activities, and we discovered ComCorp is playing footsie with the cartels."

"Really? I know the senior executives are mostly amoral psychopaths, but allying themselves with the cartels? That reeks of desperation."

Kine nodded. "Desperation is a good word for it. The hidden war is ruining many zaibatsus and their political backers. And the cartels are just beginning to feel the pain."

"Hence your rising operational tempo."

"Precisely. So, what can you tell Captain Delgado and me about the goings-on here? We received a copy of what you sent Captain Talyn but hearing it from the three of you will help us formulate a plan."

"We'll share everything with you. Where is Captain Delgado?"

"He's waiting outside the base with a wingman. I wanted to meet you first and see how we can get them in without drawing attention. They carry Marine Corps credentials."

"What's the name of Captain Delgado's wingman?"

"Sergeant Kuzek."

I called the Operations Center and warned them a pair of Marines in civilian would seek admittance in a few minutes on matters related to my investigation. Kine contacted

Delgado the moment I was done, and we engaged in idle chitchat while waiting. Soon enough, the sound of male voices in the stairwell reached our ears.

Kine popped her head out of my suite. "Over here, Curtis."

The lanky, sharp-faced, copper-haired man with a scruffy beard who entered and came to attention seemed awfully young for a Special Forces captain, especially one serving in an elite squadron. His winger, a dark-complexioned slab of a man, stayed in the corridor and assumed a relaxed but watchful posture.

"Pleased to meet you, Chief Superintendent Morrow. You as well, Inspector Galdi and Sergeant Bonta." He nodded at each of us in turn. "I'm Curtis Delgado, Erinye Company. We're Ghost Squadron's Furies."

"At ease, Captain. We don't stand on ceremony in the Professional Compliance Bureau."

He obeyed instantly, and a pleasant grin split his beard.

"Yes, sir. I understand you are in somewhat of the same business as us — removing threats."

"You could say that. But our methods differ vastly."

"There's more than one way of taking on the nasties."

Delgado came across as someone with a straightforward manner, but I could sense the steel behind those intelligent eyes.

"Agreed, sir. Ours is subtle in a different way. Can we discuss the preferred manner of dealing with Aeternum? As Aleksa probably told you, Erinye Company is here for a good time, not a long time."

I waved at the settee group filling most of my day room. "Please sit. Sergeant, would you handle the visuals?"

"Yes, sir."

Over the next half hour, I ran them through events on Mission, including the details on both the murder and professional compliance investigations. Kine and Delgado held higher security clearances than we did and were no doubt old hands at keeping secrets.

"Quite an interesting situation, Chief Superintendent," the latter said when I fell silent. "Sounds a lot like New Oberon before it blew up."

Arno winked at him. "Which you never visited because it was mercenaries who did the job."

"You may well think so, Inspector. I certainly couldn't comment." The twinkle in Delgado's eyes told us what we needed. "You're aware the New Oberon police chief there was in on it, right? Are you sure about AC Braband?"

"We vetted him to a fare-thee-well before he was appointed CO of the 24th Regiment. Besides, the Constabulary is a lot choosier with its senior officers than most planetary police forces. But we'll be looking into his personal life alongside the others, even though he's been steering clear of Mister Derzin."

"As far as you know. In any case, thank you for the briefing and the images of the Aeternum facility. Our ship is scanning the place during each orbital pass, and we can usually generate a decent three-dimensional rendering, but nothing replaces actual ground views."

"What are your intentions?"

His grin returned.

"You'd be duty-bound to arrest me if I told you. Our garbage removal operations generally violate a whole slew of Commonwealth laws, the sort the zaibatsus and cartels hide behind, which is why they exist in the first place. Let's just say that one night soon, at oh-dark-thirty, if you look to the southwest, you might see a few fireworks. You mentioned regular ships, both free trader and corporate. When is the next one due?"

I glanced at Arno, who said, "A free trader should land in the wee hours on Monday morning. They generally touch down around oh-one-hundred and lift off shortly before local sunrise."

"Are you planning on an intercept?"

Delgado nodded. "We've carried out a few in recent times. Our taking away the enemy's toys is a surprisingly effective way of bankrupting them, and we end up with more disposable ships for covert operations."

Arno cocked a questioning eyebrow at the Marine. "Disposable?"

"As in single-use, so we don't risk losing our expensive and incredibly useful Q-ships."

"Like the one in orbit right now?"

Delgado tapped the side of his nose with an extended index finger.

"You didn't hear it from me."

Kine raised a hand. "Captured data?"

"Right. We usually try to capture data cores intact, whether it's a ground target or a starship. Our analysts work their way through whatever we find and send processed intelligence to the Constabulary. Considering the situation here, I'll make sure you receive a copy of whatever we seize. That way, you can do your own processing on the spot and maybe develop enough evidence for arrests."

"That's very good of you."

Another quick smile. "Captain Talyn said we were to extend you every possible courtesy, and I can't think of a better one than that."

"Information is power," Arno intoned with a solemn expression on his face. "However, what you give us won't be admissible in court, unfortunately. Fruit of the poisoned tree. But it might point us at evidence we can hand the federal prosecutor."

"If it doesn't, call us. We can act on inadmissible evidence."

"Which means you're wiping out the cartels nowadays. The Organized Crime Division gets quite chagrined every time they're building a case against a cartel only to see their targets assassinated or outright vaporized."

"But it saves the taxpayer a lot of money and the honest part of the legal system plenty of heartaches." Delgado sprang to his feet. "Chief Superintendent, Inspector, Sergeant. You've been most gracious with your time and your findings. We will see that something happens by Monday at the latest. If it goes well, we won't meet again, at least not during this operation. But keep your communicators close at hand. We'll feed you anything we find."

We shook hands, then they left.

"Are you as chilled as I am, Chief? We just spent half an hour with people who plan on carrying out a covert military strike against what is, until proof of the contrary, a legitimate corporation. And based on intelligence that could only come from highly irregular, if not illegal means."

I gave Arno's question a few seconds of thought before shaking my head. My greater exposure to Captain Talyn's dark universe had swept away many of my scruples. A few dangerous criminals deserved removal by any means necessary in an era of increasing political instability, rife with corrupt officials who cover up any atrocity for the right price.

"We did not, in fact, spend half an hour with people who plan on carrying out a covert military strike, Arno. They were never here. And if by chance actionable information comes our way, we won't know from whom."

Arno took a deep breath and exhaled noisily. "Understood, Chief."

I glanced at Bonta, who said, "I saw no one and heard nothing, sir."

About an hour after we settled in for another day of data digging, my communicator chimed softly. I tapped it.

"Morrow."

"Aleksa Kine here. Are you still secure?"

"Yes."

"Someone followed us on our way back to the spaceport. I can't figure out exactly where we picked up a tail, but it wasn't long after we left the base. Two men, nondescript, looked like professionals, decent fieldcraft, just not good enough for us. I'm sending you the images we took. Someone in the 24th is playing for the other side or is overly curious about visitors."

"Thanks for the warning."

"All part of being on the same team. Kine, out."

I sent the images to my computer and called them up on the primary display. Neither of their faces rang a bell. My companions couldn't identify them either.

"The personnel on duty in the Operations Center are the only ones who know about a Constabulary warrant officer and two Marines visiting us, Chief. If Ops sprung a leak, we face bigger problems."

"So long as no one links them to a Special Forces company in orbit aboard a Q-ship, we needn't worry overmuch. I'll add the incident to the case file, and Commissioner Sorjonen can decide if it warrants further investigation. Looking for misconduct in the Operations Center now could give the game away."

"Shame. It would be straightforward. Trace communications, private calls included, in and out of the base between the time of Warrant Officer Kine's arrival and their departure and," he snapped his fingers, "we find our miscreant. That's the thread we pull on and unravel this case."

"Commissioner Sorjonen can pull if he wants, Arno. He has enough officers to tear through the 24th at will. Me, not so much. Besides, startling suspects when you're waiting for reinforcements is lousy tactics."

"True. I guess the idea of not being in on a kill for the first time in years irks me."

"Me as well, but orders are orders."

— Twenty-Six —

Braband seemed preoccupied as he nursed a glass of beer alone at the commanding officer's table. He barely noticed us when we crossed the Steele Club's main room, headed for our usual corner seats, far from prying ears. He answered my friendly wave with a distracted and rather curt hand gesture.

"Something's bothering that man," Arno remarked as we sat.

Bonta made a face. "The weight of command. When you're chief of police in a star system where nebulous and probably criminal affairs are stirring, and your girlfriend did a runner, things can seem a little depressing, Inspector."

"Especially with a team from the Firing Squad inside the gates. He'll be downing a few more of those beers once Commissioner Sorjonen and his inquisitors arrive."

For once, Braband didn't bother exchanging a few words with us before he left. Something was definitely eating at him. In the week and a half since our arrival, I'd never seen him so taciturn.

The next morning, shortly after we settled in our respective suites and switched on our devices, I heard a muffled curse waft across the hallway from Sergeant Bonta's sitting room.

"Someone tried peeking into our node from a terminal inside the 24th Regiment's secure network just before twenty-two hundred hours last night. Whoever it was obviously wasn't aware PCB data security measures included a tripwire. Otherwise, he or she wouldn't have tried."

"Can you track it?"

"I can try, but it might trigger tripwires our intruder left to cover him or herself, confirming we noticed."

And that would open a whole new universe of trouble just when we needed to keep a low profile while Erinye Company prepared its strike. But the intrusion proved someone on this base was playing with, if not for the other team.

"Probably the same individual who put a tail on our friends," Arno said as if reading my mind.

"Another issue for Commissioner Sorjonen's people. At this rate, his unit might need augmentation as well."

"Maybe he'll let us stick around and see this one through, Chief."

"Doubtful. The moment something becomes a head office case, we provincials are persona non grata."

AC Braband seemed no happier at lunch and barely acknowledged our presence. He struck me as someone impatient for the departure of unwanted guests. Little did he know he'd be trading the three of us for ten or twenty times that many PCB investigators next week. And from no less than the Political Anti-Corruption Unit — the scariest of them.

I repressed an urge to force my presence on him just so I could see his reaction, principally because there was no point. As we walked back across the parade ground, something akin to a giant fist punched me in the right shoulder. I spun around and fell backward, hitting my head on the pavement. Then everything went black.

I woke in a hospital diagnostic bed with the fuzzy feeling of someone high on painkillers, a sensation more familiar than I would have liked. Everything was a blur. Moments later, a bearded head swam into view, and even though I couldn't make out details, I knew it was Arno.

"Chief. How are you?"

"Hopped up and floating." My voice came out as a croak. "What happened?"

He held up a transparent bag with a dull, elongated object inside. "Railgun slug. Looks like a ten millimeter. It was likely fired from extreme range because it didn't penetrate your jacket's bulletproof weave. Chalk one up for orders making us wear the stuff while on plainclothes duty. Nothing is broken, but you're heavily bruised. That knock on the head when you collapsed didn't help either."

It took a few seconds before his words registered. "Sniper? Someone tried to assassinate me?"

"Looks like it. AC Braband has everyone scrambling to find the slug's point of origin, which is almost certainly a hopeless cause if it was fired from five or six kilometers away. The 24th is treating it like attempted murder, so be ready for the customary interview by a pair of Braband's finest detectives. I'll try to hold them off until you're out of this place."

"Where am I?"

"Ventano General Hospital. This is a private room, and there's an armed constable standing guard outside. Only medical staff and Constabulary members are allowed in. You've been out of commission for the last five hours while the doctors blasted your head and shoulder with regen therapy to reduce the swelling. They'll likely keep you overnight for observation, seeing as how it's getting late in the day. All things considered, Chief, you were lucky. Without the jacket, you'd still be in the operation room getting your shoulder rebuilt from scratch."

A nagging question floated through the fog enveloping my brain, but I couldn't see it clearly, although it seemed important, perhaps even vital.

"What I don't understand," Arno continued, "is why try to kill you? A shooting like that confirms we're almost over the target, even if we can't yet make it out. Anyone but a total fool must understand we take this sort of thing seriously enough to pull out every stop, lest people think murdering cops is a suitable way of avoiding jail."

There it was, the nagging question, put into words by my favorite wingman.

He shrugged. "Since no one in this star system besides the three of us are aware of Commissioner Sorjonen's impending arrival, perhaps it was an effort at deflection. Injure or kill you and end our prying into Mission Colony's affairs. Someone in the financial institutions or the telecoms might have warned one of our targets about the warrants."

That made sense even to my momentarily dulled thought processes. The shooting certainly stopped our work halfway through today, and with the weekend, we wouldn't be looking into any further private lives until Monday. But did we already pry into that of my shooter, or the shooter's employer? Or was it next in line?

A middle-aged woman wearing medical garb appeared in my field of view.

"Inspector, I think we should let Chief Superintendent Morrow rest now." Arno's head vanished.

"Of course, Doctor."

"Barring any unforeseen complications, you can pick her up tomorrow, say any time after oh-nine-hundred."

"Will do. Take care, Chief, and have a pleasant night. Sergeant Bonta and I will be here at nine sharp."

The woman leaned over and stared into my eyes.

"I'm Doctor Muldaur. You took quite a beating from that slug and your subsequent collapse, but nothing's broken, and I don't see signs of concussion. The generalized painkiller will wear off within the next hour, so you'll start thinking clearly again soon. I'll apply localized analgesic patches to your shoulder and skull, but you may nonetheless experience a certain amount of discomfort, especially if you move."

"How long?"

"Until you heal from your injuries? It'll be about two weeks before the bruising subsides. The discomfort, hopefully earlier, but avoid using your right arm for the next few days. If you get sudden headaches, seek medical help right away. Are you hungry?"

I thought about her question for a few seconds, then noticed my stomach seemed rather empty. Unsurprising, since it was probably past eighteen-hundred hours.

"Yes."

"I'll see that someone brings you a light meal, then you should try to sleep." I felt her stick something on my skin, both at the base of my skull and over my right breast, and two synchronized waves of numbness radiated out. "There. We'll change them in the morning, and I'll make sure you take a few home. If you need help, just call out. The AI will alert one of the duty medics."

Muldaur vanished just like Arno, leaving me alone. I tested my shoulder while remaining prone and found it stiff. Painfully so. Turning my head wasn't much better, but I found the bed's controls and raised my upper body to a sitting position, ready for what I hoped would be appetizing hospital food. The room was small, plain, and antiseptic, with a window overlooking the North Fjord and the heights beyond. Chances were good I was looking at the general area from where my would-be assassin fired, considering I was facing in that direction when the slug struck me.

But why try a kill with a railgun from a distance that would challenge even the best Marine Special Forces snipers? Why try at all? Sure, the shooter wouldn't be aware our civilian garb was made from tactical cloth, and if the slug had struck me in the face, I'd be dead. But from several kilometers away, you aimed at the center of mass, hoping to rupture something vital. Headshots were for much shorter ranges.

A medic in blue scrubs came in unannounced, carrying a covered tray. He smiled at me.

"I see you figured out how to raise the bed. Excellent." He pulled an overbed table on casters from its niche, put down the tray, then carefully maneuvered it into position before adjusting my bed so I could eat in as much comfort as possible. "Enjoy your meal."

"Thank you."

I lifted the cover from what was a bowl of stew as he left. The aroma tickling my nostrils drew an embarrassingly loud rumble from my stomach. It was tasty. The medic returned twenty minutes later and retrieved the tray, leaving me to stare at the entertainment display on the wall across from my bed. I cycled through the news nets but found no mention of the attempt on my life. Good. It meant AC Braband was taking this seriously. I'd have been royally irked if my name came up in breathless speculation about whether the wannabe-revolutionaries were back and targeting senior federal officers.

As I looked for something interesting, extreme fatigue overtook me. I turned off the display and lowered my bed. Sleep came within moments.

When I woke, after a string of bizarre, disturbing dreams, I was no longer in the hospital room. Which meant Arno and Sergeant Bonta weren't picking me up at oh-nine hundred on Saturday morning.

— Twenty-Seven —

I was lying on a hard surface in a small, bare room with concrete walls and a blank metal door. The glow globe floating in one corner gave off a harsh, industrial light that stung my eyes at first. I tried sitting up, but the analgesic patches had long since expired, and I gasped at the sudden pain shooting through my right shoulder while a bass drum beat an agonizing tattoo in my head.

When both faded to a more manageable level, I tried again, cautiously this time, and swung my legs over the side of what I saw was a field cot. I still wore the hospital pajamas, with no footwear, but my wrist device was gone, meaning I couldn't figure how much time had elapsed, let alone activate the emergency beacon it hid.

When the second round of muscular and cranial pain ebbed, a fresh pressure made itself felt — my bladder. One quick glance around the room confirmed there wasn't so much as a bucket. But there must be a surveillance device. No one with half a brain leaves a kidnap victim unsupervised.

"Hey." My voice came out as a dry croak. "I need the facilities. Otherwise, you'll be cleaning up a nasty mess."

No reply.

I took stock of my situation. Fact number one, whoever abducted me had help inside the hospital. My stew was almost certainly laced with a knockout drug. Fact number two, either the constable standing guard at my door was distracted or momentarily called away, or he was in on it. Or worse, was taken off the board by my captors. If the latter, I hoped it wasn't a terminal benching. Fact number three, whoever did this, just earned him or herself a universe of hurt. Once Commissioner Sorjonen landed, he'd take Mission Colony apart to find one of his own. With any luck, Arno would contact Warrant Officer Kine and ask for Erinye Company's help. If nothing else, they were the best hostage rescue unit within a dozen light-years.

It struck me that the sniper shot was to get me out of the base's secure perimeter and placed in a vulnerable position. But why? Why kidnap an officer who no longer presented a clear and present threat as evidenced by our withdrawal from Government House and our wind up of the Tosh murder? They, whoever that was, weren't aware of Sorjonen's imminent arrival. Other than going through the private affairs of a few administration members, we didn't do a damn thing in days. It meant one of the financial or telecom legal folks probably blabbed to the mysterious 'they' and set off events ending in my waking up here.

It would become another item for the Political Anti-Corruption Unit. At this rate, Sorjonen would need reinforcements from every corner of the Commonwealth.

The cell door opened without warning, and a burly individual wearing black tactical clothes, black gloves, and a full-face helmet stepped in. Since I couldn't see so much as a bit of skin, let alone a face, it was impossible to tell whether it was a man or a woman, but sheer size favored the former.

He pointed a large-bore blaster at me, then at the corridor. Presumably, he was my escort to the nearest facilities. I winced as I stood but let out no sound of pain. A brief wave of dizziness threatened my balance, then I took a tentative step, the concrete floor cold and rough beneath my bare feet.

The man backed away, staying well out of reach. Once in the corridor, he pointed at a door to my left, one decorated with the universal sign for bathroom. The passageway exuded the same industrial feel as my cell, and I wondered whether this was the Aeternum facility. Of course, it wasn't the only large, concrete structure on Mission. Still, if Derzin was foolish enough to abduct me, he wouldn't think twice about using his compound as my prison, believing it impregnable, mostly because of political protection. That would change with Erinye Company's strike.

The bathroom was just as starkly functional as the rest, adding further credence I was in an industrial complex. Mercifully, the guard stayed outside, leaving me free to wash and drink water from the tap as well. I almost peeled back my hospital pajama top to examine the bruising on my shoulder but didn't think my faintly upset stomach would take it. Besides, the face staring back at me from the mirror told a story on its own. I looked the way I felt.

Once back in my cell, I wondered how Arno and Sergeant Bonta reacted to my disappearance. And Assistant Commissioner Braband. A report must already be on its way to Wyvern and Cimmeria, and our Special Ops friends in orbit should know about recent events. The more I thought about it, the more this struck me as a situation spinning out of control.

Cops getting killed by criminals wasn't an uncommon occurrence. Kidnapping senior officers, on the other hand? The service made it clear it didn't pay ransoms but instead hunted the culprits with extreme prejudice. And in recent years, the service conditioned those promoted above the rank of chief inspector against interrogation.

It wasn't the most pleasant experience in the world. But contrary to popular belief, those who were conditioned didn't invariably suffer immediate cardiac arrest if injected with certain drugs or tortured. We simply wouldn't be able to answer. The danger stemmed from the interrogation itself, not the conditioning. Push a human body far enough, and it'll shut down because it could no longer go on. Cardiac arrest ensued.

No, someone was panicking, someone who didn't understand how the Constabulary worked, especially the Professional Compliance Bureau. We didn't scare easily, and there would always be another to carry on the investigation. But why not just kill me? If there was a reason, I didn't see it yet.

Several unpleasant hours passed, during which I struggled to find a comfortable position on the hard cot. My stomach soon started rumbling due to the lack of nourishment, and I asked the unseen watchers for food, but in vain.

My inner clock, reset by the previous day's sedatives, couldn't tell me what time it was, but I knew over six hours passed before the door opened again. The same anonymous guard, or at least I thought it was him, entered, blaster pointed at my midriff. Another man, this one unarmed and wearing a dark business suit, followed him in. He was in late middle age, mostly bald with a fringe of gray hair making a last stand around his shining skull. He had a pugilist's flattened nose, deep-set, dark, almost porcine eyes, and a square jaw slowly succumbing to jowls.

"Caelin Morrow." He stopped just inside the door, hands thrust into his trouser pockets, and studied me. I returned the favor. After almost half a minute, he shook his head in mock disbelief. "It's been what? Almost thirty years?"

"And you are?"

"The one who'll finally execute the arrest warrant that should have seen you disappear along with the rest of your unpatriotic, Pacifica-hating family. And once I've taken you back to our homeworld, I'll make sure you vanish forever, as a lesson for those who think enlisting in the Commonwealth services is a way to escape sedition charges."

"How charming. You realize that the warrant is worth less than toilet paper beyond the Pacifican heliopause. You attempting to enforce it on a federal colony is enough cause for exile on Parth, as a lesson for those who think they can get away with arresting Commonwealth officials on illegal charges before murdering them."

"Murder? Hardly. But keeping social and political peace is a worthy end that merits execution of anti-social elements."

"Does that mean my family is dead?"

"They were dead before you escaped Pacifica. I was part of the arresting team and bringing you to justice will be the crowning achievement of a successful State Security career."

I felt a surge of hatred rise up my throat, an acid so strong I would have flung myself at the secret police goon, were it not for the blaster aimed at my midriff and the injury to my shoulder.

"Do you understand the retaliation you face for kidnapping a federal official and murdering her on charges that would be declared illegal if it weren't for the miasma of corruption on Earth?"

"No one will know for sure, other than State Security, but the rumors will suffice for our purposes. And you Constabulary fools don't run on rumors."

"It won't be the Constabulary retaliating. The Fleet and us, we're family, and right now, Special Forces are giving filth of your sort the terminal, ten-millimeter blaster treatment all over the Commonwealth. If I vanish on Pacifica, State Security will suffer the same fate as the federal SSB last century. You can count on it."

After working with Captain Talyn and Colonel Decker, I believed in what I was saying, and it must have shown because I saw doubt in his eyes.

"Set me free and get the hell off Mission Colony, and I won't ask them to terminate you."

A mocking smirk pulled at his thin lips. "Such language for a chief superintendent. No one is terminating me because I am the hunter, and you're my prey."

"You're obviously here at someone's behest. Is it Salak? Or Derzin?"

Considering they were aware of who I was shortly after my arrival, there would have been just enough time for a fast ship to make the trip from Pacifica, perhaps a civilian version of the Navy's avisos. Those tiny hulls mated with frigate-sized faster-than-light drives reached the highest hyperspace bands, where physics became voodoo science. They made interstellar crossings in little more than half the time needed by regular liners, though it's said repeated exposure to the outer edge of hyperspace took a toll on crews and passengers alike. I couldn't imagine what it would do for someone who suffered from my sensitivity.

"That is none of your business." His smirk widened. "I'll enjoy recording your execution. A dangerous traitor who wormed her way into the federal police finally getting her just desserts."

"I was a seventeen-year-old child, you cretin. My brothers were even younger. We posed about as much of a threat to the corrupt assholes running Pacifica as pregnant jackalopes."

He wagged a sententious finger at me.

"But the whelps of rabid, violent parents such as yours grow up and become even more rabid and violent. Better we stop that sort of thing before it becomes a problem. I'm sure you feds believe in proactive policing."

"What you do isn't policing, it's state-sanctioned murder."

He made a dismissive gesture.

"Six of one, half a dozen of the other. What matters is the safety of the state. You know how progressive societies work, right? All within the state, nothing outside the state, nothing against the state."

I fought to keep my rage in check. Here was the man who took part in my family's murder, and I couldn't mete out the kind of justice my Ghost Squadron friends were visiting on his like. The Commonwealth was truly dying when the only way of suppressing government-sanctioned criminality was through military action.

"You're not hauling me back to Pacifica. Count on it. With my disappearance, the surface to orbit traffic will be tightly controlled."

A dismissive shrug this time.

"It's a big planet with a lot to cover, friendly traffic controllers, and no Navy ships in sight. Good luck with a hundred percent effective quarantine."

I briefly debated telling him about the Q-ship, or at least dropping a few hints, but decided it was better if no one knew until Erinye Company launched its attack. Then a thought struck me.

"You came aboard a Black Nova ship, didn't you? But it's not the regular run, which is due on Monday. Let me guess, that ship is parked on the Aeternum landing strip outside."

The State Security goon gave me an ironic round of applause.

"I see that contrary to expectations, our valiant Constabulary actually produces reasonably capable detectives. So you see, the local authorities won't interfere with my transport. The way I understand it, Black Nova's owners practically run Mission Colony, despite your ineffectual police regiment."

"And next you'll tell me they still run Pacifica from the shadows."

He stretched out his arms, palms upward, and laughed with unseemly glee.

"The Pacifican Deep State lives, Chief Superintendent, even after the outrage perpetrated against it by what we know are rogue Fleet elements. ComCorp isn't just a plaything of the late Amali clan. No, you're mine, and nothing can change that now."

— Twenty-Eight —

"Stand up and hold out your arms, wrists together." He produced a set of standard police manacles. "We're leaving this shitty star system."

When I didn't immediately obey, the goon said, "My brief is bringing you back alive. No one said anything about unharmed. I could slice through your spinal cord and turn you into a quadriplegic for all that my superiors care, so long as you're still breathing when we hang you in the basement of the State Security HQ building."

I knew instinctively he'd take great pleasure in crippling me as a precursor to execution, so I obeyed and held out my wrists in the approved manner while suppressing a fresh bout of agony from my right shoulder. "How about footwear?"

"Why?" He slapped on the manacles and tested them by tugging on both wrists. Another burst of pain coursed through my body, but I kept a straight face. There was no way I'd give him the satisfaction of wincing. "Traitors walk to their deaths in bare feet."

He gestured at the guard, turned on his heels, and left the cell. The guard waved his blaster toward the open door as a signal I should follow, and we made our way through a warren of bare corridors before stepping out into a starless night. I took a deep breath of damp air, tinged with the scent of vegetation and the tang of recently fired starship thrusters.

I'd guessed correctly. An aviso with massive hyperdrive nacelles bearing Black Nova markings sat on the Aeternum landing strip we'd studied from the heights a week earlier. Sandwiched between goon and guard, I trudged up the belly ramp, the soles of my feet by now freezing cold and aching from thousands of tiny pinpricks thanks to the tarmac's rough surface.

Once inside, the State Security officer waved me through an open cabin door.

"It's nicer than you deserve, but this ship doesn't have a brig. We'll make up for it when we reach Pacifica."

The moment I was inside, the door slid shut, cutting me off from the rest of the ship. I heard the faint sound of a mechanical latch falling into place and knew testing the lock would be futile. I climbed into the narrow bunk and searched in vain for the most comfortable position. With manacled hands, the options were limited.

Less than ten minutes later, the public address system came on, and an anonymous voice told everyone aboard they should take liftoff stations. Shortly after that, I heard a soft whine and felt the subliminal vibrations of thrusters coming to life. Then, a giant hand pushed me down as the ship rose into the night air.

Now, my only hope was Erinye Company and their Q-ship. But would they seize a clearly marked, civilian, corporate aviso on a legitimate departure vector? Doing so could easily be construed as piracy under Commonwealth law, without the fig leaf of a Navy vessel arraigning an unmarked freighter on suspicion of smuggling or piracy.

When the giant hand finally gave way, replaced by the tug of artificial gravity, I knew we'd reached orbit. If nothing happened in the next thirty minutes, I might as well kiss my life goodbye. Only an anti-ship missile could overtake an aviso accelerating toward the hyperlimit. And once that aviso went FTL, it was gone. But thanks to the ship's inertial dampeners, I wouldn't be able to tell when it broke out of orbit, leaving behind any chance of rescue. By now, I felt genuine fear worming its way past the ingrained stoicism that served as my last line of defense.

A series of dull thuds broke through what I suspected was a descent into self-pity, and I allowed myself a glimmer of hope. Starships didn't make noises like that unless they were docking at a space station, or something was docking with them. Operating purely on instinct, I pivoted my body ninety degrees, so my feet faced the door, then I folded my knees, ready to kick anyone entering the tiny cabin. If a rescue was in progress, the State Security thug might decide to execute me before a boarding party could stop him. He struck me as the sort of fanatical sociopath the Pacifican government preferred.

My ears picked up the faint sound of the door unlatching, and I coiled my legs for one last, defensive strike. It slid open. But instead of my would-be killer, I faced someone wearing an unmarked, pressurized armor suit and carrying a scattergun, the sort preferred by boarding parties. The helmeted head tilted to one side, in the unconscious gesture of someone using the built-in transmitter.

Moments later, a voice came from the blank helmet visor.

"I'm with Aleksa Kine. We've come for you."

Unexpected relief threatened my composure, and for a second or two, I felt light-headed.

I stood awkwardly, hands still shackled in front of me.

"There's a bald goon with a squashed nose aboard. He's Pacifican State Security and has the code to unlatch this."

Others wearing the same armor stood in the corridor while men and women in merchant spacer coveralls knelt on the deck, hands behind their heads, the State Security thug among them. One of the boarders quickly raised and lowered his visor so I could identify him. Captain Delgado. Curtis.

He pointed at my captor. "Is this him?"

"Yes. They abducted me at his behest so he could take me to Pacifica and execute a thirty-year-old arrest warrant for treason against me."

"Meaning execute you upon arrival."

"Precisely. He was one of the State Security gangsters who arrested and murdered my family when I was seventeen."

Delgado nudged him with his scattergun. "The code for those shackles, asshole."

When he didn't respond, Delgado butt stroked him in the chest. "I won't ask again."

"Seven, two, three, zero."

The trooper who'd opened my cabin door reached down and entered the digits. The manacles fell to the deck with a loud clatter.

"What happens now?"

"This ship was carrying a kidnap victim who would have been murdered by the Pacifican government upon arrival. And not just any victim, but a senior ranking Commonwealth officer. That means the crew is headed for Parth where they'll be tried by a military court, and since the evidence is incontrovertible, they'll spend time in a penal colony. The ship, of course, has just undergone a permanent change of ownership. Vessels involved in criminal activity are automatically confiscated. And this piece of shit?" Delgado tapped the barrel of his scattergun on my abductor's bald dome. "He earned himself a one-way ticket to the Infinite Void. We don't play around with his sort anymore. Nowadays, we practice *lex talionis*, an eye for an eye. The only remaining question is who puts a ten-millimeter blaster hole in his skull. Since he was one of those responsible for your family's death and planned on killing you as well, you get first right of refusal."

I stared at Delgado for a few seconds, processing his words. Did a Commonwealth Marine Corps officer he just offer me the chance to carry out an extrajudicial execution? Me, a thirty-year veteran of the Commonwealth Constabulary, not only sworn to uphold the law but responsible for hunting those among us who broke it. Yet part of me thirsted for revenge, and the events of the last few hours made that thirst unbearable.

Delgado noticed my hesitation.

"He's a dead man no matter what. We can't let planetary secret police bastards kidnap people at will across the Commonwealth. His execution, extrajudicial as it will be, is a necessary evil, *pour encourager les autres*. Besides, object lessons are becoming rather effective in these increasingly violent times. We'll be returning his credentials as well as a picture of his corpse to Pacifica. Speaking of which," he held up a small card, "since he strikes me as the sort who don't introduce themselves when they commit crimes against humanity, this is Senior Special Agent Idris Orloski, soon to be the late Special Agent Orloski."

I'd killed before, in the line of duty, to save my life or that of others and knew I wasn't squeamish in the face of dire need. But my life was no longer on the line, nor were the lives of anyone else. Orloski didn't present a danger. I shook my head.

"Very well. I can't say I'm surprised, based on what I heard about you." Delgado gestured at the trooper beside me. "Take the Chief Superintendent aboard our shuttle and give her the spare pressure suit."

The trooper touched my arm and pointed aft, where an airlock stood open. I stepped through it and came face-to-face with Warrant Officer Kine, whose helmet visor was raised.

She smiled at me. "Glad you're safe, sir. It was a close-run thing. The idiots almost decided running was the better choice."

Kine pointed at a neat bundle on one of the jump seats.

"This is for you. Take your time. We're not leaving until the prize crew is happy, and the prisoners are secured. We'll be bringing them with us. Our ship has a nice, comfortable brig."

"Except for the Pacifican special agent."

"You were a Constabulary liaison officer with the Special Forces and know the score, sir. Some individuals aren't destined for the legal system because the legal system will let them off the hook. Pacifican State Security officers will be high on the list of quasi-untouchables, considering the power Pacifica wields over the federal government."

"I know."

The pressure suit fit me like a glove, and I no longer felt as vulnerable as I did barefoot and in my hospital pajamas.

I sat on one of the benches and looked up at Kine. "So how did you intercept the aviso?"

"We spotted it coming in and landing at the Aeternum facility. Since it broadcast a Black Nova beacon, we figured it might be related to your disappearance. ComCorp wouldn't send one of its precious avisos to Mission Colony just for shits and giggles. We kept a watch on the facility, and sure enough, shortly after the ship touched down, our eye in the sky spotted you coming out, escorted by Orloski and an anonymous guard, probably one of Luca Derzin's men. *Sorcerer*, that's our ride, transformed into a Navy frigate and aimed her targeting sensors at the aviso the moment it came within range. Captain Pirillo laid on his standard 'surrender or die' speech. They surrendered, and here we are."

"What if they'd chosen death?"

"The gunnery officer would have surgically sliced off their port hyperdrive nacelle. Besides, corporate crews don't believe in dying for the company flag."

"How did you hear about my abduction?"

Kine let out a brief chuckle.

"We've been monitoring the 24th Regiment's operational network since arriving. It's pandemonium on the surface, as you might imagine. The hospital raised the alarm when the night shift took over and realized you were gone. As soon as I found out, I contacted Inspector Galdi, who told us you might be inside the Aeternum compound if they hadn't killed you. Since we would hit it within forty-eight hours of your disappearance, Captain Delgado amended the plan to include a rescue on the ground. Then the aviso showed up and made our lives a little easier where you're concerned."

"And a little harder for the planned raid on Aeternum. Derzin and company will know something's up."

She shook her head.

"Doubtful. We jammed the aviso's communications before ambushing it. They couldn't send a warning signal, and there's no one else in orbit who saw the seizure. As far as the opposition will know, their ship vanished without a trace. Its crew will mysteriously appear on Parth in a few weeks, charged with abetting a kidnapping. If Black Nova sends them decent lawyers, they might escape with a slap on the wrist. If not too bad, so sad. But they're just foot soldiers, so the outcome doesn't matter to us. Our job is terminating the enemy command structure."

I gave her a smirk. "Our? Did you forget you wear gray, not black?"

She grinned at me. "In these times, 'our' includes gray, black, blue and green, sir."

"One for all and all for one?"

"Oo-rah!"

— Twenty-Nine —

Fifteen minutes later, the aviso's six crew members, blindfolded, shackled at the ankles and wrists, with duffel bags slung over their shoulders, shuffled through the airlock. The Marines strapped them in for the ride back to *Sorcerer*, then took their own seats. Senior Special Agent Idris Orloski was conspicuous by his absence, but I'd already decided this was one of those times when 'don't ask, don't tell' was in the best interests of the service. Officially, he never visited Mission Colony, nor was he involved in my kidnapping. The latter was nothing but the truth. I knew Derzin did it. What I needed now was proof.

Shortly after we undocked from the aviso, I felt the artificial gravity in the shuttle shift slightly and knew we were entering the Q-ship's hangar. The gentle bump of our craft settling on the deck confirmed my guess moments later. The aft ramp dropped, and Warrant Officer Kine stood.

"If you'll follow me. You need new wearables before we discuss getting you back on the surface with Captain Pirillo, who's the overall operational commander. You certainly can't keep wearing that tin can or go around in pajamas."

Kine led me to the accommodations deck and into an unoccupied cabin where a pile of civilian spacer clothes waited. I stripped off the pressure suit and the pajamas, then glanced longingly at the cabin's heads.

"Is there time for a quick rinse?"

"Of course, sir. This is your cabin for the duration of your stay aboard. You'll find toiletries in there."

A few minutes later, clean and dressed like the average tramp starship passenger, I felt more civilized. And alive. Just then, my stomach made a loud and embarrassing noise. Kine gave me an amused look.

"We'll stop by the mess on our way to Captain Pirillo's day cabin. There's always something on offer."

"Since my last meal was hospital stew over twenty-four hours ago, at this point, even emergency rations would do wonders."

"The ship's galley can do a lot better than rat bars. You seem a bit stiff. Do you want to see the ship's physician before meeting Captain Pirillo?"

"It's nothing that time won't heal. Other than wandering around barefoot, I've not been injured since the shooting. Mind you, my shoulder feels pretty stiff, and I still have a background headache." I glanced at the low quarter spacer's boots. "But the soles of my feet are feeling better by the minute. Nice choice of socks."

"Everything comes from the ship's fabricator. You're wearing what we wear during undercover operations."

"How about you take me where I can eat what you eat during undercover operations before my stomach complains again?"

"After we see the doc for analgesic patches, perhaps?"

"Sure."

The doc, a physician's assistant, had a brisk but pleasant manner. He listened to my story, then pulled out a twelve pack.

"This should keep you for the next few days. If things worsen while you're with us, see me right away."

"I will. Thank you."

"My pleasure."

The ship's mess, a combined facility for everyone aboard, including the embarked Special Forces company, kept a simple cold buffet available twenty-four hours a day. It was make your own sandwich, reheat your soup, and nibble on raw vegetables with spicy dips. Tasty, filling, and delightfully civilized.

Wolfing down a heaping plate under Kine's amused gaze must have been quite the sight, though she didn't comment. A cup of coffee topped off the meal, and I sat back contentedly, examining the mess for the first time. Nothing of its decor betrayed the ship's status as an undercover Navy combatant. No crests, plaques, or other naval mementos. I could have been in a corporate freighter's mess and not known the difference.

Kine, noticing my interest, said, "Q-ships keep even the insides as sterile as possible, in case play-acting demands they allow inspection parties to board."

"Did that ever happen on your watch?"

"No. The Fleet changed its operating procedures in the last few months and put Special Operations Command units on a more aggressive footing. I daresay things changed a lot since your time." Her communicator buzzed softly. "That's our signal."

After disposing of my plate and cup, Kine led me up a deck and along another unadorned passageway to a door marked 'Captain's Day Cabin.' It lay just aft of one marked 'Bridge.' The day cabin opened at our approach, and Kine ushered me in.

Both Curtis Delgado and a lean, gray-haired man wearing a merchant spacer's rank insignia stood.

"Chief Superintendent Morrow," the latter extended his hand in greeting, "welcome aboard MV *Red Harvest*, as we are currently known. *Sorcerer* only comes out when we unmask our guns."

We shook. "Thank you for the timely rescue. If that aviso had escaped, I'd be a dead woman walking. Pacifican State Security never forgive and never forget."

"Neither do we, sir," Delgado said. "Their time will come, as will that of many organizations like it."

Pirillo gestured at a chair.

"Please sit, Chief Superintendent. As Warrant Officer Kine no doubt told you, we must discuss your return to the surface. There are a few factors we should consider. Erinye Company's strike on the Aeternum facility is timed for the next freighter's arrival, which I believe you folks said was Monday, and I'd rather your miraculous reappearance not make the opposition suspect the Navy is lurking in orbit.

At this point, it would be prudent if we assume the only people we can trust on the surface are your team."

"Agreed. My abduction pretty much proves the point. But I'd still be happier if I could let Inspector Galdi know I'm okay. He's an old hand at keeping secrets."

Pirillo nodded. "We'll arrange for it right after we finish here. That being said, I'd be happier if you stay with us until Erinye Company launches. Will doing so imperil your investigation?"

"No. We're at a standstill anyhow, and when Commissioner Sorjonen arrives with a PCB team from HQ in a few days, we're off the case."

"I understand you were a Constabulary liaison with the 1st Special Forces Regiment."

"Yes, and so was Sergeant Bonta, but that doesn't mean I'll gladly step off a perfectly functioning shuttle in low orbit at this point. My jumping days are long gone. Not that I enjoyed the experience overmuch anyhow."

"We won't be jumping in," Delgado said. "Ghost Squadron's operations are based on the principle of strike hard, strike fast, and vanish the moment we're done. For that, we use stealth dropships that can approach a target undetected and lay down devastating cover fire. What we were thinking is this. You go with us on the raid, enjoy a firsthand look at what Aeternum is hiding, and collect any evidence you need in your corruption case. On the way out, we drop you off near Ventano and let Inspector Galdi know where he can find you. Then you can spin a cover story that'll help advance your investigation. How does that sound?"

Reappearing at oh-dark-thirty in the wilderness didn't hold much appeal, but if they landed me at the spaceport or on the base's parade square, it would raise too many questions. Besides, I couldn't let anyone other than Arno and Sergeant Bonta know about the aviso and Erinye Company's raid. That meant telling everyone I'd been held at the Aeternum facility and escaped when unknown raiders flattened the place, which contained an element of truth. Always a good thing if you plan on lying to your superiors.

"Sounds like a plan."

"We'll set you up with a tin suit and a sidearm. The suit we'll take back when we drop you off. The sidearm is yours to keep. Ever handled a Shrehari blaster re-bored for fifteen-millimeter human ammo?"

"You mean like the one Colonel Decker owns?"

Delgado nodded, grinning. "His favorite, though I understand he kept losing them when he was working for intelligence. We always carry a few untraceable spares in case of need, such as equipping an unexpected passenger. I'd rather you didn't wait in the dark for Inspector Galdi without a weapon, not when all hell will be breaking loose, and I'd rather not leave you with something that can be connected to the Fleet. There's a simulator on board. You can practice handling the blaster as long as you want between now and when we launch."

"I gratefully accept your gift."

"Then it's done. Warrant Officer Kine will be your guide, aide, and personal assistant until we part ways." Delgado glanced at Pirillo. "If there's nothing else, sir, then maybe we can ping Inspector Galdi's personal communicator."

"I'm good. Just make sure we ping it in a way the opposition can't figure out what's happening. You never know who might have the right decryption keys."

"Veiled speech." Delgado turned to me. "Can you think of something that will tell the inspector it's you but seems like gibberish if anyone else reads the message?"

I thought for a few moments, then nodded. "Send a message that says, 'Montague Hobart came through once more.' He'll understand."

When Pirillo gave me a questioning look, I elaborated.

"A Fleet agent who went by the alias Montague Hobart saved my life on Aquilonia Station during an investigation involving Captain Talyn, a commander at the time. Inspector Galdi was there, and he'll know right away you folks rescued me."

"Understood. I'll see that the message is sent right away. In the meantime, Warrant Officer Kine can get you equipped and settled in."

My guide took me to the ship's stores, where a helpful bosun's mate issued unmarked combat armor, a substantial Shrehari blaster, ammo, and spare power packs. I studied the weapon for a few moments, knowing it would be a two-handed stance if ever I faced a threat. The bosun's mate politely showed me the safety check sequence, then the loading and powering procedures, after which Kine helped me carry everything to my cabin.

Delgado showed up a few minutes later.

"Inspector Galdi received your message. His reply was 'An honorable man, even from beyond the grave.' I'm curious. What did he mean by that?"

"Montague Hobart was one of Admiral Ulrich's officers, a Lieutenant Commander by the name Garrett Montero. Enemy agents murdered him on Scandia during the attempted putsch."

"Oh." He gestured at the armor and weapon. "Everything's good?"

"Yes, but I'll need time in your simulator tomorrow. Right now, I'd wipe out the entire Pacifican State Security for a dram of single malt and eight hours in a clean bunk."

"The bunk, you already have. The dram, I will organize. Don't leave your cabin."

Delgado vanished into the corridor. He returned less than two minutes later with an amber bottle and three tumblers. After serving us, he raised his glass.

"To a successful rescue and an equally successful raid on Aeternum."

The Glen Arcturus burned a welcome path down my throat.

— Thirty —

Although my cabin was small and plain, the bunk was a narrow slice of heaven. I managed eight hours of uninterrupted sleep and woke refreshed, ready, and raring to go. The mess was empty when I entered, looking for breakfast, but the ship's cooks had refreshed the buffet overnight, and I piled a healthy amount of food on my plate. Kine found me as I was finishing my second cup of coffee.

"Good morning, sir. How was your night?"

"It was excellent. So was breakfast. Kudos to the galley."

"The Navy eats well." She poured herself a mug of coffee from the urn and sat across from me. "Everything is quiet planetside. The 24th seems at its wit's end looking for you if our communications intercepts are anything to go by. No one noticed the brief appearance of a Navy frigate in orbit, nor the disappearance of a Black Nova aviso, which is nearing interstellar space by now, headed for parts unknown."

"I can easily picture Inspector Galdi and Sergeant Bonta watching the 24th, trying to hide smug expressions. They've probably figured out I'll be coming back via Erinye Company's raid on Aeternum."

"Which means they'll be expecting a call within the next twenty-four hours. Good. Are you ready for a bit of simulator time, so you can get used to the armor and gun? As in your shoulder and head feeling no pain?"

"Sure. The analgesic patches work like a charm."

We drained our mugs and headed for my cabin, where I donned the tin suit under Kine's critical gaze. It had been a while, and this configuration wasn't the same as the one we used back in my younger days, but I managed. I checked the blaster, added a power pack but no ammo, and holstered it.

"Ready."

Kine led me to the hangar deck, which doubled as simulator range when not actively engaged in shuttle or dropship operations. The serried ranks of unmarked, armed spacecraft were impressive.

"That's what we'll be taking on the raid. They can carry twenty armored passengers and take out any ground-based weapon emplacement. Two per troop, one for company HQ and one for the prize crew. They're not quite the standard Marine Corps and Army issue, for obvious reasons," Kine said, noticing my interest, "but they're almost twins under the skin and just as lethal."

"No doubt."

Kine handed me a simulator plug for the blaster and watched as I installed it. Then, for the next hour, she led me through a series of firing drills until I was comfortable handling the heavy handgun from every possible firing position. And I was reasonably accurate at close range. But my arms and wrists ached from the strain of the unaccustomed weight, never mind my bruised shoulder. However, beggars can't be choosers, and my regular sidearm was, hopefully, in Arno's care at the moment, along with the clothes I wore when I was shot.

Kine established I wasn't a menace to Erinye Company, that I remembered basic tactical communications and fieldcraft, and that my armor and its built-in electronics worked. Once she was satisfied, we returned to my cabin, where I put everything away until it was time for the raid. A quick lunch, this time in a mess teeming with Marines, then it was back on the hangar deck for orders.

None of the assembled troopers looked much like Marine Corps recruiting posters, other than they were fit and exuded an aura of danger. Longish hair, scruffy beards, and civilian spacer clothes were the order of the day. Erinye Company could pass for one of the many mercenary outfits selling their military expertise throughout the Commonwealth, and that was precisely the point.

What they were planning, indeed what they did most of the time, violated any number of laws, but since our feckless political class refused to let us cops clean up the Commonwealth through legal means, the job was theirs. But leaving the slightest bit of evidence that pointed at the Fleet would cause a constitutional crisis beyond imagining.

Curtis Delgado, with a shorter, stockier, and older man at his side, marched to the front of the company, standing in a broad circle between the facing rows of dropships.

"That's First Sergeant Emery Hak with the CO," Kine whispered for my benefit. "He's second in command. A good man, so long as you don't cross him."

"Good afternoon, Erinyes." Delgado's voice rang out loud and clear.

"Good afternoon, sir," the Marines replied in perfect unison.

"For those of you who didn't meet her yet," Delgado pointed at me, "that's Chief Superintendent Caelin Morrow of the Commonwealth Constabulary's Professional Compliance Bureau standing next to Aleksa. The chief superintendent is in the same business as we are — taking out the trash — and she's the reason we made a detour here on our way home. She'll be coming with us on the raid because for now, she's in charge of investigating the ComCorp corruption in this star system and needs every bit of evidence we find inside the target area. Chief Superintendent Morrow will travel in my call sign with Aleksa as her winger. Now that the introductions are over let's go through the operation one last time. Once we're done here, the company is at one hour's notice to move, so if you were planning on a cold beer later, forget it."

No one so much as blinked, proving Delgado's warning was merely for form's sake. These were the most professional troopers in human space. They didn't need reminding alcohol and black ops don't mix.

A three-dimensional projection of the area around Aeternum appeared on the center of the hangar deck, and Delgado took us through the entire raid, from start to finish, after which he opened the floor for questions. I had many, but none of them were proper for someone who, by and large, would be a passenger.

"One last point. When we extract, my call sign will head north for a few klicks, nap-of-the-earth, to drop off Chief Superintendent Morrow before rejoining the flight." The projection's scale changed, and a red dot appeared by an intersection on the main road back to Ventano. "Once that's done, the ship will contact Inspector Galdi and let him know where he can pick up his CO."

He glanced at me, and I nodded.

"That's it, folks. Dismissed."

I hadn't accompanied a Special Forces operation in almost twenty years, and my apprehension grew with each passing hour while we waited for the regular Monday ship from beyond the Rim Sector's outer frontier. But curiosity at what we would find inside the Aeternum facility provided a welcome counter. Since I didn't want to be a burden on Warrant Officer Kine, I stayed in my cabin and sampled the ship's extensive entertainment library. Meals came and went. Then, shortly after I fell asleep, the public address system startled me awake.

"Now hear this. The presumed target ship is on final approach. Notice to move is now thirty minutes. That is all."

The announcement drove away any further thoughts of sleep, so I climbed out of bed and slipped on my clothes, then sat, unsure what I could do while waiting. Enjoying a fresh cup of coffee came to mind. I wasn't the only one with that idea because Erinye Company troopers, Warrant Officer Kine, among them, filled the mess.

"This is always the hardest part," she said when, coffee cup in hand, I sat at the table she shared with Curtis Delgado, First Sergeant Hak, and two others who gave me friendly nods. "Waiting for the right time to launch."

Delgado raised his mug by way of greeting. "The approaching ship matches what you provided us, but I'll wait until we see it land on the Aeternum strip before pulling the trigger. We should know in about an hour."

"May I ask a dumb cop question?"

"Sure."

"If we'll know in an hour, why is the notice to move now thirty minutes?"

Delgado's infectious grin made an appearance.

"It gets everyone out of the rack and dressed, ready for one last coffee or tea along with a bite." He nodded at the buffet. "If I say go right now, in thirty minutes, my Marines will be formed by troops on the hangar deck, armed and armored, ready to board while the dropship pilots will see that their craft are ready for departure. We live for this stuff, Chief Superintendent. No one wants to be late."

For the next hour, we chatted about inconsequential things and swapped war stories, and it seemed like I was once again a keen young staff sergeant heading into danger with my comrades from the 1st Special Forces Regiment's Charlie Squadron. They said you can never go home again, but some homes weren't the same as others.

Since I was part of the broader tribe because I wore the same wings and had earned the same dagger, they treated me as one of their own, and that cheered me more than I expected. However, the only one at the table who wasn't still in high school when I jumped out of perfectly good shuttles from low orbit with Charlie Squadron was First Sergeant Hak. It meant recounting twenty-year-old missions made me feel more than a little superannuated. And even Hak had been a 'leg' back in the day, a regular infantry trooper.

Delgado's communicator finally buzzed.

"CIC to Erinye Niner."

"Delgado here."

"The suspect ship landed at the Aeternum facility."

"We launch in thirty minutes."

"Aye, aye, sir. CIC, out."

A klaxon sounded, followed by a female voice.

"Now hear this. Erinye Company launches in thirty minutes. Crew and Marines to your stations. That is all."

As one, the troopers downed their drinks and left in an orderly fashion after dropping their mugs and plates at the cleaning station. I followed suit and returned to my cabin, where I donned the armor, checked my blaster's power pack, and loaded the magazine with pure copper disks, though I knew better than to put one up the spout. Getting ready for launch seemed eerily natural, even after almost twenty years. There were things you just never forgot.

I joined the orderly rush of troopers headed for the hangar deck and made my way toward the command shuttle where Captain Delgado, First Sergeant Hak, Warrant Officer Kine, and the two Marines with whom I'd shared a table waited, helmet visors up. Because I'd done this before, I knew there would be a ritual, so I joined the command team and stood at ease beside Delgado, after exchanging nods with him and the others. I might be the most senior Commonwealth officer on deck, albeit Constabulary rather than Marine Corps, but he was the operational commander, and my rank didn't matter in the slightest.

When the stream of Marines crossing the main airlock into the hangar deck died away, Delgado drew himself to attention.

"Erinye Company, report."

A powerful, basso voice rang out. "Alpha Troop, present and ready."

Seconds later, "Bravo Troop, present and ready."

"Charlie Troop, present and ready."

"Delta Troop, present and ready."

"Prize crew, present and ready." A dozen spacers under one of the Q-ship's lieutenants, indistinguishable in their combat armor, would seize the trader and sail it home.

Delgado raised his right arm and made a circling motion. "Mount up."

I followed Kine into the dropship's aft compartment, along with the rest of the company HQ troopers, while Delgado remained outside. He would be the last to board. Kine pointed at the flight deck.

"Curtis would like you to take one of the two jump seats behind the crew."

I understood Delgado was giving me a place of honor, although I suspected it was at least in part so he could keep an eye on me to make sure I didn't leave the shuttle and run into battle with his people. Taking non-combatant passengers on black ops raids was never entirely comfortable for those in charge.

Two Navy petty officers, part of the Q-ship's complement, occupied the flight deck — pilot and gunner. I took the seat behind the gunner and strapped in. Delgado joined me moments later, and I heard the aft ramp close. A red strobe light gave the hangar deck a hellish hue while a klaxon sounded, then the space doors on either side opened, leaving the glowing film of a force field in their wake.

One by one, the ten dropships lifted, pivoted, and nosed through one of the two openings. Ours was last, and my trepidation increased when I saw Mission Colony's night side through the flight deck windows. Though clouds covered most of the Tyrellian Sea, they glowed in many spots where light from the main settlements seeped through. The largest would naturally be Ventano, where my two wingers waited for news of my safe return.

Our dropship joined the formation, and we entered a long lazy spiral that would take us to the surface.

— Thirty-One —

We soon plunged through the clouds, and everything turned black beyond the dimly lit flight deck. That sudden change meant our vector would quickly shift from a steep downward angle to nap-of-the-earth flying. It brought back old memories, the sort that woke butterflies in my stomach and made my mouth run dry. I took a quick sip from my armor's built-in water pouch before realizing I'd done so instinctively. Muscle memory was a fascinating thing. I wouldn't have thought it could resurface effortlessly after so much time.

The texture of the darkness changed abruptly, and within moments, my eyes picked out the distant glow of Ventano beyond the hills separating it from the interior. Our target was still almost a hundred kilometers away since the plan was to fly in undetected by Aeternum's ground-based sensors. We'd pop up and destroy the suspected weapon emplacements at the last moment, just before landing on the tarmac beside the grounded free trader.

Try as I might, I couldn't see any of the other dropships through the flight deck windows, nor did they show up on the gunner's targeting display. Ghosts indeed. Derzin's people and the trader's crew wouldn't know what hit them. No one spoke during the descent, but I could feel the tension like a palpable presence and reminded myself it was a good thing. Troopers who became complacent eventually screwed up. It was best to view every operation as the toughest one yet.

I saw our airspeed drop precipitously on the pilot's console and knew we were almost there, though I couldn't see the light from the Aeternum facility outlining the treetops in front of us. We crested yet another hill, and I finally saw faint emanations ahead. Unlike a conventional spaceport, Aeternum didn't cover its tarmac with artificial daylight.

"Linking Erinye Flight," the gunner announced in a soft tone. A few seconds passed. "All dropships are linked, and weapons are ready to execute Fire Plan Alpha."

"Attack zone in thirty seconds." Our airspeed slowed almost to a crawl. Now that the ships were linked, they appeared on the gunner's console, and I saw a U-shaped formation capable of engaging the target's entire perimeter in one devastating salvo.

"Still no sign they detected us."

"The contrary would chagrin me," Delgado said, flashing his customary grin. "Our approach was as slick as always."

"Ten, nine..."

I flipped my visor down and switched it to night vision.

"Eight, seven..."

"Lock and load."

I pulled out my blaster, thumbed a disk into the combustion chamber, and made sure the safety was on, then re-holstered it.

"Three, two, one…"

The dropship's abrupt vertical rise pushed my stomach into my lower gut. At least that's what it felt like, and the world beyond the flight deck windows turned into a vision of hell. Countless streams of plasma, fired by half a dozen multi-barrel guns from each shuttle, chewed through the space between both fences, obliterating the bumps that hid remote weapon stations.

Seconds later, we landed between the ship and the Aeternum facility under the stunned eyes of civilians wearing coveralls. Delgado climbed out of his seat, pointed at me, and said, "Stay. I'll let you know when it's safe."

Then he joined his troopers outside as they quickly disarmed the civilians and shackled them. A few of Derzin's guards made the mistake of firing at the Marines and died instantly. One of the troops ran up the trader's belly ramp, a second entered the facility via open freight doors, and the other two deployed around the building. The eeriest part of the operation was the total radio silence. Erinye Company did everything with hand signals.

A Marine came down the belly ramp again and raised an armored fist over his head. Moments later, the prize crew's shuttle landed and disgorged its passengers, who ran up the ramp while their craft lifted off again to resume its overwatch duties. Though I'd seen it before, the speed with which Erinye Company seized the ship and facility left me breathless.

It seemed like mere seconds had elapsed when the gunner turned toward me.

"Chief Superintendent, Captain Delgado, who's by the freight door, just pointed at us and made the hand signal for lieutenant colonel, by which I presume he means you."

"Thanks, PO." I stood and made my way aft, where Warrant Officer Kine waited at the foot of the ramp. "I've apparently been summoned."

"It means the facility is secure, and Curtis wants to show you something."

We jogged over.

"The place is ours," he said by way of greeting. "You'll want to see what we found while my people extract their computer core."

"Sounds ominous."

"Not the worst I've seen, but Aeternum isn't doing much pharmaceutical research and development if any." He led us into a wide passage lined with open freight doors giving onto separate, yet still cavernous stockrooms. "This place is a smuggler's haven, but it's what that ship out there brought in, which makes this a bit stomach-churning."

We entered a room with countless stacks of small plastic crates.

"According to our sensors, these containers are filled with human tissue. Organs, to be precise — hearts, livers, kidneys, you name it, adult and child-sized, everything perfectly preserved by miniature stasis bubbles. So long as the stasis fields are on, the organs stay fresh and ready for their intended recipients. Either someone is running an illegal, and therefore unsupervised organ cloning operation or..."

Delgado's voice trailed off, leaving me to finish his sentence.

"Aeternum is involved in organ harvesting. There are many unregistered human colonies in the Protectorate ruled by warlords, thugs, and assorted criminals, and harvesting organs is a lot cheaper than cloning them."

"Indeed. But harvesting them from children?" Delgado shook his head. "I think it's time we made an agreement with the Shrehari and divided the Protectorate between us. At least the boneheads will keep crap like that from happening in their half, and we can clean up."

"We're recording as much as we can, although it'll never be accepted as evidence even if the Fleet makes it public. One of the other storerooms contains crates of so-called pharmaceuticals with Aeternum markings, except our sensors show the contents as having a chemical signature remarkably close to that of a particular illegal drug which is usually manufactured from substances found on certain Protectorate worlds." He gave me the drug's street name, and I recognized it at once.

"Nasty stuff."

"That's not everything. We found evidence they keep large numbers of humans confined."

"Slavery? Is ComCorp mad?"

"Just trying to keep up with the cartels, I suppose. We also found something unexpected." He led us out of the warehouse section and deeper into the facility until we reached an airlock-like door with biohazard markings on it.

"Behind this door is something with the hallmarks of a biosafety level 4 laboratory. Every level 4 lab in the Commonwealth is registered and routinely inspected. Mission Colony does not have an authorized level 4 lab. There's no evidence it's in use, but I can't take chances."

I grimaced behind my helmet visor. "Ugh. What will you do with this?"

"Rods from God."

"Pardon?"

"Kinetic bombardment. Tungsten rods fired from the ship will turn this facility into a smoking crater, without leaving behind any proof we did it. We'll take samples from the storerooms with us for analysis, but the rest will be vaporized."

"What about the people who work here, and the trader's crew? We can't just murder them with your rods from God."

"The crew is coming with us as prisoners. They brought in those human organs, which is proof enough for a lengthy stay on Parth. We disarmed the Aeternum folks and stripped them of everything but their clothes. We're driving the lot beyond the ridge in one of their own trucks, where they'll be safe from the kinetic strike. They can walk toward Ventano from there until the day shift shows up and gives them a lift home."

"How do you know it'll be the day shift and not Derzin's people already on their way here? Or should I avoid asking?"

He hesitated for a fraction of a second.

"Since you already saw most of our tactics and procedures, I guess there's no harm in telling. A place this far from town won't be connected by a landline. And the dropship carrying the prize crew? It's a Growler, an electronic warfare shuttle. We jammed their radio and satellite communications from just before we opened fire until we destroyed their communications center, which, by the way, was equipped with military-grade gear, some of it likely stolen or diverted from the Fleet."

"I see. Well, I'm glad you're letting the workers go."

"We don't kill civilians out of hand, Chief Superintendent. The State Security goon was an exception, and he deserved summary execution. Luca Derzin's employees, not so much. Derzin himself yes, since running a large-scale human organ smuggling ring, especially if the organs were harvested and not cloned, is a capital crime deserving at least exile for life on Desolation Island, if not execution. And I won't even mention the possibility he was running slaves. But my brief isn't going after Aeternum's senior leadership. That job belongs to the Constabulary."

"Which will be difficult without admissible evidence, and anything seized here, tonight, is about as far from admissible as it gets, never mind revealing the Fleet's intervention."

Delgado nodded. "That goes without saying. What we hope is the evidence we find, especially the data we'll extract from their computer core, is enough to point you at other, admissible sources. And if it isn't, cosmic karma will eventually catch up with Derzin and the others involved, I promise."

"Cosmic karma being?"

"That would be telling, Chief Superintendent. Remember, we're not having this conversation since we're not actually here. Rival gangsters or an unhappy cartel put Aeternum out of business tonight, and you just happened to escape along with the workers. What happens next is your call." He turned on his heels. "Extraction time is almost upon us."

When we emerged from the warehouse section, Erinye Company's troopers were already loading up under First Sergeant Hak's supervision. The ship's belly ramp had vanished, and I could hear the whine of its thrusters spooling up.

"Time to get out of that tin suit, sir." Warrant Officer Kine gestured at Delgado's dropship.

My last glimpse before climbing aboard was of the command sergeants raising their hands one after the other, confirming their readiness to lift. Kine helped me strip off the armor, then tighten the gun belt and buckle it around my now vulnerable waist. When Delgado finally appeared, he handed me a palm-sized metallic cassette.

"We copied their entire computer core onto this. Enjoy."

"Thank you for everything, Captain. Watching professionals of your caliber at work is a privilege."

"It's been a pleasure working with you, Chief Superintendent. I hope what's on that cassette will help you clean this place up."

"Give Captain Talyn and Colonel Decker my best."

"I will. Take care of yourself. The ship will warn Inspector Galdi of your position the moment we drop you off. Goodbye."

He tossed off a jaunty salute, then vanished into the flight deck while I sat beside Kine near the now-closed aft ramp. I felt the dropship lift seconds later and make a sharp turn. Within minutes, it slowed and gently settled again.

Warrant Officer Kine offered her hand. "Take care, sir. Hopefully, we'll get a chance to work together again. I didn't think much of PCB officers before this, but you're okay. Heck, you're better than okay."

Instead of the aft ramp dropping, a person-sized door at its center popped open. I undid my seat belt and climbed out onto a deserted country intersection. The moment I was clear, the door slammed shut, and the dropship lifted. It vanished behind the treetops seconds later, just as a loud rumble two dozen kilometers to the south reached my ears. I watched the captured free trader rise on columns of pure light until it disappeared into the clouds.

Curious about the rods from God, I found a reasonably well-camouflaged observation post allowing me both a view in the direction of the Aeternum facility and the road from Ventano. Reasonably well camouflaged for oh-three hundred, that is. The combat helmet's night vision visor would have been quite useful. As I settled in, the last few hours seemed unreal, as if I'd experienced a particularly vivid dream.

The unexpected explosion fifteen minutes later — a bright flash followed by a rumble that shook the very ground I sat on — made the events of tonight all too real. Luca Derzin's Aeternum was gone, vaporized by a vengeful Fleet. Twenty minutes after the flash died away, a car coming from the north slowed as it neared the intersection, then stopped. Two figures climbed out, and even deprived of a night vision visor, I easily recognized Arno Galdi and Destine Bonta.

"Chief?"

"I'm here, Arno."

"Thank the Almighty and our friends in secret places."

— Thirty-Two —

"I'm sure you have quite the story to tell, Chief." Arno settled in beside me as Bonta closed the doors and turned us around for the return trip.

"And I'll tell it where I'm sure no one is listening."

"The good sergeant swept our car before we left Ventano. It's as clean as our suites. How are the shoulder and the old noggin?"

"The shoulder is stiff, but the noggin is fine. The ship's doc gave me a supply of analgesic patches, so I mostly don't think about it unless I make a wrong move."

"Good. What's your plan for returning from the dead?"

"You smuggle me into my quarters and let me sleep for a few hours. Tomorrow, we enjoy a peaceful and leisurely breakfast while the colony loses its collective mind over the destruction of the Aeternum facility by persons unknown."

"What will our theory about the perpetrators be?"

"Cartels. I'm sure ComCorp has experienced a few dustups with them in recent times, seeing as how its executives like to throw their weight around. What interests me is how the various players will react upon seeing my smiling face. Oh," I pulled the cassette from my pocket, "a copy of the Aeternum computer core, courtesy of Ghost Squadron's Erinye Company."

"Yes." Arno pumped a fist in the air. "Now, we'll nab the smarmy bastard."

"Only if we find actionable evidence."

As we drove, I recounted events from when I first woke up in my cell to the moment when I witnessed the kinetic penetrators vaporize Aeternum.

"Wow. I think you just beat your previous record for strange, Chief."

"I'm hoping this new record will remain unbroken, though I'll confess taking part in a raid with a unit from the 1st Special Forces Regiment took me back to simpler and happier days. You'd have loved it, Sergeant. It was like old home week, but with friends I just met."

"I'll bet. Next time, I should make sure the kidnappers take both of us."

"There won't be a next time. Not if I can help it. Your turn. What happened once the night shift came on and found an empty bed where a sore chief superintendent should be?"

"Ever seen what happens when you kick over an insect colony's nest, Chief? It was that but several orders of magnitude worse. Sheer bloody panic."

"What about the constable on duty outside my door?"

"He was snoring like a New Tasman sand devil with polyp problems. The hospital staff found him in a linen cabinet, drugged. Poor chap suffered from the mother of all headaches when he woke. Never noticed a thing, but they found a needler mark on his neck, like the one on Tosh's. Perhaps Mayleen Allore is still in town, shooting at people. But at least he'll live."

"Thank the Almighty for that."

"A nurse and two orderlies on the evening shift vanished and haven't been seen since. They were recent arrivals on Mission, hired through an employment agency which—"

I raised a hand. "Belongs to a ComCorp subsidiary."

"Got it in one, Chief. Naturally, the investigation is focusing on them. AC Braband's been dancing attendance on the governor since Saturday morning. The Rim Sector PCB commander vanishing on their watch isn't sitting well with either of them. Now about smuggling you into the base, the main gate's security AI will detect three bodies in this car."

"Tell me you brought my credentials."

"Along with your clothes and your sidearm. By the way, that piece of hand artillery is interesting." Arno pointed at my left hip.

"A gift from Ghost Squadron. They keep these on hand after re-boring them for human ammo. Untraceable."

"How nice of them. Will you keep it?"

"Of course, although it'll be a gun cabinet queen when we're back home. That thing is heavy. Sergeant, please find us a quiet lay-by. I'll change into my normal clothes and stow the Shrehari blaster in favor of my own gun. Our best bet to seem so boringly normal that whoever's playing for the other side will notice my tracks in the base's security system and suffer a brain aneurysm. But I don't think they'll try the long-range railgun sniper again. That was purely to get me beyond the perimeter and into the Pacifican State Security's hands. When I reappear in fifteen minutes or so, the guilty party will realize they failed and that I know who did it."

"Derzin."

"Without a doubt. The challenge now is finding proof."

"May I conclude we won't keep a low profile until Commissioner Sorjonen's arrival, Chief?"

"No one will fault us for going in hard after the events of the last forty-eight hours. I could say it's personal, but that would be sheer indulgence. How about we beat the iron while it's hot, to use an ancient cliché?"

"Beat it, we shall, and with enthusiasm."

Driving through nighttime Ventano wearing the business suit I'd worn when I was shot and carrying my much smaller, though no less deadly pistol, felt more than a little surreal after the events of the last two days. The city seemed so peaceful, so prim and proper, anyone but us wouldn't know about the rot beneath the surface. But rot there was — enough to threaten the integrity of the colonial government.

What would I do about it? That was another question altogether. It was still only three against an entire star system. Our Ghost Squadron friends would have broken out of orbit by now, headed for Caledonia and Fort Arnhem with another success under their belts. As per Captain Delgado, what happened next was my call. Commissioner Sorjonen wouldn't arrive until Wednesday or Thursday at best. That gave me three days.

We found sentries standing guard at the base's main gate for the first time since arriving on Mission. They stopped us and scrutinized our credentials. The duty sergeant's eyes widened when he recognized me.

"Not a word to anyone. You never saw me. Is that understood?"

"Yes, Chief Superintendent." He stepped away from the car and saluted, then waved us through.

"There wasn't anyone when we left," Arno said. "The strike on the Aeternum place must have everybody spooked. By the way, Chief, chances are the Ops Center will know you're back among us by now, despite you scaring the poor sergeant. They'll have your credentials red-flagged."

"Let's hope they don't or that the duty staff shrugs it off. The last thing I want right now is to run across AC Braband, let alone answer questions."

"And what will you tell the folks investigating your disappearance?"

Bonta pulled the car into its usual parking spot by the officers' quarters and switched off the power plant.

"That's what I've been wondering ever since the Marines rescued me. If I say I escaped Derzin's facility during the attack, then the investigators will immediately haul him in, and I'm not ready for that. I think it's simpler if I don't speak with them for now. Besides, the only one who can force me to answer questions is DCC Hammett, and when he arrives, Commissioner Sorjonen."

"In that case, we have to wrap this up before the Grand Inquisitor lands."

I never thought I'd be so happy to see my suite again, but I was. After stowing my Shrehari blaster and the data cassette in the gun safe — I decided it would be best if I kept my regular sidearm within reach — I took a quick shower, slapped on fresh analgesic patches, and slipped under the covers for a few hours of blissful sleep.

A gentle knock on the door woke me sometime after sunrise. I glanced at my timepiece. Oh-seven-thirty. Only half an hour left before the dining room closed until midday. I slipped on my gym clothes and lit up the hallway video feed. It was Arno and Sergeant Bonta, the latter carrying a covered tray.

"Good morning, Chief," Arno boomed as I opened the door. Sergeant Bonta chimed in.

"Good morning, and if that's my breakfast, you two are most welcome." I stepped aside and ushered them through. Bonta placed the tray on the table and produced a flask of coffee from a tunic pocket. "To what do I owe this unexpected and delightful delivery?"

Arno sat across from me and let out a snort of irritation.

"Everyone knows we brought you back in the middle of the night, so naturally, the investigators tasked with your disappearance buttonholed us when we entered the dining hall, demanding answers and to interview you right this morning — annoying little sods. I said you'd speak with them when you were ready and they should, under no circumstances, badger you, but they're probably waiting in ambush downstairs. They also asked where we picked you up, and I gave them the old no comment along with my best PCB stare. I think you're safe for now."

"What about Braband?" I took a bite of the breakfast sandwich. It tasted wonderful.

"He's heading for Government House shortly to attend an emergency committee meeting which will discuss the attack on Aeternum. I wager your abduction is the least of his worries right now. There's something else that might amuse you. A Navy patrol frigate, a proper one this time, is inbound. It contacted the Operations Center from the hyperlimit an hour ago. The dining hall was abuzz with the news."

I swallowed my bite and chased it with a sip of coffee. "Could be a coincidence, or maybe Captain Talyn diverted the frigate here at the same time as she rerouted our friends."

"Let's see." Arno scratched his beard. "Special ops do a hit and run on Mission. A few hours later, a patrol frigate unexpectedly appears. Nope. That's no coincidence. I think the Navy's here to control all in and outbound starship traffic and contain the situation."

"The inspector has a point, sir." Bonta, who'd been busying herself at my computer, looked up. "The Ops Center has satellite and drone imagery of the Aeternum site. I'll call it up on your display."

When the first image appeared, Arno let out a low whistle.

"There's nothing left but a gigantic hole. Doesn't even look like there's any debris worth mentioning around it. I don't think I've ever seen such comprehensive destruction. Braband's folks won't find much evidence. Certainly nothing that could point at Derzin's nefarious activities, which leaves the computer core dump they gave you."

"Only as a way of finding admissible evidence, don't forget."

We watched the images and videos with a sick fascination. There would probably not even be a trace of organic material left, which was just as well if the level 4 lab contained dangerous organisms. The road itself simply stopped short of where the outer perimeter fence once stood.

"Any idea what happened with the workers our friends dropped off on the other side of the crest?"

"The Ops Center log doesn't mention them, sir."

"Could be Derzin's people raced toward the facility right after it blew, picked the workers up along the way, and hid them. We passed a few large vehicles headed the other way after we retrieved you, Chief. No witnesses capable of telling the galaxy what was happening inside the place. No evidence of it either. Not that inconvenient for Derzin, if you except the countless millions of creds that went up in smoke."

"But it screwed up their plan to take control of this star system. Mission Colony now wears a big red target. It will suffer the scrutiny of the Colonial Office, our lot, and apparently the Navy if that frigate is here because of my message to Captain Talyn."

I shoved the rest of the sandwich into my mouth and chewed on it, mind racing, while I parsed the possibilities and their implications.

Was ComCorp really trying to take control of this star system by corrupting the administration? The Mission star system was a crossroads of sorts, and what I witnessed inside the Aeternum building represented a vast sum of untaxed, untraceable profits from illegal imports. In effect, Aeternum wasn't just a money-laundering operation, it engaged in product laundering. A brilliant idea if it weren't for meddlesome PCB investigators. Or rather, a sour-faced governor complaining about the local police chief's rudeness toward her, which resulted in nosy investigators showing up unannounced.

Derzin's operation must have been putting a lot of money in the ComCorp coffers already. With the local government under his thumb, that flow of income might have turned into a torrent. Perhaps even enough to help replenish zaibatsu coffers suffering under the double whammy of increasingly powerful cartels and a Fleet hellbent on cleaning up the Commonwealth against Earth's wishes.

"Let's look at what was in Aeternum's computer core."

— Thirty-Three —

"Military-grade encryption, sir," Bonta sat back, frowning. "This won't be simple."

"It never is." I had carefully changed into my work clothes, the ones with the puncture-proof weave, while she and Arno took their first stab at Aeternum's data. The bruises were still vivid, though the pain was receding.

"I'm running it against known ciphers. With any luck, we'll find a partial match that can give us a starting point."

"How long?"

"Hours. Perhaps even days."

Arno gave me a curious look. "I know that expression, Chief. You're contemplating something that would make a normal cop's hairs stand on end."

"Maybe."

I couldn't quite see the idea forming in the back of my mind just yet, but I felt an unbearable urge to use the current crisis as my lever and break the case wide open. The question was finding the right fulcrum.

Go at it the wrong way, and I could bugger everything up, which wouldn't put me on Commissioner Sorjonen's good side. I either backed off now and handed everything over, or I presented him with a neatly wrapped solution, ready for prosecution. Anything in between simply wasn't worth contemplating.

"What say I join the emergency committee meeting?"

Arno rubbed his hands gleefully. "A splendid idea. I'll drive. The good sergeant certainly doesn't want us breathing down her neck while she wrestles with corporate cryptography."

The sergeant at Government House's front gate was both apologetic and a tad fearful as he told us no unauthorized personnel were allowed past the guard post, even after scanning our credentials.

"Inspector Galdi and I are hardly unauthorized. Surely someone with your years of service knows the PCB can enter any federal installation without requiring special permission."

"Yes, Chief Superintendent. But Assistant Commissioner Braband gave strict orders no one except the governor's staff could enter Government House."

"His orders don't include us because he has no jurisdiction over PCB officers. Now let us in and don't call ahead. I enjoy surprising people and become annoyed when said surprise is ruined by loose lips."

The sergeant hesitated for a fraction of a second, then drew himself to attention. He gestured at the guard to open the gate, then saluted.

As we entered the grounds, Arno chortled and said, "It must feel good to be known as the Lady High Executioner."

"Our reputation has its uses." We parked alongside AC Braband's staff car and climbed out. "Best if I go into the meeting alone. Snoop around a little and spread some of that grandfatherly charm. I'm curious about the mood in the administration this morning."

"Will do."

We split up inside the lobby. I headed for the conference room while he sauntered off toward Brionne Milton's office. The door was ajar, and Governor Peet's voice reached my ears before I got there. She did not sound happy.

I pushed the door wide open and walked in. Peet fell silent, staring at me in disbelief. Whether it was because of my miraculous return or my rudeness at crashing her meeting, I couldn't tell. The folks around the table seemed equally stunned, though I thought I saw amusement in Rudel's eyes. Braband, on the other hand, kept a stony expression, showing neither approval nor disapproval.

"Good morning, everyone. Considering the events of last night, I think it's proper that an officer from Rim Sector HQ participates in this little conflab." I took one of the empty chairs and sat, uninvited. "Please go on, Madame. I'm only here as an observer."

I could see Peet swallowing choice words as her jaw muscles worked, but in the end, she realized I wasn't leaving. And no Constabulary member would escort the sector PCB commander out of the room under duress. She cleared her throat, visibly irritated, and wishing I would vanish in a puff of smoke.

"Well, then. As I was saying, this is the worst incident on Mission Colony since the Shrehari war last century, an attack that destroyed one of our leading industrial facilities."

More like leading smuggler's nest, but it wasn't yet time for the truth. I listened to Peet spout platitudes for almost ten minutes and wondered what this emergency committee thought it was doing in the first place. She noticed my sardonic expression because her face became even more pinched.

"Any insights you'd like to share with us, Chief Superintendent? As a Sector HQ officer, you surely know more about this sort of thing than the rest of us."

"Insights? No. Theories, yes. Commercial warfare is as old as humanity, and endemic on the frontier, especially nowadays. My guess is a cartel involved in the pharmaceutical business, legal or otherwise, struck Aeternum to remove a powerful rival. The money involved in pharmaceuticals is astronomical, more than enough justification for hiring a mercenary outfit. Now that they accomplished their goal, taking Aeternum off the board, they won't be back. If you're worried about the colony's immediate safety, don't be. Especially not with a Navy frigate on final approach."

I met Braband's eyes and saw nothing in them. His gaze was as stony as that of the founder's statue in the main square. Was he annoyed that the governor called on an officer he outranked, one imposed on him by a distant HQ and who enjoyed the reputation of abruptly ending careers? Or was something else bothering him?

"You're remarkably well informed." I didn't know whether Peet meant it as a comment or a snide remark. Her sour expression never wavered. "Would you care to tell us about your mysterious disappearance on Friday, abducted by parties unknown, and your equally strange reappearance this morning, as if nothing happened?"

"No."

She went from ordinary sour to antimatter sour. "What do you mean, no?"

"The events since I was shot on Friday, including the assassination attempt, are under PCB investigation. We do not discuss our cases outside of the Bureau, for obvious reasons."

"They might be obvious to you."

"Revealing information about the cases we investigate before we make arrests might pervert the course of justice."

Peet sat back and stared at me with basilisk eyes. "Pervert the course of justice. Heavens above, what a bizarre choice of words."

"That is the term used by the Commonwealth Criminal Code, Madame. It covers acts that could compromise enforcement of the law or compromise investigations into lawbreakers. For example, once I arrest whoever is responsible for my abduction, perverting the course of justice is one of the charges I will lay. The same will apply to any member of the colonial administration involved."

"Surely you don't think—"

I raised a restraining hand.

"What I think is neither here nor there. The facts are what they are. Something stinks on Mission Colony, Madame, and I will find the source. It's what we do, and we're exceedingly good at rooting out corruption. The Constabulary doesn't take an assassination attempt on a senior officer lightly either, let alone a successful kidnapping." I turned my gaze on Braband. "Right, sir?"

He gave me a tight nod. "Right."

"In fact, we take official corruption so seriously, my superior, Deputy Chief Constable Hammett, has dispatched a full PCB investigative team from the Political Anti-Corruption Unit. This unit is under the command of Commissioner Taneli Sorjonen, a legend in my branch of the service." I could have sworn I saw the blood drain from Braband's face, though his deep tan played tricks on my perception. "The commissioner and his people will arrive in a few days."

Peet gave me a silent sniff. "I'm sure your commissioner will find this colonial administration has nothing to hide."

"On the contrary, Madame. There are dark secrets on Mission, the likes of which I've rarely seen. Never, in my decades with the Constabulary, have I been an assassin's target. Nor did I ever see a large-scale industrial complex obliterated by unknown forces from orbit."

I looked around the table, watching for reactions. Rudel still seemed slyly amused; Peet appeared even more offended; Braband stonier and the rest of the senior staff thoroughly puzzled.

"I resent your insinuations about my governance of this star system, Chief Superintendent, and I shall make my displeasure clear when this commissioner of yours arrives, be sure of it."

"That is your prerogative, Madame." If Sorjonen had earned Arno Galdi's undying respect, I figure he'd take Peet's displeasure and turn it into a full-blown inspection of her private life. But why say so and spoil the surprise? "Will you and this committee interview Mister Derzin to determine the effect of last night's attack?"

"Since you're an intruder and not a member, this committee's intentions are none of your business."

I gave her a sad smile. "And here I thought we were getting along so well."

Peet reared up. "I never encountered anyone as impertinent as you."

"That's because I'm the first PCB chief superintendent you've met. We're a force of nature which respects neither rank nor position."

"I noticed. Assistant Commissioner, is there nothing you can do to restrain this officer?"

Braband gave me a look I couldn't interpret, then shook his head.

"Different chains of command and lines of authority, Madame, the sort I cannot cross. If you wish, I can lodge a complaint with Commissioner Sorjonen when he gets here. Not quite the same chain of command, but the lines of authority are there."

"Please do."

Now that was a fascinating development — Braband helping Peet sideline me after she complained to Maras about him. What did I do that offended him? Other than name his now-vanished lover, a prime person of interest in Amaris Tosh's murder?

I speared Braband with my patented internal affairs stare. "Will the 24th search the impact site for clues, sir?"

He gave me a look that combined exasperation and fatigue.

"We are negotiating with Mister Derzin for access."

"Under the circumstances, Mister Derzin has no say in the matter. His facility, or rather the crater that replaced it, is a crime scene, which means we enjoy unfettered access despite any objections he might raise."

"His certificate of exemption from the Commonwealth government proves otherwise."

Why was Braband going along with Derzin and Peet's charade suddenly? Something didn't add up. Then, another piece of the puzzle clicked into place. But I didn't know what it meant. Could the exemption be related to the level 4 biohazard facility whose airlock-like entrance I saw? Was a faction in the federal government running or subsidizing rogue bioresearch? If so, why and to what end? Captain Talyn would surely pursue the matter with her resources once Delgado sent her his after-action report. I pulled out my communicator and placed it on the table.

"Why don't we call Mister Derzin right now and let him know that what was his exempt premises is now our crime scene, and investigators are on their way."

A faint scowl appeared on Braband's face.

"This is my jurisdiction, Chief Superintendent, and last night's strike on a commercial facility is not in the PCB's remit. I will, therefore, decide how we handle that crime scene."

"I could construe anything less than a full forensic examination of the site as a dereliction of duty."

"Then it seems I am stuck between a rock and a hard place, Chief Superintendent. Because of the exemption, I cannot send my people to examine the crime scene absent Mister Derzin's cooperation. Yet, by not overriding Mister Derzin, I place myself in your crosshairs. Is that an accurate summation of our current standoff?"

The air of disbelief on Peet's pinched face as she watched me apply pressure on a superior officer would have been amusing at any other time.

"To a point, sir. As I am not under your command and don't care about Derzin's exemption, I will investigate the scene with Inspector Galdi and Sergeant Bonta. I would appreciate your placing a forensics team under my command."

He stared at me in silence for several heartbeats. "And if I refuse or try to stop you, I suppose you'll unleash the full power of the PCB on me."

"You know how this works, sir. Your cooperation is unnecessary, though it would be much appreciated."

"Then I ask for a written statement I warned you about the exemption, but you proceeded nonetheless."

"Certainly."

— Thirty-Four —

"I suppose it's too soon for a proposal they rename the site Aeternum Crater," Arno muttered when Sergeant Bonta stopped our car in the same spot as almost two weeks ago. At the same time, the forensics van, with Inspector Kosta aboard, pulled in behind us.

The images and video feed didn't do justice to the degree of devastation. There was simply nothing left. The building and adjoining tarmac were gone, vaporized, both the inner and outer fences along with the remote weapon stations had vanished, as had several meters of topsoil and rock. I estimated the crater's diameter at a good two hundred meters — rods from God. Heaven help us if someone ever uses them against population centers.

"You realize we won't find a damn thing, Chief."

"Yes. But we're not here because I expect Inspector Kosta to uncover something we can use as admissible evidence. I know perfectly well what happened. We're here as a matter of principle and as a way of rattling Derzin. The more I think of it, the more I figure the exemption is related to the illegal level 4 biohazard facility. Organ and drug smuggling

279

were highly profitable sidelines, if not a deliberate cover in case nosy cops smelled something. But the only way we'll find out is by cracking the data dump's encryption or convincing someone to talk."

"We'll need both, Chief. You know, if I were Derzin, I'd be looking for a quick starship out of here, now that his operation is history."

"Him and others, no doubt. However, I'll wager the frigate is here so that none of the principal actors in this drama escape before we close the net."

"Captain Talyn is thorough, I'll say that for her."

I turned my head and smiled at Arno. "Captain Talyn considers us on her team, working for the same ends, albeit less radically and more lawfully."

"Do you think DCC Hammett knows?"

"Possibly. I'm sure we're not the only sector PCB unit working with the Fleet." I waved at the crater. "Let's go as far as we can and watch Inspector Kosta take sensor readings."

We parked a few meters short of where the road ended abruptly. The forensics van did the same, then Kosta and six technicians climbed out. We joined them at the crater's edge.

"Kinetic strike from orbit," Kosta said by way of greeting. "It's the only explanation. Impressive, but I fear our trip here is in vain. Nothing will have survived. We'll run a full sensor survey nonetheless, if only for due diligence."

"Thank you."

As they deployed, I tried to reconstruct the facility and recall where everything once was, yet without any visual markers, not even the bare ground, my attempt failed miserably. Part of me wished our friends hadn't thoroughly destroyed the place if only so we could show the galaxy what sort of criminal enterprise Aeternum really was.

Yet I understood the need to terminate operations of this sort with extreme prejudice before more innocents were hurt. Especially in the face of a legal system that was, to a certain extent, compromised by both zaibatsus and organized criminals and could, therefore, not be entirely trusted. Working as a cop these days wasn't for the faint of heart, and I realized my own long-standing principles had taken a beating since I first encountered Captain Talyn and learned about the secret war for humanity's future. Needs must when the devil drives, and he's been running rampant across our insignificant part of the galaxy in recent times. The low whine of an approaching aircar reached my ears, and I figured it could only be Derzin. Good. Time for the next act in this little drama.

I turned my back on the crater and watched the sleek, expensive aircar glide to a gentle landing behind our vehicles. As expected, when one of the aft doors opened, Luca Derzin stepped out. As usual, he was expensively dressed, but his face no longer wore its usual half-mocking, half-sardonic expression. I walked up to where he was parked, so Kosta and his people couldn't overhear our conversation.

"You are trespassing, Chief Superintendent. Didn't Braband make it clear this is an exempt site, one which even the Constabulary cannot enter without my express permission?"

"When an exempt site becomes a crime scene, the senior officer present can override the exemption."

"You're not the senior officer on Mission Colony. Braband is."

"I'm the senior PCB officer on Mission and not in Braband's chain of command. Ergo, I can override the exemption in the interests of justice." We locked eyes. I didn't know what he saw in mine, but I could read cold fury in his. "Besides, whatever you were hiding is gone, so I don't see why you're still insisting. You of all people should realize it only makes me dig around even more."

"Leave before I see that your career ends in disgrace."

I laughed derisively. "You couldn't even arrange for my career to end in an unmarked Pacifican State Security grave. Why should I worry about empty threats?"

"I'm sure I don't understand what you mean, Chief Superintendent."

"Please don't insult my intelligence, Derzin. I'm sure hearing about my return from the dead gave you quite a shock, although perhaps not as big a shock as hearing about Aeternum's eradication. You and I both know what happened last Friday, and what you intended for me."

An ugly smile appeared. "The abyss between knowing and proving is often unbridgeable, such as now. Very well. Play your little police games, then leave."

"Thank you. And please don't try to leave the planet without my permission. Until we sort this out, you're a material witness."

"Witness or victim?" He gestured at the crater behind me. "I'd say the latter. Besides, you can't restrict my movements without a warrant."

"I don't need a warrant. If you disregard my order, I will arrest and jail you."

Rage flared in his eyes as his nostrils whitened. "You do not understand who you're messing with, Morrow."

"Apparently, neither do you. Aeternum is gone forever and the Pacifican State Security goon — what was his name again? Senior Special Agent Idris Orloski? In any case, his body is in a decaying orbit around Mission and will eventually burn up on re-entry. Think for a moment what it means that I'm alive, still running my investigation, and he's as dead as your business. Surely you were told the moment the Black Nova aviso with Orloski and me aboard lifted off Saturday evening. Yet here I am, alive and well, taunting you. What happened to your employees, by the way? They were last seen on the road to Ventano, far from the facility when it was vaporized."

"None of your business."

"On the contrary. They witnessed last night's events." I jerked my left thumb over my shoulder. "We must speak to them."

"The exemption covers my employees."

"Which isn't worth the paper it's printed on at this point. Either grant us access to your employees, or I will arrest you for perverting the course of justice."

He sneered most unattractively. "You don't have the power."

"And you still don't understand. In this star system, I can wield as much power as a deputy chief constable, and I can call on friends in high places." I pointed at the sky. "Trust me when I say I know precisely what Aeternum was up to. Fortunately for you, there's that abyss between knowing and proving, but I always nab my man. Let me make one thing crystal clear. If anything happens to me from now on, you will disappear without a trace. My people will ensure it."

"Oh, dear." He made a face. "Now that sounds like a threat your bureau should investigate."

He pulled out his communicator. "Thankfully, I recorded our conversation for the benefit of whoever will investigate you for misconduct."

"Try listening to the recording. Go ahead. I'll wait."

Derzin tapped the screen, but nothing more than static came through. He looked up at me with an angry, albeit puzzled expression. I pulled my favorite jamming device from my coat pocket.

"Surely you didn't believe I'd engage in an open conversation without taking precautions. You've underestimated me at every turn, Derzin. Stop while you're ahead. I'm sure ComCorp will pay for the best lawyers once I charge you. Don't compound your list of mistakes. You wouldn't enjoy meeting the people who seized that aviso, which, by the way, is no longer registered to Black Nova."

I tapped my chin with an extended finger.

"Now that I think of it, your ComCorp bosses might not spring for the best lawyers. Thanks to your hubris, that expensive facility with its lucrative contents are gone, as is an equally expensive and oh so useful aviso along with any chance of ComCorp turning Mission Colony into a wholly owned fief. Now you're facing the inevitable consequence — nemesis."

He made a dismissive hand gesture. "You're rambling like an idiot, spinning ludicrous theories out of thin air. As I said, you have no proof. Be smart. Declare victory and go home."

"Tell me, which federal agency is covering for you? That unregistered and therefore illegal level 4 biohazard facility was surely the reason for the exemption certificate. Your top cover must be pretty high up in the federal government." I enjoyed watching him blanch at the mention of the level 4 lab. "Like I said, you don't understand who you're messing with."

"Again, no proof, since everything is gone."

"Say, you wouldn't be playing footsie with the SecGen's *Sécurité Spéciale* now, would you? That seems to happen a lot inside your zaibatsu." Judging by his expression, I'd hit another bullseye. "You realize they don't like loose ends, especially failures. If I were you, I'd reflect on my future, and what I could do so I had one. You have until tomorrow to produce the employees working here at the time of the attack. Enjoy the rest of your day."

I turned on my heels and rejoined my team, all the while feeling Derzin's eyes burning holes in my back.

"How did it go, Chief?"

"I hope I scared him into doing something stupid. By the way, if ever his minions try to kill me again, take Mister Derzin out of circulation."

"You mean—" Arno made a slicing gesture across his throat.

"No. But I hope he saw you do that just now. I told him you and the sergeant would make sure he vanished for good if ever something did happen. I'd rather not spend the rest of our stay here wondering when the next sniper round will come."

We heard the aircar lift off and fade into the distance.

"I got what I came for. Let's head home and work on that data dump."

When we reached the base's main gate, the duty sergeant informed me AC Braband wanted a minute of my time the moment I returned.

— Thirty-Five —

"That was quite the performance you put on in Government House this morning, Chief Superintendent." Braband studied me with eyes devoid of emotion. He pointedly did not offer me a seat, but I took one of the chairs in front of his desk, nonetheless, triggering a brief frown of displeasure.

"Sir?"

"I am debating whether I should lodge a formal complaint against you with DCC Maras, for onward transmission to your superior."

"That would be your prerogative, sir. Keep in mind you opened yourself to dereliction of duty charges and an investigation into why you weren't taking control of the crime scene. I understand the dilemma you faced and solved it for you. That will be in my report to DCC Hammett."

He sat back and briefly glanced down at his desktop. "Well, perhaps it's not worth a formal complaint, but I will discuss the matter with Commissioner Sorjonen."

"You may do as you wish, sir."

"When were you going to tell me about his arrival?"

"When I deemed it appropriate. Turns out that was this morning."

"What happened to you over the weekend? I don't believe in miracles, not even when they involve the sainted PCB." A hint of sarcasm? That was new. "Why do I suspect you were somehow involved with the people who destroyed Aeternum?"

"I couldn't tell you, sir. My policy is avoiding unfortunate involvements."

"Someone kidnapped you on Friday, late in the evening, and somehow you reappeared in the middle of the night a little over forty-eight hours later, as if you'd merely been on a weekend getaway. The investigation into your disappearance is active and under my jurisdiction. You owe me answers."

"And I would like to cooperate, but any answer I might give is covered by a security classification so high that no one in this star system, save for my team, has the right clearance. Sorry, sir. There's more to PCB investigations than anyone can imagine, and they sometimes take us into the rarefied realm of Top-Secret Special Access."

Exasperation finally broke through his icy mien.

"You truly are a law unto yourself, Morrow, aren't you? How is it we wear the same uniform but don't share the same values? You wouldn't get away with ninety percent of what you do if it weren't for the PCB mantle."

I shrugged.

"Search me. Life choices, I suppose. Since becoming a garbage collector doesn't pay as much as a PCB chief superintendent, I figured taking out human trash was the better choice."

He gave me a surprised look.

"Is that what you think of your fellow officers who've made a misstep? Trash?"

"Trust me. By the time I cuff them, they've made more than a mere misstep. We're talking terrible life choices piled one on top of another. Bent cops, corrupt bureaucrats, venal politicians, they usually carry on for years until they make one fatal mistake which attracts my attention, and that mistake is always because of hubris. No, Commissioner, those I've arrested deserved their fate, including the ones who were executed for capital crimes. My calling them trash is proper. They swore an oath and then crapped on it for personal gain."

Yes, I was provoking him. Something about his demeanor in the last few days bothered me. I wanted to see how far I could take it before he snapped.

"And PCB officers wonder why everyone in the service hates them. I hoped you were better than this, Morrow, but I was wrong."

"I'm no better or worse than any other member of the Constabulary. My team and I do a necessary job and do it to the best of our abilities. If the PCB didn't exist, you'd be fighting corruption with one hand tied behind your back and wonder why civilians don't trust the Constabulary. By the way, I've ordered Luca Derzin to stay on Mission Colony under pain of arrest and incarceration."

He reared up. "You what? Under whose authority? Or did you forget I run the police in this system? Derzin is a civilian and, therefore, not part of your remit."

"He's a material witness and showed up at the site while we were there, so I took advantage of the moment. You'd do the same under the circumstances, no doubt. I also gave him until tomorrow to produce the Aeternum employees who mysteriously vanished after escaping their attackers."

"How do you know they escaped and weren't vaporized?" I gave him a knowing look, and a faint air of disgust briefly twisted his features. "Your Top-Secret Special Access classification covers the answer, no doubt."

"You're catching on, Commissioner. Luca Derzin is not a nice person. You already know that. But he's actually a worse human being than you can ever imagine, and I'm worried he might consider the survivors of last night's attack unwanted witnesses."

"Do you seriously figure Derzin would murder the Almighty knows how many of his employees? That's preposterous."

"Aeternum's parent zaibatsu is ruthless and has a lengthy history of tying up unfortunate loose ends. We've just never found proof that would satisfy a prosecutor, assuming we could find one willing to go up against ComCorp." For a moment, I caught a glimmer of worry in his eyes.

"We? Wouldn't that sort of thing belong to Major Crimes rather than the PCB?"

I gave him a wintry smile. "You'd be amazed how many federal officials are corrupted by the zaibatsus and cartels. A few even live long enough to face a judge, though most become loose ends."

"You mean some of them are assassinated? I find that incredible."

And I couldn't fathom an assistant commissioner so naïve, but then, I saw the seamy underside of the federal leviathan every day. At his current level, he was no more than an administrator with a badge.

"Either killed by the people who paid them handsomely or taken off the board by a Fleet sniper because they might escape justice altogether. Yes, Commissioner, it's becoming chaotic and violent. The side that stands for law and order will lose if it doesn't adopt the enemy's tactics, techniques, and procedures."

For a moment, I couldn't quite believe I was saying it aloud in front of anyone other than my team. He obviously couldn't either.

"Aren't you appalled by that state of things, Chief Superintendent? You spoke of bent cops crapping on their oath. I don't see how condoning the adoption of criminal TTPs is any different."

"It hinges on the outcome, I suppose. The zaibatsus, ComCorp chief among them, are part of a faction that wants to make the Commonwealth something you and I would neither recognize nor wish to serve, a corpocratic empire. Those fighting them in the shadows, so we don't face a third migration war, are winning, but only because they act with more ruthlessness than the enemy. And make no mistake, Luca Derzin belongs to the enemy faction, as do those who fall for his blandishments and sell out."

He said nothing for several seconds. "You make it sound like we're already in a civil war."

"That's because we are. Only the battles are still being fought in the background, by black ops units and undercover agents. Remember the New Oberon incident?"

"Yes."

"That was one of those battles."

He tilted his head to one side and narrowed his eyes. "Are you saying last night's destruction of the Aeternum facility was another battle in this hidden civil war?"

"I can neither confirm nor deny it. However, Mission Colony is a battleground, though I didn't realize it until recently. In that light, my abduction was not a criminal undertaking but hostile action by an enemy who feels threatened. Unfortunately, I still don't know who is on their side other than Luca Derzin and his minions."

Braband shook his head. "I can't figure whether I should be alarmed or recommend you see a psychiatrist. What you're telling me is rather hard to swallow."

"I felt the same when I first came across one of the black ops people fighting this war and who is now a senior Fleet officer. Yet hearing her put it the way I just did, made sense of so many strange events and trends I'd noticed. Give it some thought, Commissioner. You might find my words easier to digest." My communicator pinged at that moment. Arno. I flicked it on. "What's up?"

"We just received the detailed background check on Mayleen Allore from New Tasman, Chief. If you're still with the AC, he might find this interesting."

I glanced at him and saw his face light up with curiosity.

"I'm with the AC. Go ahead."

"There is no Mayleen Allore. Someone created a legend for her on New Tasman, but she's only ever existed in the government registries. Those who supposedly lived next door to the Allore family or attended school with her never heard that name." Which confirmed Captain Talyn's advice to forget about Mayleen. "Thank you, Inspector. Was there anything else?"

"Nothing that can't wait until your return."

"Morrow, out." I put the communicator away and studied Braband, searching for a reaction. "Does that help you believe me? The woman who called herself Allore is another soldier in the secret war. But on the opposite side."

Braband let out a heartfelt sigh. "Which means I was literally sleeping with the enemy."

"You weren't the first and won't be the last." I stood. "If there's nothing else…"

"No." He swiveled his chair to face the windows without so much as a thank you or a goodbye. This was clearly a troubled man.

As I crossed the parade square, my heart beat a little faster than usual, in large part because I instinctively feared a repeat of last Friday. The attempt to see me murdered by Pacifican State Security might have failed, but Derzin wasn't the sort who would heed my warnings. He possessed the overweening arrogance of a sociopath who thought he was untouchable. I felt an uncomfortable twinge of relief upon entering the officers' quarters.

Once in my suite, I recounted the conversation with Braband almost verbatim for my team's benefit.

"I'm curious, Chief. Why tell him about the black ops shenanigans?"

"Instinct. Something about Braband's been bothering me since last week, and I can't figure out what. Perhaps I decided a jolt of ugly reality might help."

"Your instincts are better than most investigators' intellects. That's what makes you such a fearsome PCB unit commander."

"Flattery will get you everywhere. Anything new on cracking the data dump's encryption?"

Bonta shook her head. "Sorry, sir. The algorithm comparison is still running."

"Then back to the data dig so rudely interrupted by Derzin's sniper."

— Thirty-Six —

"I will hazard an unprovable theory, Chief," Arno said when we settled at our usual table in the Steele Club that evening. "If colonial administration members are being corrupted by Derzin, then the currency isn't necessarily wealth. We've run through the affairs of most garden party attendees, save for the topmost officials, and found bupkis."

"You figure influence instead of numbered accounts in distant star systems, right?"

"Or perhaps both. Derzin, through his ComCorp masters and their pet politicians, can reach into the machinery of government and make good things happen for those who cooperate. For example, get Peet a promotion to assistant colonial secretary or Bisso an associate judgeship on the supreme court. Ambition has been the downfall of many previously honest officials. More so than greed for filthy lucre, and easier to feed without leaving traces for inquisitive inquisitors such as we three. Plus, maneuvering people they own into positions of influence gets them a tighter grip on government. It's a win-win all the way. If

Derzin gave them hush money as well, it'll be as insurance and only accessible upon retirement."

Our drinks arrived at that moment, the bartender by now preparing them the moment he saw us enter. When he left, I took a sip of my gin and tonic before staring into the glass as an uncomfortable idea, triggered by Arno's words, surfaced.

"We should look into the career prospects of the 24th Regiment's senior officers."

"You figure Derzin is whispering sweet promises of promotion into the ears of those with poor advancement prospects after a tour here?"

"It is one of the oldest forms of police corruption. We've encountered many a chief superintendent who'd gladly mortgage his or her soul for one final chance at assistant commissioner. And from there, a coveted star on the collar."

"True. Do you figure Braband might sell his for that star?"

"The notion has crossed my mind in recent days. We can vet an officer's career to a fare-thee-well and declare him clean without knowing his deepest aspirations and most crushing disappointments. Perhaps Maras told him the 24th would be his last command, and Derzin offered to put in a kind word just because he could, and Braband seemed like a splendid fellow. Demands for quid pro quo would come later. Braband's relationship with Derzin might not be as advertised."

"Or Mayleen Allore served as go-between as well as a honey pot, to provide plausible deniability. Braband spoke of pillow talk. Perhaps he shared his dreams and ambitions with her and gave Derzin a way in, even if it wasn't directly. Remember, we only have his word about his dealings with and opinion of Derzin. Or of Peet, for that matter. She's unpleasant and entitled, but that doesn't make her bent. Otherwise, half the federal bureaucracy would finally do hard labor, but in a prison colony on Parth."

I took another sip. "Are we guilty of hubris, Arno?"

"By giving Braband a pass because we vetted him, and we never make mistakes? Quite possibly. We forgot everyone has a price. For most of us, fortunately, the price is such no one can pay it. Others might enjoy blameless careers until someone makes them an offer they can't refuse."

"Derzin meeting Braband's price is an unpleasant thought. I hope we'll not face our nemesis because of it."

"How do we figure this out, sir?"

I gave Bonta a helpless smile. "By doing what we always do. Keep digging, prodding, and pushing until the weakest link snaps."

"Ah, but finding the weakest link, now that's the challenge, Chief. Shall we open a betting pool on who it might be?"

"Are you suggesting we gamble in a Constabulary mess? I'm shocked, Arno, shocked."

He put on a mock wounded expression and placed his hand over his heart.

"I'm hurt you'd even consider for a second I was proposing we'd gamble for money. Bragging rights, that's what I meant."

"Let's dig a bit more, then we can speculate on who might break."

Our first potential candidate showed up in the middle of the night when my communicator woke me with an urgent call from the Operations Center.

"Morrow, here."

"The captain of the Commonwealth Starship *Rodrigo Diaz* wishes to speak with you, Chief Superintendent."

It took me a few seconds before remembering *Rodrigo Diaz*, nicknamed *El Cid*, was the patrol frigate in orbit.

"Put him through."

A few seconds passed, then, "Chief Superintendent Morrow, I'm Commander Tiberius Archer. I was sent here with orders we intercept and inspect all ships arriving or leaving and look for certain people and certain things. We just arraigned a private yacht, registered to a Black Nova subsidiary, which lifted off from the Ventano Spaceport carrying one Luca Derzin, whose name is on the list. My orders say I should contact you if we get a hit."

"Thank you, Captain. Derzin is indeed a person of interest. Less than twenty-four hours ago, I forbade him from leaving Mission Colony, since he's a material witness in a serious incident. Could you please place him under arrest, see that he trades his clothes for coveralls and deck shoes from your stores, then arrange for his transfer to the 24th Constabulary Regiment's detention facility? And when you hand him over, I'd rather they didn't see his face. A pillowcase as hood would do. I'll be at the landing pad and take care of him from thereon."

"Extraordinary rendition protocol, eh? With pleasure. I've not come across a snottier yacht owner or passenger in my entire career. Threatened to take my stripes, if you believe it."

"Oh, I do. Mister Derzin is a nasty customer. I'll warn the 24th they should expect a shuttle on the pad before daybreak."

"Excellent, Chief Superintendent. My apologies for waking you."

"No apologies necessary. You did me an immense favor by intercepting Derzin. What happens with his yacht?"

"Since it didn't cooperate at first, then was found to carry someone who shouldn't be leaving Mission Colony without authorization, I'm seizing it as a prize."

At this rate, I'd be responsible for Black Nova losing a fair amount of tonnage, and that just broke my heart.

"If we should ever meet in person in or near a place dispensing fine drinks, the first few rounds are on me."

"I look forward to it. *Rodrigo Diaz*, out."

"Operations Center, this is Chief Superintendent Morrow."

A pause.

"Inspector Lestrade. I have the duty."

"*Rodrigo Diaz* will send down a shuttle carrying a man arrested at my orders. Give it priority landing on the base's pad and see a proper escort meets it and accompanies the detainee to the base's cellblock. I will be in attendance, so please inform me the moment you know the shuttle's estimated time of arrival."

"Yes, sir. What is the prisoner's name?"

"Since I'm detaining him under a national security certificate, his name will remain classified until further notice."

"Understood, sir. Was there anything else?"

"No, Inspector. Thank you. Morrow, out."

I was fully awake by now. The dumb bugger tried to run, as sure an admission of guilt as anything. Did Derzin not know about the frigate in orbit, or was he so arrogant he believed the yacht could outrun it? And did I wake my team now or wait for the Ops Center's ETA on the shuttle? I opted for the latter. Just because I was keyed up by the idea of interrogating Derzin on Constabulary turf didn't justify interrupting their sleep prematurely. First, fill in that national security certificate and fire it off to both Wyvern and Cimmeria.

Inspector Lestrade called back half an hour later with the ETA. I woke Arno and Sergeant Bonta and brought them up to speed. When we reached the base's landing pad, a sergeant and two constables were waiting patiently in the early morning gloom. Upon seeing me, the sergeant called his people to attention and saluted.

"Detainee escort ready, Chief Superintendent."

I returned his compliments with a formal nod since we were in civilian clothes.

"Thank you, Sergeant."

We kept our eyes on a night sky devoid of clouds. I spotted the shuttle first — a black shape occluding the background stars — but I didn't say a word. Call it conceit if you like. I've always worked at keeping a better situational awareness than most, something I learned from my early years looking over my shoulder for Pacifican State Security goons.

Moments later, the shuttle fired its thrusters, a sure giveaway. We watched it land in silence. Contrary to Erinye Company's dropships, this one bore a registration number along with markings identifying it as one of *Rodrigo Diaz*'s small craft.

Once the thrusters spooled down, the aft ramp dropped, and three figures emerged from a red-lit passenger compartment. Two spacers in naval battledress and one figure in coveralls with a cloth hood over his head. Derzin. I recognized his shape. He was manacled at the wrists, but his legs were free. I heard indistinct sounds coming from beneath his hood as if he were muzzled.

The sergeant nodded, and his constables met the spacers at the foot of the ramp where they took charge of Derzin and a bag containing his personal effects. The constables marched him off while the spacers retreated into their craft. Its aft ramp rose, and I heard the whine of spooling thrusters. We turned away and followed the sergeant to the cellblock.

When we entered, the duty NCO, sitting behind a waist-high counter, stood.

"I am Chief Superintendent Caelin Morrow, head of the Rim Sector Professional Compliance Bureau." I pointed at Derzin. "I am detaining this individual under a national security certificate. You will not enter him into the records. I want him held in solitary confinement, where no one other than myself, Inspector Arno Galdi, and Master Sergeant Destine Bonta enter his cell or communicate with him. You will handle food and water under no-contact protocols. If the detainee suffers a medical emergency, you will contact one of us for instructions and not enter the cell without permission. Do you understand my orders?"

He didn't seem happy, but he nodded once. "Yes, Chief Superintendent."

I sympathized with his lack of enthusiasm. No one with a functioning set of ethics and values liked national security certificates. They circumvented several laws protecting citizens from overzealous police and military personnel. In Derzin's case, I was stretching not only my authority to issue one but also the limited circumstances in which they were permissible without a judge's prior approval. And I could keep Derzin under the certificate for only seventy-two hours, after which I would either charge or release him.

The duty NCO came out from behind the counter. "If you'll follow me."

He led us, Derzin and the two constables, into the cellblock and along a corridor, which ended at an airlock-like door. We went through it and found ourselves in the isolation wing were the cells were vacant. The NCO pointed at the first one on our left.

"In there, please, Chief Superintendent."

The constables escorting Derzin led him in, handed the bag with his clothes to Sergeant Bonta, then left along with the non-com. When I heard the airlock close, I walked up to Derzin and removed the hood from his head. Chalk one up for Captain Archer. His people had slapped a muzzle across Derzin's mouth, so he couldn't speak and identify himself. I left it on for the moment but prodded him to sit on the cell's single bunk.

"Luca Derzin, I am holding you on a national security certificate, which means for the next seventy-two hours, you don't exist. No one knows where you are, and you do not have the right to an attorney. I warned you about staying on Mission. You disregarded my orders. This is what happens when someone like you crosses the line. I was in the Aeternum facility shortly before a kinetic strike from orbit obliterated it and saw for myself that it was, in large part, nothing more than a smuggling transshipment warehouse. The importation of human organs alone is worth twenty years in a prison colony on Parth. Add illegal narcotics on top of that, and you're looking at life. If the analysis proves those human organs were harvested and not laboratory-grown, the penalty for trafficking them is death, as is engaging in the slave trade. Yes, we found evidence of that as well. Then there's the matter of that unregistered and illegal level 4 biohazard containment area."

I watched his eyes widen with every word I spoke and saw a hint of fear for the first time.

"Sure, my eyewitness account and any evidence taken are inadmissible in court, but I have a copy of the Aeternum computer core, as do other federal authorities. We will find admissible evidence, enough to put you away for a long time and arrest both the upstream and downstream actors in the smuggling chain. With any luck, we might even connect Aeternum's malfeasance to the most senior ComCorp executives and their political enablers."

I paused and studied him.

"You don't believe me. I can see it in your face. But the rules are changing. Your sort can no longer hide behind laws designed to enable corporate criminality. If I arrange for your disappearance, no one will come looking. No one will find you. Forget about compliant prosecutors and judges letting you walk away from the charges. Those days are over. We are at war, your sort, and the side of law and order. Aeternum's destruction was a strike against an enemy, and you are a prisoner of war. The only way you can salvage something is by cooperating with me. I'll let you mull it over for a few hours. Sergeant?"

"Sir." Bonta stepped forward and removed Derzin's wrist manacles, then pulled off the muzzle while Arno kept a bead on him with his blaster.

To his credit, Derzin did nothing more than glower at us, which proved he understood his situation.

— Thirty-Seven —

At breakfast, a few hours later, a somewhat agitated and angry AC Braband buttonholed me. His voice, though low enough it wouldn't carry to any nearby table, held a rough edge.

"What's this about a national security certificate detainee in my cells? Who is it, and who issued the certificate?"

"I did."

"How can a mere chief superintendent issue herself national security certificates without so much as a judge's approval?"

"They gave PCB commanding officers that authority last year in response to the increasing unrest and judicial corruption across the Commonwealth."

"I never heard about it."

"That was by design, sir."

"And the identity of the detainee?"

"I can't tell you. The whole point of holding someone under a national security certificate is to make him or her vanish for a brief period while we investigate corruption capable of destabilizing an entire star system."

His frown deepened.

"You think the situation on Mission Colony is that dire?"

"Again, sir, I can't tell you at the moment."

Braband gave me a hard look before walking away.

"I don't think he likes you anymore, Chief."

"Can't say I'd feel any different if I were in his position. A more junior officer with extraordinary powers running roughshod over my patch would tick me off as well."

"When are we talking to our guest next?"

"Around noon, I'd say. In the meantime, we keep working on the data dig and that wretched computer core dump."

Arno rubbed his hands. "Another bout of good, old-fashioned police work, defined as ninety-nine percent perspiration, one percent luck. Speaking of which, when will we search his two residences?"

"After the first interview, if I think it necessary. We can pretty much assume he left nothing compromising behind."

We were back in the cellblock shortly after eleven-thirty. A different NCO sat behind the counter, but he recognized us instantly and jumped to his feet.

"What's the status of the security certificate detainee, Sergeant?"

"Life signs are normal for the circumstances. He ate his breakfast, and we're preparing his midday meal. No one entered the cell since your departure. I can show you the log."

"That won't be necessary, thank you. We will interview the detainee in the cell."

"I'll handle the doors from here, Chief Superintendent. Please go ahead."

We found Derzin lying on the bunk, right forearm draped over his eyes. It fell away as he turned his head to look at us. "I was wondering when you'd be back."

"Did you think about our earlier conversation?"

"Why bother? I'm a dead man, whether I satisfy your curiosity or stay silent. The moment my employers find out the Constabulary held me on a security certificate, they'll disavow me with, as you people like to say, extreme prejudice. There won't be a safe place for me anywhere, not even on Desolation Island."

They sounded like the words of a defeated man. However, his tone and the look in his eyes were anything but those of someone resigned to his fate.

I dropped into the cell's single chair, an uncomfortable, shiny plastic thing.

"Where are the people who worked at your facility the night of the attack?"

"No idea."

"Try the other one, sunshine," Arno growled from behind me. "Nothing happens around here you don't know about or aren't manipulating in some way. You were turning Mission Colony into your own little fief so you could become neo-feudal baron on behalf of perfumed ComCorp princelings."

"My security chief takes care of such matters."

Arno didn't even pull out his tablet to check the name. "Azfar Kozyrev, right?"

"Yes. Good luck finding him. I told my people they should make themselves scarce after my departure."

"Are the employees in question even still alive?" I asked.

Derzin shrugged, then placed his hands behind his head to prop it up.

"If Azfar gave into his usual paranoia, they probably ended up as pseudo-plesiosaur food before sunrise yesterday."

"You certainly have interesting human resources policies."

"I don't hire model citizens."

"Let's talk about the colonial government people you were corrupting."

"Let's not. You're the hotshot internal affairs investigator. I'm sure you can identify them without my help."

"I think Mister Derzin still hopes he can salvage something from this mess, Chief. Officials who sold their souls to ComCorp will be useful even with the Aeternum operation destroyed."

The flash in Derzin's eyes told me Arno hit a bull's eye, and that he still expected to walk away unscathed, provided he didn't sell out his superiors.

"They won't be useful once I collar them, and I will, Mister Derzin. No one expects us, no one escapes us. How about I tell you a story, and you tell me if it's fiction."

Another shrug. "There's nothing else on my agenda right now."

"Let's see. ComCorp has been hemorrhaging wealth in recent years because of certain unnamed factions in the federal government who escalated the secret war against zaibatsus engaged in criminal activities. As a result, your parent company decided it would take a leaf from the cartels' playbook and set up, as Inspector Galdi put it, neo-feudal fiefs in strategically located frontier star systems by corrupting officials."

"Your ability to conjure conspiracy theories out of thin air is astonishing, Chief Superintendent."

"Somehow, your superiors are friendly with one of the federal agencies reporting directly to the Secretary-General and wangled that nice exemption certificate you've been dangling in front of everyone. I figure it's because of the unregistered level 4 biohazard lab hidden at Aeternum's heart. What were you doing there? Research on tailored viruses for the *Sécurité Spéciale*?"

"The lab wasn't actually in operation yet, and I couldn't begin to guess what it would work on. You see, my job was managing the import-export part of the business. The lab would have been run by someone else entirely. I don't know who or from what organization."

Arno let out an amused chuckle. "Sounds like a matryoshka doll, your Aeternum. A secret level 4 lab inside a large-scale smuggling operation which itself hid inside a seemingly legitimate pharmaceutical research and development facility. Did you do any legitimate R&D in there?"

"Why bother? The import-export business was fantastically lucrative, even though it wasn't yet running at full capacity. Besides, ComCorp's pharmaceutical subsidiaries already run plenty of R&D facilities. But it was a great cover, considering no one would question our penchant for secrecy." He snorted softly. "With the evidence gone, you can't prove any of this. And even if the attackers were part of your unnamed federal government faction, anything they took is inadmissible in court. Not that secret squirrels would risk unmasking themselves by bringing court actions in any case. This is fascinating, Chief Superintendent, but it won't help you root out the imaginary corruption of Mission Colony government officials. I'm sure you've been busily investigating the personal affairs of the leading figures and found nothing."

"Influence peddling doesn't leave traces if it's well done, Mister Derzin. I'll wager you promised ambitious but disappointed government officials a chance at further promotion and a way out of this star system at the Commonwealth's hind end if they reciprocated your friendship offers and ignored Aeternum's activities. Perhaps you sweetened the offer with a little anonymous retirement fund for those who showed the usual signs of venality. In fact, I'll go even further and say Aeternum was just the beginning. ComCorp probably planned on expanding its questionable operations over the next few years. You don't infiltrate agents on a long-term basis if you don't have a long-term plan."

"Agents now? Your imagination is definitely overactive."

"The zaibatsus run their own intelligence and security services, and we're aware they often cooperate with the *Sécurité Spéciale.* Let's take Mayleen Allore, for example. She doesn't exist. Our own criminal intelligence branch investigated her past on New Tasman. They found her in government registries, but no one remembers a Mayleen

Allore at school or in the community. It can only mean she belongs to ComCorp's undercover network. Here's how I see it. Allore weaseled her way into the heart of Government House, and when Elden Braband replaced Kristy Bujold, she ran a honey pot sting on him. There are no doubt more ComCorp agents inside the colonial administration. Commissioner Sorjonen and his unit will find them, be sure of that. What happened? Did Amaris Tosh figure out what you were doing? Is that why Allore murdered her?"

He gave me a bloodless smile. "You may well think so; I couldn't possibly comment."

"I see Mister Derzin knows the classics, Chief."

"He also likes to entertain folks. We watched your garden party earlier this month and are even now checking on the colonial government officials who attended. Am I right in assuming you expected us? We stuck around long enough after the party to see your men come out of the glen's far end, where Gustav Kerlin's assassin hid."

"Congratulations, Chief Superintendent. Yes, I expected you. And if you'd played your part properly, we wouldn't be having this conversation because I'd have lodged a formal complaint and ended your investigation."

Arno scoffed. "Keep underestimating the Chief, and you might find there are worse things than arrest under a national security certificate."

"Noted, Inspector, though you can't keep me here indefinitely without a judge's approval."

"And you know I didn't obtain a judge's approval how? Because you corrupted Justice Bisso and a few others? What did you promise Bisso? An associate supreme court judgeship?" Not quite a bullseye this time, based on his reaction. "Or were you blackmailing him?"

"I wasn't doing anything of the sort, and I'll be out in a few days, Chief Superintendent. You have a reputation as a straight shooter. So does AC Braband for that matter, and these are evidently his cells."

"Then what? You run from your own side for the rest of your life? Or was that mournful soliloquy earlier just a load of manure? You're a survivor, Mister Derzin. I've met your sort many times before in my career. At this point, your focus is salvaging what you can, and a colonial administration in ComCorp's pocket is worth saving. But satisfy my curiosity. Why did you do a runner after I told you to stay?"

"So I didn't end up having a lengthy conversation with someone like you. Leaving the Constabulary puzzled at what happened seemed like a splendid idea."

"Methinks he hoped the folks he corrupted would clam up when they realized there was no one and no evidence that pointed at misconduct, Chief. Keep them in reserve for the next try here, or for when they received the promised promotion and gave ComCorp more tentacles inside the federal government. Owning an associate supreme court justice would be so useful. Am I right, Mister Derzin?"

"Shall I quote another classic line, Inspector? No?" He glanced at me. "Are we done here? This discussion is tiresome, and I believe mealtime is upon us."

I understood by then Derzin wouldn't give me any names. Officials whose corruption remained undetected were valuable assets and his ticket back into ComCorp's good graces. I stood and stared at him.

"Enjoy the rest of your day, Mister Derzin."

Once outside, Arno asked, "Do we visit his residences this afternoon?"

"Yes." We wouldn't find much, if anything, but I felt an urge to stay on the move while Bonta's code-cracking algorithm kept poking at the computer core dump. We didn't have much time left and needed a lucky break.

— Thirty-Eight —

That noon, the members of the 24th Regiment gave us an even colder shoulder than usual in the dining hall. Word of a national security certificate detainee on their base had clearly made the rounds, even though everyone knew you didn't discuss the matter. Most cops hated the security certificate concept and considered it a way of circumventing the laws we swore to uphold. They weren't wrong. I disliked using them as well, but Derzin represented a clear and present danger, and I'd run out of options. Us waiting for Sorjonen and walking away was no longer on the table and hadn't been since that sniper sent me to the hospital.

We found a key card among Derzin's personal effects and drove to his townhouse in Ventano's most expensive central neighborhood. Sergeant Bonta scanned the place from inside our car before we even tried the front door. She found nothing, and the key card gave us admittance. Another scan before stepping in proved no booby traps waited for the unwary.

As I expected, we found nothing of use after an extensive search, though it didn't look or feel like Derzin simply walked away. Perhaps he counted on returning once everything calmed down.

"You called it, Chief. Nice digs, though. Derzin likes living large, and he has a certain amount of taste. Did you see his bar? Nothing but the best. That collection of bottles would fund an inspector's pay for a year."

"Let's visit the countryside next. His estate might hold more clues, though I doubt it."

Derzin's key card opened the mansion driveway's ornate, forged iron gate just as smoothly as it admitted us into the townhouse. Everything seemed quiet from the outside — windows shuttered, no cars in the driveway, none of the occupancy aura we investigators could detect with experience. A cop knowing whether a place was empty when he or she didn't have a handheld sensor saved lives.

Sergeant Bonta did her usual thing, though this time, she let out a thoughtful grunt.

"Full-scale active surveillance system, sir. Makes you wonder whether it's connected to miniature remote weapon stations. If Derzin planted a belt of the full-sized version around Aeternum, why not the estate?"

"Nervous in the service, Sergeant?" Arno asked in a good-natured tone.

"You want to take point, Inspector?"

Before they could engage in an endless back and forth, I opened the door on my side.

"We'll take point as a team. Arno and I can be the lookouts while you scan the property, Sergeant."

We slowly wound our way around the main house's exterior, stopping on the patio to find our observation post and the place from where Colonel Decker shot Gustav Kerlin. When we turned the corner around the larger of the outbuildings, our nostrils picked up a depressingly familiar odor of decomposition. Arno pointed at a flat, black box, the size of a typical ground car, a few meters from the barn.

"If I'm not mistaken, that's a macerator. You can make human bodies disappear in them, but it's a lengthier process than the more popular alternatives."

Taking care of the unpleasant things was a commanding officer's job. The reek of putrefaction increased as I neared the macerator to the point where I could only breathe through my mouth. I slipped on the gloves I always carried in my pocket for just such an occasion and lifted one of the lids. I found myself staring at the faces of two partially decomposed human beings. One appeared to be a match for Mayleen Allore, the other was a swarthy, thickset male who Arno identified as Azfar Kozyrev, Derzin's head of security.

"It seems our Mister Derzin took care of his loose ends before leaving, Chief. Give it another two or three weeks, and the macerator would have liquefied these two specimens beyond anything recognizable as human."

I pulled out my communicator and called the Operations Center.

"Chief Superintendent Morrow here. We're at Luca Derzin's country estate and found two sets of human remains in a macerator. They've been dead for perhaps a day or two. I need forensics and body recovery."

"Understood, sir. Can you stay on site until they arrive?"

"Yes."

"Thank you."

"Morrow, out."

Sergeant Bonta, stony-faced, was taking detailed records of the bodies in situ when I rejoined her and Arno by the macerator.

"Are you charging Derzin with murder, Chief?"

"Yes. As soon as we return to the base. Maybe it'll make him change his tune, though I doubt it."

Derzin's key card let us into the mansion without triggering alarms. Like the townhouse, nothing seemed out of place, as if the owner were on an extended vacation, fully intending to return. It proved Derzin was a cool customer, not someone who panicked. He knew the jig was up in the wee hours of yesterday morning and moved quickly so he could vanish without a trace, leaving the edifice he built for another day. That he murdered at least one of the two was beyond question. Perhaps Kozyrev executed Allore at Derzin's orders and was killed in turn after he dumped her body in the macerator. In retrospect, it was so predictably sordid.

The crime scene folks would give the mansion a once-over anyhow, so we retreated to our car and waited until they and the homicide investigators arrived. I showed Inspector Kosta the macerator, assured him I wore gloves when I lifted the lid, and let him know we went through the house and outbuildings, the three of us gloved. Then we returned to Ventano and another interview with Derzin.

He was once more lying on his cot when we entered and gave us only a cursory glance. I took the sole chair again while my wingers leaned against the wall behind me.

"Macerators take a few weeks to dissolve human bodies, Mister Derzin. You should have disposed of Allore and Kozyrev differently. We got a whiff of decomposition the moment we neared it."

"I don't know what you're talking about." Something in his voice and the look in his half-open eyes said otherwise.

"I will charge you with the murders of Azfar Kozyrev and Mayleen Allore when your period of detention under the national security certificate ends. That, on top of everything else, will make sure you don't escape a hard sentence on Parth, no matter what your employers might wish. That's if they don't abandon you altogether. Mind you, using the macerator would have worked if you'd made good on your escape, so I'll give you points for thinking it through. I suppose your man Kozyrev killed everyone connected with your import-export business before you did unto him. No witnesses, no loose ends, just fertile ground that can be tilled once irritating pests like us are gone. That's a lot of people on your conscience, even if you only pulled the trigger once, murdering Kozyrev, after he killed Allore, and you helped him dump her body into the macerator. The crime scene investigators will reconstruct events with pinpoint accuracy. They're good at it, better than you are at hiding your traces."

I let that sink in before continuing.

"The way I see it, the only choice open to you is minimizing the pain. Tell me who in the colonial administration has been covering for you and your operation, and I'll see that the prosecutor cuts you a deal for a reduced sentence. Life instead of death or perhaps even twenty-five years on Parth instead of lifelong exile on Desolation Island."

"Sorry, Chief Superintendent. No deal."

Arno pushed himself away from the wall and stood behind my chair.

"I figure Mister Derzin is counting on his good friends in the Ventano courthouse to save his sorry skin once he's out of detention, and we charge him with murder."

Derzin gave Arno a poisonous glare.

"Perhaps your inspector isn't as thick as he seems."

"Many people make that mistake. They generally take early retirement under a cloud or spend a few years as guests of the federal government."

"No doubt." He turned his eyes back on the ceiling. "I just had an intriguing thought, Chief Superintendent. Why would you charge me with murder? Isn't that Braband's job? You're internal affairs. A civilian accused of murdering other civilians, that's an ordinary police matter. What if Braband's people can't come up with evidence tying me to the scene? Your entire case is looking shakier by the second. I think once you release me from this unlawful confinement, I will sue the Constabulary for depriving me of my civil rights."

Mere bluster? Or did we miss something? The Derzins of the galaxy possessed wonderfully twisted minds that moved in ways ours could only imagine. Or did he have another unidentified asset? Then an ugly thought reared its head. I stood.

"We'll continue this conversation later, Mister Derzin, once you've contemplated a future with murder charges on top of corruption and perverting the course of justice, to name just a few."

Arno and Sergeant Bonta gave me strange looks once we were back in the corridor.

"What didn't we do when we arrived?"

Both thought for a moment, then Arno snapped his fingers.

"We didn't check the desk sergeant's log. You think someone visited Derzin? He sounded entirely too confident for a man accused of murder."

When we entered the front office, the duty NCO looked up from his terminal and, upon seeing the thunderous expression on my face, stood with alacrity.

"Yes, sir?"

"Show me the log."

"Sir?"

"The log, Sergeant. I want to see it."

He touched his terminal, then spun it around for my benefit. Assistant Commissioner Braband had visited the cellblock shortly after I called in the bodies of Allore and Kozyrev. I scrolled backward and found no instance of his name in the last four weeks. Interesting.

"Who did AC Braband visit?"

The sergeant seemed distinctly uncomfortable. His eyes shifted from side to side as he avoided my gaze.

"He said his visit was confidential, and I shouldn't discuss it with anyone."

"You know who I am, right?"

Arno cleared his throat.

"The good sergeant is probably thinking an assistant commissioner beats a chief superintendent on matters affecting his career. Well," he leaned forward, "if that's the case, you're betting on the wrong officer, my friend. Chief Superintendent Morrow has ended more careers than all Constabulary regimental commanders put together. Perhaps you should try again."

"He visited the national security certificate detainee."

"Against my specific orders, only we three were allowed in his cell?" The look of sheer misery on his face made me relent. "We will discuss this later, Sergeant. For further clarity, you will note the following in the log, so every duty NCO knows. I will arrest and charge whoever lets anyone visit that detainee with dereliction of duty, which, upon conviction, means the end of the member's career. Not even the Chief Constable is allowed in without my say so. National security certificates are as serious as it gets. Do you understand me?"

He snapped to attention.

"Yes, sir. Loud and clear."

Once outside, I allowed myself a few choice words, but sotto voce. "Braband is bent, isn't he? How did we miss that?"

"Hubris. Just like you said. He *was* clean. But perhaps Derzin met Braband's price, and I'll bet it was for a guaranteed commissioner's star, giving ComCorp a tame flag officer deep within one of the major headquarters. But what did Braband give in return? It had to be something that would bind him forever."

"Yet we found no actual proof. Everything is circumstantial. If I charge Braband for violating the certificate, he'll counter with this being his jurisdiction and his responsibility, and Caelin Morrow overstepped her bounds for the hundredth time. Well, I'm about to overstep my bounds even further."

"Which means you're headed for his office, where you'll exchange a few sharp words."

"Naturally."

— Thirty-Nine —

Chief Inspector Wuori was with Braband when I entered the latter's office unannounced and uninvited. I pointed at her.

"Out. Now."

She glanced at Braband, whose face was unexpectedly turning paler than I'd seen so far. He nodded.

"Best do as Chief Superintendent Morrow says, Kalle."

Once we were alone, I glared at him.

"What the hell were you thinking when you violated my orders concerning the national security certificate detainee? The restrictions I imposed cover everyone in this star system. I thought you were smarter than that. No wonder the detainee suddenly feels like he'll walk away from his misdeeds unscathed."

Braband half rose from his chair.

"Never use that tone with me again, *Chief Superintendent*. You arrogant PCB folks aren't immune from disciplinary charges."

"Lay them when Commissioner Sorjonen arrives. But do so before I tell him you violated the security certificate.

323

He'll take a dim view of that. In the meantime, would you care to explain yourself?"

"No. Now leave this office."

"Then I'll explain matters. You know I've taken custody of a national security certificate detainee from the Navy, but not who that was. Yet at the same time, Luca Derzin, who I've been eying for an extensive list of crimes, vanished. When the Operations Center informed you we'd found the bodies of Mayleen Allore and Azfar Kozyrev at Derzin's country estate, you figured he must be the detainee and violated my orders. Why risk my wrath and that of DCC Maras? Is Derzin holding something over your head?"

"Out. Come back when you can show proof of misconduct, something you won't find. Harass me again, and it won't go well for you. You're reaching, Morrow and your antics will end now. Leave my office. That's an order. If you disobey, I will lay charges of insubordination."

"If you suffer from a guilty conscience, sir, best you consider making a voluntary statement. It'll go easier." I turned on my heels and left.

When I entered our section of the senior officers' quarters, both Arno and Sergeant Bonta stuck their heads out of their suites.

"And?"

"The man is thoroughly spooked, perhaps even on the edge of full-blown panic, which can only mean he compromised himself. Why do I suddenly wonder whether Peet isn't one of the few innocents in this? Derzin and Braband did their best to make her seem on the slippery slope. One by being a smarmy used starship salesman and the other a deeply concerned cop?"

"Could be ComCorp wants her gone, replaced with someone they own, Chief. What better way than to make her seem corrupt, so she comes under our scrutiny. Even if we only found peccadilloes stemming from an overly developed sense of entitlement, the Colonial Office would recall her at hyperspeed, especially after the New Oberon business revealed no end of uglies."

"Not a bad theory, Arno. But absent proof… Hopefully, Commissioner Sorjonen's people will find something."

A beep sounded from Sergeant Bonta's suite. "That's the decryption algorithm. It found something."

"Maybe our proof, Chief."

"From your lips to the Almighty's ears."

Bonta vanished into her sitting room. Arno and I followed.

"We broke through the first layer of encryption, sir."

"First? How many are there?"

"I can see at least three, but each of them might hide several subordinate layers." We watched in silence as she parsed the decrypted files. "Looks like accounting records, inventories, that sort of thing."

"Shift a few files over to me," Arno said. "I'll examine them."

"Done."

I made myself a tea, lost in thought while they diligently scanned file after file. Finally, Arno poked his head into my sitting room.

"I just love it when criminals keep accurate records. The amount of smuggled goods and organs that passed through here since Derzin set up his operation is staggering. Too bad this stuff is the fruit of the poisoned tree, but the criminal intelligence folks will have a field day tracing it. And they won't encounter problems developing admissible evidence. Unfortunately, it doesn't help us with the corruption problem."

"Sirs?" Sergeant Bonta's voice floated across the corridor. "I broke through another layer of encryption. You need to see this."

When Arno and I entered her sitting room, she pointed at the large wall display. We studied it in silence for a minute or so.

"There's one of those for every month since Aeternum started operating," Bonta said.

Arno let out a grunt.

"Bogus status reports for Derzin's nominal superiors at Pure Breath Inc. Not a single mention of his so-called import-export operations. What's the point?"

"That's what I thought, Inspector, so I looked a little closer and found a further layer of encryption embedded in each report. Now that we found the basic pattern, breaking through is getting easier." She touched her screen. The report dissolved, and a new document took its place.

"Oh, dear. The 24th Regiment's cellblock will overflow by the time we're done, Chief. How did Derzin compromise so many people?"

"Let's look at each monthly report in chronological order. That might tell us how this mess unfolded."

And it did. By the time we noticed the dining hall was about to close, we knew everything except why so many people in high profile positions let themselves fall from grace. After a hasty meal, we reconvened in Bonta's suite.

"Derzin is quite the artist, Chief. He didn't just dangle shining career advancement promises in return for increasingly compromising quid pro quos. Who'd think Justice Bisso is a sexual predator? He probably uses the yacht as his personal dungeon." An air of disgust crossed Arno's face. "I bet we'll find a lot of disturbing audio and video files beneath those deeper encryption layers."

"Notice which name is absent from the friends of Derzin list, Arno?"

"Yep. I'll bet for all her faults, he couldn't put the squeeze on Peet, even with agents embedded deep in Government House. Hence Operation Make Peet Look Bad. The one thing they didn't expect was Maras asking you to investigate personally straight off. I expect we'd have received a report from Braband a few weeks after Peet's complaint, alleging she seemed on the take and found ample, albeit planted evidence the moment we investigated her private life. Too clever by half, our Mister Derzin."

"They didn't plan Tosh's murder, nor did they expect me to show up unannounced and volunteer as SIO, something Braband couldn't refuse because it would have seemed strange under the circumstances. I'll bet Tosh stumbled on something by accident, perhaps evidence of Derzin's plot against Peet, or that Aeternum wasn't an honest R&D facility. At this point, we'll probably never know since her killer is dead, and Derzin won't talk. I'm sure Braband wasn't in on it. His reaction to the news seemed genuine."

"What now, Chief?"

"We look for the audio or video records that are surely hidden somewhere in there and build cases against each. We know this evidence isn't admissible, but they won't know when we arrest and interview them. I'm convinced most of the people Derzin corrupted will confess when presented with the facts. And those voluntary confessions will be admissible in court. Even if they recant later, their careers will be over."

Bonta broke through the deeper encryption a few hours later, time Arno and I spent writing up the individual case files we would use during our interviews. What we found wasn't pretty. The videos Derzin used to blackmail Justice Bisso were downright nauseating.

Rudel, despite his complaints, would have enjoyed a comfortable retirement with the funds Derzin placed in a numbered account on Arcadia, as would Braband's second in command, Chief Superintendent Sorem. The only one for whom I felt a modicum of sympathy was Terrence Salak. Derzin forced him to cooperate by threatening his family with a visit from the Pacifican State Security Police.

As for Braband, the honey pot had worked. He overindulged with the pillow talk, revealing things about the 24th Regiment's internal workings and its investigations that should have remained confidential. More importantly, he revealed his price. That's when Allore, on Derzin's orders, reeled him in. She made Braband believe Peet was bent by innocently dropping hints and complaining about the governor's behavior.

Then, Allore convinced him exposing Peet would secure his promotion to commissioner, but that meant creating conflict between him and her, so both the PCB and the Colonial Office take notice. I might have felt sorry for Braband under different circumstances. But he'd let his paramour lead him around by the nose, and that wasn't forgivable, even if he didn't accept payoffs or offers of influence peddling.

I went to bed after oh-one-hundred hours, both exhausted and elated we'd broken the case wide open before Commissioner Sorjonen's arrival.

The next morning, shortly after breakfast, we barged in on Braband, who was sitting behind his desk, staring out the window with a preoccupied frown. He swiveled his chair and faced us.

"Go ahead. Do what you must."

"Assistant Commissioner Elden Braband, I am Chief Superintendent Caelin Morrow of the Rim Sector Professional Compliance Bureau. I am charging you with perverting the course of justice. You do not have to say anything. But it may harm your defense if you do not mention when questioned something which you later rely on in court. Anything you do say may be given in evidence. Do you understand?"

"Yes."

"Here is what will happen next. I will show you the evidence we uncovered and allow you to make a statement. Should you take that opportunity and tell us everything, I will release you on your own recognizance until DCC Maras decides whether you should face disciplinary action or be allowed to retire. I am, however, relieving you of command no matter what."

"Then Cyndee Sorem gets a premature step up. Good for her."

His comment underlined what we already suspected. Derzin had kept his victims compartmentalized, so that none of them knew about their fellows.

"I will arrest Chief Superintendent Sorem after we're done here. She has been taking bribes from Luca Derzin and will trade her quarters for a cell. Since I can't trust any senior officer at this point, I will temporarily take command of the 24th Constabulary Regiment until Commissioner Sorjonen's arrival. Now, will you make a voluntary statement?" I pulled out my official recording device and placed it on his desk.

Braband sighed.

"Let's get this over with. I screwed up, and that's all there is to it. I need not see your evidence."

— Forty —

"Very well." I switched on the device. It would capture both audio and video. "The following is a voluntary statement given by Assistant Commissioner Elden Braband. Present are Chief Superintendent Caelin Morrow, Commanding Officer, Rim Sector Professional Compliance Bureau."

"Inspector Arno Galdi, Rim Sector Professional Compliance Bureau."

"Master Sergeant Destine Bonta, Rim Sector Professional Compliance Bureau."

Braband spoke in a measured tone, essentially confirming Derzin's reports to his superiors.

"Governor Peet and I clashed almost from the day I arrived. She doesn't understand how colonial governors interact with the star system's senior Constabulary commander and was downright unpleasant in private. She apparently had a vastly different relationship with Kristy Bujold if you get my meaning. It made me despise her. When I began seeing Mayleen, my relationship with Peet worsened. It was just one of those things, you understand. Personalities that rub each other the wrong way. Where I stepped into it was listening to Mayleen's stories about Peet. I now realize she fed me a load of manure to make Peet seem corrupted by Derzin. It was her idea I act rudely with Peet in private so that she lodges a complaint that would attract the attention of the Colonial Office and my superiors. When Maras asked me for an explanation, I would pass along my suspicions and prove myself the good guy. Mayleen figured it would give me a few more points when the promotion board met."

"You never discussed Peet with Derzin?"

He shook his head. "No. Never. I honestly believed Derzin was corrupting Peet. It's only in the last few days that I realized what I'd done. Your finding Mayleen's body on Derzin's property confirmed they had used me as Derzin's puppet."

"Governor Peet is just about the only senior official in this star system who brushed off Derzin's attempts at influencing her."

"It certainly didn't seem that way."

"Peet has her flaws, and she's susceptible to flattery, but Derzin couldn't pay her price. Instead, he decided she must go. That's where you came in. Derzin used Allore to manipulate you, while he suggested to Peet she should complain about you. A clever scheme which could have worked, except for the fact of our vetting you at DCC Maras' request, something only she and we knew about."

Braband let out a heartfelt sigh. "How did you find out about Derzin's plot?"

"We obtained a copy of the Aeternum computer core. Our Mister Derzin kept meticulous records of his activities for the benefit of his superiors. Encrypted, of course, but we broke the code last night. You're our first stop because I need you out of the way. If it's any consolation, my report will state they duped you rather than corrupted you."

"It won't save my career."

"No. Your career is over. A sergeant or an inspector who demonstrates such a lapse of judgment might walk away with a letter of reprimand. Assistant commissioners answer to a higher standard. Why did you visit Derzin's cell against my orders?"

"Because it felt like everything was unraveling, and I wanted answers." Braband met my gaze openly. "Derzin threatened me with exposure by revealing my part in the attempt to compromise Governor Peet if I didn't help him."

"And were you going to help?"

He let out a humorless laugh. "No. I told him he could go to hell and that I'd take my lumps."

"Funny. Derzin seemed pretty confident after your visit."

"Probably because he figured I'd cave. A man like him always gets what he wants." Another sigh. "I feel like such an idiot right now, Chief Superintendent. I can't understand how this happened."

"Everyone has weaknesses and a price. Luca Derzin is extraordinarily skilled at finding both. He's a bit like Mephistopheles that way. Unfortunately, he was able to exploit your weaknesses via Mayleen Allore, and she dangled your price in front of your nose — promotion. At this point, I would ask for your credentials, badge, and service weapon. I'm suspending you with pay. You will leave the base and not communicate with any member of the 24th Constabulary Regiment until DCC Maras decides your future."

He handed them over, then left without looking back. I watched his car pass through the main gate from what was now temporarily my office.

Chief Superintendent Cyndee Sorem wasn't quite as rueful as her former superior. She blustered, threatened, and even cursed us. But in the end, she too gave a voluntary statement when I showed her information about the numbered account Derzin set up, including the current, somewhat healthy balance. Sorem filled in a few blanks for us.

She was the one who put a tail on Kine and the Marines, fearing, with reason, they were a threat, and she tried to access our node the night before Allore shot me. And her motives for taking Derzin's money? Greed. Sorem knew she would retire as a chief superintendent and wanted a comfortable post-Constabulary life. While socializing with Derzin as part of her outreach duties, she unwittingly let him peer into her soul, and when he needed favors from the police, he bought it, bit by bit, until she was under his thumb.

After taking Sorem's credentials, badge and service weapon, Arno and Sergeant Bonta escorted her to the cellblock while I informed Chief Inspector Wuori I was her new commanding officer.

Then, I checked Braband's agenda and saw Governor Peet was holding another emergency committee meeting that afternoon, one which would bring together half a dozen of the people on our arrest list. I arranged for a full platoon of constables from the 1st Battalion, under a master sergeant, along with half a dozen cars to go with us. I also warned the cellblock's duty NCO he should expect an influx of customers.

Shortly after lunch, my team and I met in the hallway outside our suites, and we inspected each other with a critical eye. I couldn't remember when we last made an arrest in uniform, but this time it seemed proper even though I wasn't much for theatrics. Arno, Sergeant Bonta, and I wore more medal ribbons on our high-collared, gray service dress tunics than most officers, and none of them were of the 'I was there' variety. As a bonus, both Bonta and I wore Pathfinder wings with combat jump stars above our ribbons and Pathfinder daggers on our black gun belts. The general effect was pleasantly menacing.

"You're good to go, Chief."

"So are you, Inspector." Master Sergeant Bonta, fit for a recruiting poster when in uniform, needed no last-minute checks. Her turnout was perfect.

The platoon was assembled in front of our building, and when we stepped out, the sergeant called them to attention before saluting me with parade-ground precision.

"Master Sergeant Devine reporting with twenty constables as ordered, sir."

I returned the salute. "Place them at ease, please."

When he'd done so, I let my eyes meet their unabashedly curious gaze. They knew I'd relieved their commanding officer and arrested his deputy a few hours earlier.

"Folks, we're heading to Government House, where I will arrest several senior officials on charges of corruption and perverting the course of justice. You will escort them back here and hand them over to the cellblock duty NCO. Questions?" When no one dared raise a hand, I turned to the sergeant. "Mount up."

I felt the usual, slightly disturbing rush of power when we climbed out of our car and up the Government House front steps. The constable standing guard snapped to attention and saluted, though his eyes were bugging out at the sudden invasion led by a PCB officer.

Our boot heels clicked loudly on the marble floor as we crossed the lobby and headed for the conference room. Once again, the door was slightly ajar, and I pushed it open. The sounds of conversation ceased as the assembly stared at me.

"I am Chief Superintendent Caelin Morrow, Commanding Officer, Rim Sector Professional Compliance Bureau. Demetrius Rudel, I am arresting you on charges of corruption and perverting the course of justice. You do not have to say anything. But it may harm your defense if you do not mention when questioned something which you later rely on in court. Anything you do say may be given in evidence."

Rudel stared at me with a stunned expression, though he didn't offer any resistance when a pair of constables pulled him up and cuffed him. I repeated the process with Terrence Salak, Justice Bisso, and three more officials who worked for Rudel. There were more in the administration, but I'd leave them for Commissioner Sorjonen, who was expected in just over twenty-four hours.

Peet, who'd remained silent during the arrests, looked around the table at the few who remained, then at me.

"I presume there's a good explanation for this, Chief Superintendent."

"Madame, my team and I uncovered evidence of widespread corruption in the colonial administration stemming from Luca Derzin. The individuals I just arrested are merely the tip of the iceberg. Further arrests will be forthcoming in the next few days. You should know that Derzin, along with several others, was scheming to see you relieved of duty on suspicion of misconduct."

She gave me a startled glance. "But Luca is my friend."

"He never was your friend, nor anyone else's. Derzin is a criminal, a vile and violent creature, hellbent on using Mission Colony as the main base for his illegal activities. Fortunately for everyone in this star system, especially you, Madame, his plan misfired, and he will now meet his destiny. If I may leave you with a piece of advice. Don't listen to silver-tongued flatterers and be nicer to the honest, hardworking people around you. They'll have less incentive to wish your removal and cooperate with another Derzin."

We spent the rest of the day interviewing the prisoners. Upon seeing the videos Derzin kept so he could blackmail him, Justice Bisso collapsed. I ordered him taken to the hospital, but his heart gave out on the way there. The medics couldn't revive him. The others, when confronted with the evidence, made voluntary statements. Those six, plus the two from Braband and Sorem, would make sure Derzin was convicted even if we found nothing else.

Salak would probably receive a caution, while Rudel and his three subordinates, who took healthy payoffs in exchange for ignoring Aeternum's activities and regular starship traffic, faced a few years on Parth. None knew what was going on, but they shared the same disillusionment with their careers and a sense they were entitled to a better retirement fund for their hard work at the hind end of the Commonwealth.

After speaking with them, I figured the Colonial Office faced a bit of a morale problem along with a pay scale that didn't reflect reality. Nothing new in my universe, though I would mention it in the report.

After the last confession, we visited Derzin while still in uniform. This time, he sat up and stared at us with undisguised curiosity.

"To what do I owe the honor, Chief Superintendent? I didn't know PCB officers owned uniforms. And so many medals. Well done."

"I'm releasing you from national security certificate detention and arresting you on charges of corrupting public officials, smuggling, drug trafficking, illegal transportation of human organs, perverting the course of justice, and murder. I already collected eight voluntary statements from individuals you suborned."

"Bull crap."

"No. They couldn't confess fast enough when I presented them with the evidence we found in the Aeternum computer core dump."

"How did you obtain—" he fell silent, then swore under his breath. "The attackers were Fleet, right? In that case, anything from them isn't admissible in court."

"True. But the statements made by Braband, Sorem, Bisso, Rudel, Salak, and Rudel's directors are. And the investigation is far from over at this point. We will find more evidence based on what we know so far. The next time, invest in better encryption. And don't bother applying for bail because it'll be denied. You won't even get a hearing. This is your home until a judge, one of those you didn't corrupt, passes sentence. ComCorp won't save you. They won't even try. Your attempt at turning this star system into a wholly-owned fief failed miserably because you overplayed your hand."

"Oh? How so?"

"If you hadn't been hellbent on getting rid of Peet and learned to work around her, you'd still be lording it over the locals. But you were greedy and wanted the entire administration. I doubt we will speak again. My replacement is arriving tomorrow with an army of PCB investigators who'll tear Mission Colony apart and hunt down every rotten soul while we return home. Farewell, Mister Derzin. Say hi to your ultimate boss, the devil, when you see him because, at this point, the death penalty is almost assured."

We left him to contemplate his fate. The death penalty wasn't, in fact, assured, but I thought he deserved a bit of added worry. Men like Derzin thought they would never fail. Until they did. And for many, it was too much. Perhaps in a few days, he might offer a voluntary statement of his own, in return for taking the death penalty off the table. That, however, would not be my concern.

After a long evening dealing with regimental administration issues, I hung my uniform tunic on the bedroom door and stared at it while sipping a glass of Glen Arcturus. Although I enjoyed the rush of arresting bent officials, the sordidness of the individual confessions was a drain on my soul. Humanity would never stop committing the seven deadly sins, but at that moment, I wondered whether I should stop hunting sinners and hang up the uniform permanently.

— Forty-One —

The following day, I decided we should greet Commissioner Sorjonen in uniform. When we received notice the Constabulary cutter *Frank Preston* was on final approach, Arno, Sergeant Bonta, and I changed before heading to the Ventano Spaceport. Since we solved a large part of the corruption problem despite our orders we should lie low, I fully expected a rebuke. Showing proper humility by receiving the legendary commissioner in uniform might go some way in deflecting what I was sure would be considerable irritation on Sorjonen's part.

Imagine my surprise when he and his unit marched off the cutter also wearing service gray. I called my team to attention, and when Sorjonen approached, we saluted as one.

"Welcome to Mission Colony, sir."

Sorjonen, a tall, bony man with intense blue eyes and short, silver hair, returned the salute.

"Thank you." He held my gaze for a few seconds as if he were peering into my soul. It felt a tad unnerving, but I finally understood why he was a legend in the PCB. I could only imagine how senior officials with guilty consciences reacted to that stare.

"I've arranged for transport and quarters on the base for you and your people, sir."

"Excellent. But why are you here and not AC Braband?"

"I charged him with perverting the course of justice and relieved him of duty yesterday, sir. I also charged and arrested his second in command. She's in a cell right now."

Sorjonen's eyebrows crept up. "I shall listen to your verbal report with great interest. If the CO and his number two are in prison, who commands the 24th?"

"I do."

"What about the regiment's other chief superintendents?"

"At this point, sir, I believe the senior officers need fresh vetting. The degree of official corruption on Mission Colony is difficult to fathom."

"I see. Well, we will take care of matters from here on. Lead us to our transport."

By design, there was nothing subtle about the Political Anti-Corruption Unit's arrival, and we received plenty of worried looks as I led Sorjonen through the headquarters building to the CO's office, which he could commandeer for all I cared. I offered him Braband's former chair, but he sat on one side of the conference table, across from me.

"Go ahead, Chief Superintendent. I'm listening."

For the next ninety minutes, I recounted everything, including Erinye Company's intervention. When I fell silent, he gave me that unnerving look again and sat back.

"Impressive. Only the three of you, but half of my work is already done. And in the space of a few days." A smile I couldn't interpret softened his angular features. "I'm equally impressed that you can call on friends in strange places. They can be handy. Oh, don't look so surprised. I'm sure you expected harsh words from me because you disobeyed DCC Hammett's orders to lie low. But under the circumstances, you did precisely the right thing, and I will tell the DCC personally."

"Thank you, sir."

"You've been running the Rim Sector PCB unit for several years now, right?"

"Yes."

"And done well. DCC Hammett considers you fearless, ruthless, and stubborn, qualities the best PCB officers need. He also sees you as the best of the sector PCB commanders. Did you ever consider looking for fresh challenges?"

"Sir?"

"The Political Anti-Corruption Unit is expanding yet again. At this rate, I expect a second star on my collar within the year. I have a team lead vacancy, an assistant commissioner's slot. We don't lack for tough cases and rack up the most light-years traveled in the entire service. It's yours if you want it, and in two or three years, an officer of your caliber can easily earn her first star, especially if we keep expanding." My astonishment must have shown because he chuckled. "Arno Galdi told you about me, and you expected the worst for disobeying DCC Hammett. I adapted one of my fundamental principles from something a famous pre-diaspora military leader said. No PCB investigator can do very wrong if he or she roots out official corruption in the most effective way possible. You can even bring your two wingers with you if they agree. I know Arno's not looking for promotion, but there's a vacant chief inspector's slot in the team you would command, along with one for a warrant officer."

To say I was speechless would trivialize my reaction. I had expected to spend the rest of my career running the Rim Sector unit. It was a job I enjoyed, working with sound, selfless people who cared for law and order. And taking up new responsibilities on Wyvern, where I would no longer answer directly to DCC Hammett, seemed like a step back, even though it was a promotion, with the chance of a commissioner's star down the road. But it would be an honest star, not one earned by pandering to the well-connected or falling for doe-eyed lovers.

"The Rim Sector will never be more than minor cases," he continued. "This mess on Mission Colony is an exception, and with our arrival, no longer your responsibility. Considering the way things are headed nowadays, the central units, such as mine, will face increasingly complex and far-ranging official misconduct cases. You'd be taking on investigations like never before with resources beyond anything you've imagined and make a much bigger difference to the Commonwealth's future, especially with your Naval Intelligence and Special Forces connections. The service needs you on Wyvern, Caelin. Your most senior superintendent is surely ready for a step up to replace you."

I knew Ange Rowan would jump at the chance of taking command, and she was a superb investigator who enjoyed the respect of the entire unit. A wise man once said, living well was the best revenge. Getting promoted into one of the Constabulary's elite PCB units met the living well concept when considered in light of the Pacifican State Security Police still looking to murder me for thirty-year-old thought crimes.

"I accept, sir."

"In that case, you can put up an AC's third diamond right away. I'll make sure the paperwork confirms your promotion as of today. You'll ride *Frank Preston* back to Cimmeria with your people in a few days once I've absorbed the situation and feel confident we can complete the work you started. There, you can hand the unit over. And to who would that be?" He cocked an eyebrow.

"Superintendent Angela Rowan. She's the senior team leader and will do an excellent job as my replacement."

"Chief Superintendent Rowan it is. I'll arrange for the promotion orders so you can pin on her second diamond the moment you arrive. Then, pack up your life and head for Wyvern, which will probably be your home until retirement, many years from now. I'll let you speak with Inspector Galdi and Sergeant Bonta, but if they accept, his promotion to chief inspector and hers to warrant officer become effective today." He smiled again. "As you might have noticed, AC Morrow, I don't screw around, a quality we share."

Sorjonen calling me by my new rank felt both strange and pleasing. It was vindication for the times I pushed the envelope, angered senior officials, and overstepped my bounds.

"That is certainly clear, sir."

"Since it's late in the day, why don't we meet as an extended team tomorrow morning. This place must have an auditorium big enough for everyone. Then you can brief your new colleagues on the situation."

"Yes, sir. There is a secure auditorium at the back of this building. What about command of the 24th?"

"I'll take over from this moment on until DCC Maras sends out a replacement, though I fear she'll trust no one in this job again, after two abject failures like Bujold and Braband."

"We forgot everyone has a price, even those with the cleanest service records. Braband's price, unfortunately, was lower than we imagined."

"Indeed. Once you settle in on Wyvern and I'm back, we'll discuss your price. I enjoy knowing the value of my officers."

"My price can only be met with a time machine, sir. And they don't exist."

"Your family on Pacifica."

"Yes, sir. I would give anything to rewind the clock and escape with all of them instead of becoming the Morrow family's sole survivor."

He gave me a thoughtful nod.

"Find yourself a third diamond, then talk with your team about their futures. Should they accept, we can discuss the next steps around the evening meal."

"Yes, sir." I stood and came to attention. "With your permission?"

"Dismissed, Assistant Commissioner."

When I left the office, I stopped by a still stunned Chief Inspector Wuori's desk.

"Commissioner Sorjonen is taking interim command of the 24th Regiment effective immediately."

"Understood, sir."

"You wouldn't have a spare rank diamond tucked away somewhere, waiting for the next promotion ceremony?"

"I do."

"Could I please have it?"

Her eyes widened as she understood. "I suppose congratulations are in order, Assistant Commissioner?"

"Thank you."

She rummaged in a desk drawer and produced the small silver pin, also called a pip in the Army and Marine Corps.

"Shall I affix it, sir?"

"If you'd be so kind."

A few minutes later, I found Arno and Sergeant Bonta in deep discussion with Political Anti-Corruption Unit people in the senior officers' quarters. They and the others fell silent at my appearance.

Arno jumped to his feet with surprising agility. "Attention on deck. Assistant Commissioner Morrow arriving."

"At ease. I accepted Commissioner Sorjonen's invitation to join his unit as a team leader. It came with a third diamond."

"I can't think of anyone more deserving, Chief. Congratulations." Arno put on a comical frown. "I'll need a new nickname for you. Assistant commissioner is as much of a mouthful as chief superintendent, and after so many years, old habits will be hard to break."

"So long as it isn't commish or something of the sort." I looked around at my new colleagues. "If you'll excuse us for a few minutes, I must discuss something with Inspector Galdi and Sergeant Bonta."

We entered my suite, and I shut the door.

"What's up?"

"If you'd like a taste of the high life and a slightly bigger paycheck, there's a vacant chief inspector billet on my new team in the Political Anti-Corruption Unit, as well as a vacant warrant officer position. Commissioner Sorjonen said they're yours if you accept, with the promotions effective immediately."

Both stared at me as if I'd grown a second head.

"Good heavens, Chi—Commissioner, you're asking me to forsake my vow of eternal inspectorness."

Bonta made a face. "You'll never break the record anyhow, so why bother trying. I accept the offer, sir."

Arno glanced at us in turn. "Then in the interests of keeping our little band of merry inquisitors intact, so do I. Besides, Cimmeria no longer holds any secrets for me. I've eaten in every good restaurant, seen every worthwhile sight, and arrested all the interesting miscreants."

"Then find yourselves proper rank insignia. Our new boss is doing this one in uniform to make a point. He already took over the 24th from me."

"That means your term is the shortest regimental command in Constabulary history."

"At least I left it with a promotion, not in disgrace like my two predecessors."

"True." He looked around the room. "Do you still have enough of the Glen Arcturus for a little celebration?"

"Of course."

Once the three of us each held a glass with a healthy serving of liquid amber, Arno raised his.

"A toast to the three finest inquisitors in the entire Commonwealth Constabulary. Long may we hunt."

— Forty-Two —

That evening, we three new Political Anti-Corruption investigators ate with our colleagues after taking over an entire section of the dining room.

I discovered Commissioner Sorjonen's people were scarily smart and perceptive, and those I spoke with not only knew who I was but what I'd accomplished as head of the Rim Sector unit. The mystery of why was soon answered when a chief superintendent mentioned Sorjonen shortlisted me as one of the new team leads even before leaving Wyvern.

Interestingly, I felt as much among family with the PACU officers as aboard *Sorcerer* with Erinye Company. Years of running the Rim Sector PCB unit in splendid isolation, cut off from my Constabulary peers at Sector HQ, and far from my professional peers on Wyvern, made me forget I was part of a larger clan. But now, knowing I was no longer alone proved to be a pleasant sensation after the events of the last two weeks.

Leaving the hard decisions to Commissioner Sorjonen suited me as well after such a long time on my own, wondering whether I would earn the wrath of the universe every time I poked my nose into high-level corruption.

He and I met a strangely subdued Governor Peet the next morning. Bereft of personal staff and the colony's top administrators, she struck me as a lost soul, and I felt sorry for her.

"Did you appoint a replacement for Mister Rudel yet, Madame?" Sorjonen asked after I made the introductions.

She shook her head. "I don't know who I can trust."

"Then let me help." Sorjonen pulled a sheet of paper from his tunic pocket and placed it on her desk. "These are the names of Colonial Office employees under investigation by the Constabulary's Political Anti-Corruption Unit. Based on the wealth of data Assistant Commissioner Morrow dug up, you can be reasonably sure any senior official not on this list is suitable."

Peet, who didn't notice the third diamond on my uniform collar, looked at me with incredulous eyes when she heard Sorjonen refer to my new rank.

"You've been promoted?" Peet raised her gaze to the heavens and let out a theatrical sigh. "I suppose congratulations are in order rather than a complaint about your behavior since the commissioner obviously approves."

"I do, Madame. AC Morrow is one of the finest investigators in the Professional Compliance Bureau. You and the Colonial Office owe her your thanks for bringing the massive amount of official corruption on Mission Colony to light. She saved you from a fate worse than that which befell New Oberon."

Peet waved his words away. "I fully expect a missive from Earth telling me my application for early retirement was approved by the Colonial Secretary."

I repressed a smile. Even now, it was all about Jeanne Peet. No wonder Derzin couldn't add her to his stable of tame bureaucrats. Peet considered his flattery and attention her due, and as the scion of a comfortably well-off family, she didn't need extra funds. The unlikeliest, and in her case least likable people, sometimes had the highest price.

After leaving Government House, Warrant Officer Bonta drove us to Braband's residence. Sorjonen wanted a few words, but not in Braband's former office.

He didn't answer the door when we rang, and I sent Bonta out back to look through the garden door. She returned a few minutes later with a somber expression on her face.

"I'm afraid AC Braband might have done the unthinkable, sir."

"Can you open the lock while I call the Operations Center?"

Sorjonen gave the newly minted warrant officer a curious look when she nodded. We were inside within minutes and discovered Braband had indeed done the unthinkable.

We found him, wearing his dress uniform, complete with full-sized medals and sword, sitting in his home office chair. A small charred hole marred his right temple. It matched the bore of the blaster dangling from his right hand.

A note with only two words lay on his desk. *I'm sorry.*

Sorjonen cursed beneath his breath. A fellow officer committing suicide, even if he was under a cloud, always hit us cops in the gut.

"Damn fool. He wasn't even facing a disciplinary board. Forced early retirement would have been the worst of it."

"Shame is a powerful emotion, sir, especially in a man with a solid, reasonably distinguished record in the uniformed branches. We can lay his death at Derzin's feet, along with the others."

"Aye. I'll see that he gets a regimental funeral with full honors. Just because the man was a sucker once in his life doesn't negate decades of honest, loyal service."

I was beginning to like Commissioner Sorjonen. A genuine leader with a heart hid beneath the scary reputation as Tomás de Torquemada's most recent incarnation. Perhaps serving under his command would prove more interesting than I expected.

We stayed until Inspector Kosta and his team showed up, leaving him with explicit instructions he and the morgue people were to treat AC Braband's remains with the utmost respect.

"It's time I spoke with our Mister Derzin," Sorjonen said once we were in the staff car. "Please take us back to the base, Warrant Officer."

Derzin looked up from his bunk in surprise as Sorjonen, Bonta, and I entered his cell. Contrary to Peet, he noticed the extra silver on my and Bonta's uniforms and gave us an ironic round of applause.

"Congratulations. I'm glad my arrest profited someone, even if it wasn't me."

"I'm Commissioner Sorjonen of the Political Anti-Corruption Unit, Mister Derzin. This is now my investigation."

"Well, then, congratulations to you too. As Assistant Commissioner Morrow no doubt mentioned, I'm not the sort who'll make a voluntary statement, so start digging and good luck. By the way, since I'm no longer a national security certificate detainee, I expect my lawyer here today."

"Did you give your lawyer's name to the cellblock duty non-com?"

"No."

"Then it'll be rather difficult for us to summon him or her."

"Him. Raimundo Hennessy, Esquire. And you best start thinking about bail, Commissioner."

"Oh, you won't be granted bail by any judge in this star system. Justice Bisso died the day before yesterday, and your other friendly judges are cooling their heels elsewhere in this cellblock. In any case, the charges against you are such that no judge will grant bail."

Derzin scowled at Sorjonen. Whether it was because of the commissioner's words or his deliberately condescending tone, I couldn't tell.

"Besides, you now have a target on your back, Mister Derzin. If you believe your superiors don't consider you a loose end at this point, you're more naïve than I thought. My letting you out into the community would merely speed up your execution, and I'd rather enjoy the satisfaction of seeing a judge put on the black cap before sentencing you."

"Good luck with that."

"We don't need luck, Mister Derzin. But you should get reacquainted with the Almighty."

Sorjonen turned on his heels and left the cell. After one last look at Derzin, Bonta and I followed. My last glimpse of the man showed me someone who finally understood he'd been utterly defeated. Before leaving the cellblock, I ordered the duty non-com to put Derzin on a suicide watch.

I spent the next two days in discussions with Sorjonen and the team leaders he'd brought with him from Wyvern and sat in on his interviews of those I'd arrested. None would dare recant their confessions after meeting him. Even the lawyers who represented them could only encourage cooperation in the hopes of a reduced sentence once the PACU investigators dug up admissible evidence based on the decrypted Aeternum computer core data.

The following Monday, Arno, Destine, and I said our goodbyes and boarded the Constabulary cutter *Frank Preston*. The next time we saw Sorjonen and the officers with him would be on Wyvern, several weeks, if not months down the road.

Strangely, I didn't experience the old dream while in hyperspace this time around. Perhaps because Orloski's death at Delgado's hands gave me the closure I'd sought my entire adult life.

When I announced our departure to the team upon arriving on Cimmeria, there were a lot of long faces. Still, Ange Rowan couldn't stop beaming when I pinned a chief superintendent's second diamond on her uniform collar. The combined promotion and farewell party that followed would stay with me forever.

Leaving a unit and the people you loved was never easy, but the farewell that touched me most was from Maras. We'd enjoyed a better relationship than many in our respective positions. Though she wasn't one for sentimentality, I fancied I saw sadness in her eyes when we embraced for the first and last time.

"Take care of yourself, Caelin. Where you're headed is more dangerous than here."

"I know. But someone must do the dirty, dangerous jobs. Why not me?"

"I suppose."

"Ange Rowan will pick up where we left off. You can trust her as much as you trust me. She's one of the best. Don't be surprised if I recruit her in a few years."

"Just make sure her replacement is cast from the same mold."

For the first time in a long time, and despite the twinge in my shoulder, I came to attention and gave Maras a salute that would have made the Constabulary Sergeant Major weep with joy. She returned it in the same spirit.

"With your permission, sir?"

"Godspeed and good luck."

I poked my head into the Rim Sector PCB offices one last time before joining Chief Inspector Galdi and Warrant Officer Bonta at the spaceport. We'd be taking one of the Navy transports that continuously crossed the Commonwealth, connecting Armed Services and Constabulary installations in far-flung star systems.

Even though it was mid-morning, the place was mostly empty. My former investigators were out pursuing their individual cases. Those who remained seemed as busy as usual, and I decided I wouldn't disturb them. We'd said our farewells.

But I felt my heart sink nonetheless at leaving what was my home for so long. I might never see this place, or the people working here ever again.

Arno, Destine, and I didn't speak much at the spaceport or aboard the naval shuttle taking us and our worldly goods up to the transport *Normandie*. They, too, found our departure an emotional event.

But once she broke orbit and Cimmeria faded in the distance, we allowed ourselves a small, private celebration, reminiscing about the past and speculating about the future.

After all, we who wear the gray were mostly nomads, going where the service needed us. And right now, that was with the Political Anti-Corruption Unit on Wyvern.

Our lives were about to become more interesting than ever.

About the Author

Eric Thomson is the pen name of a retired Canadian soldier with thirty-one years of service, both in the Regular Army and the Army Reserve. He spent his Regular Army career in the Infantry and his Reserve service in the Armoured Corps.

Eric has been a voracious reader of science fiction, military fiction, and history all his life. Several years ago, he put fingers to keyboard and started writing his own military sci-fi, with a definite space opera slant, using many of his own experiences as a soldier for inspiration.

When he's not writing fiction, Eric indulges in his other passions: photography, hiking, and scuba diving, all of which he shares with his wife.

Join Eric Thomson at http://www.thomsonfiction.ca/
Where you'll find news about upcoming books and more information about the universe in which his heroes fight for humanity's survival.

Read his blog at
https://ericthomsonblog.wordpress.com

If you enjoyed this book, please consider leaving a review with your favorite online retailer to help others discover it.

Also by Eric Thomson

Siobhan Dunmoore
No Honor in Death (Siobhan Dunmoore Book 1)
The Path of Duty (Siobhan Dunmoore Book 2)
Like Stars in Heaven (Siobhan Dunmoore Book 3)
Victory's Bright Dawn (Siobhan Dunmoore Book 4)
Without Mercy (Siobhan Dunmoore Book 5)
When the Guns Roar (Siobhan Dunmoore Book 6)

Decker's War
Death Comes But Once (Decker's War Book 1)
Cold Comfort (Decker's War Book 2)
Fatal Blade (Decker's War Book 3)
Howling Stars (Decker's War Book 4)
Black Sword (Decker's War Book 5)
No Remorse (Decker's War Book 6)
Hard Strike (Decker's War Book 7)

Constabulary Casefiles
The Warrior's Knife
A Colonial Murder

Ashes of Empire
Imperial Sunset (Ashes of Empire #1)
Imperial Twilight (Ashes of Empire #2)
Imperial Night (Ashes of Empire #3)

Ghost Squadron
We Dare (Ghost Squadron No.1)
Deadly Intent (Ghost Squadron No.2)

Made in the USA
Middletown, DE
13 February 2023